Whispers in the Hearts of Men

Robert John Goddard

Seek refuge in the Lord of men, the King of men, the God of men, from the mischief of the slinking prompter, who whispers in the hearts of men... (Koran 114:5).

PROLOGUE

"Nice to be with you again, dad," the boy said. "I thought we'd go up this way and we can have a chat. Is that OK with you?"

Picking up the walking stick, he took off across the fields to Rydal House, up to Nab Scar and over the fells towards Fairfield. He paused on the summit and, with a wind tugging at his rucksack, he ate his sandwiches.

"Yes, dad, I thought you'd like it up here. You must've thought about this place so often when you were out there. I've often wondered what you were thinking when the end came. What were you thinking, dad? Yes, I can imagine, 'Look, you're making a mistake. I'm an innocent man.' And you were innocent, weren't you? So, tell me, dad, do you hate them now – those Arabs and Israelis? Do you hate them all after what they put you through? Perhaps you don't hate them all. Perhaps you hate some of them though, don't you, dad? What about those men who took you to the city? Should I hate them after what they did? Should I, dad? Please tell me. Should I hate them too?"

CHAPTER 1

Richard was about to slip the key into the lock and close the door to his room when he felt a tremor. It was delicate at first, the flutter of a butterfly's wings shivering up his legs to his belly. By the time it reached his hands, the flutter had become a tremor and it was strong enough to make him miss the keyhole.

"Oh, damn. Not now, please, no…"

The tremor had found his voice, hovered in his breathing before dropping to his belly again. Bending from the waist, Richard rested his forehead on the door while his hands stroked his tummy. He was taking deep and healing breaths when the words he might use to explain his non-appearance at the conference appeared unheralded in his head. The British Council staff would understand the misery of funny tummy or Montezuma's revenge. But no sooner had these words appeared than the discomfort melted away on a sigh of relief.

"Stage fright," he muttered. With a flicker of a frown, he added, "And at my age too." Decisively, he turned the key in the lock.

He dropped the key into his trouser pocket, felt it cold against the skin of his thigh. Wiping the palms of his hands on his jacket, he reflected on his nervousness, knew it was right and proper before an important plenary. He might be a respected academic, but that was no excuse for complacency. His lectures still needed the edge that anxiety could bring. He shrugged his shoulders and lifted his elbows to allow the air to dry his armpits. The trick was to turn that anxiety into a positive energy that you could throw back at a delighted audience. Hearing their applause in his head, he strode down the corridor and opened his arms to capture the predicted love and appreciation. He was still smiling and nodding his thanks to the imaginary audience when the butterfly wings fluttered up his legs again. Suspecting CCTV cameras, he glanced upwards. He saw one on the ceiling near the

3

staircase. Its lens was winking at him, was pointing right in his direction. Passing underneath it, Richard waved a salutatory hand at person or persons unknown. It was a childish gesture, but in that foreign land, he felt the need to express his cultural heritage with its strong individuality and its contempt for authority.

Approaching the top of the stairs, Richard returned his mind to his presentation, mentally rehearsing the opening lines. *In the 1990s, the countries and peoples in the Middle East faced two major problems. One of these problems was economic and social. The other problem might be described as political and social...*

He had spent some of the afternoon learning the first part of his lecture by rote. The words of his presentation came easily - too easily to prevent the language of his thoughts from assessing and reflecting on his emotional response to his surroundings. The little wave into the camera was a consequence of his uneasiness. Gestures like that were manifestations of a humour that the English adopted to deal with difficult or uncomfortable situations.

Richard allowed his stride to falter. He had passed the CCTV camera but there was still tightness in his bowels, and he was conscious of every breath he was taking. As a lecturer, being on stage and absorbing the thrill of eyes settling on him was a familiar sensation, but he had never before experienced that excitement in the empty corridor of a hotel. When he adjusted the rhythm of his feet, prepared them for the flight of stairs, the weight of self-consciousness descended, and he knew he was the object of someone's attention.

He stepped onto the first stair. The palm of one hand rested on the banister, its fingers drumming the cold metal. He held the other arm akimbo, the knuckle of the hand kneading his hip while beads of sweat ran from his armpits. A murmur rose from the lobby, a babble of voices swelling and hushing in the spaces around him while bursts of laughter rocketed into the air over his head. Seen from above, the hotel lobby was patterned with human connections and disconnections. Hands reached out, were clasped or released in greeting or farewell while legs danced one way and then another, circling the suitcases that waited in rows for removal. The scene was reflected in the mirrors that covered the lobby walls. Richard noted that nobody seemed to be looking in his direction.

He tried to bury his concerns in the nationality guessing game. But he soon tired of body language and communication style, of clothes and the way people wore them. That afternoon, he found the distance of the English irritating, the formality and seriousness of the Germans absurd, and the effusive and involving body language of the Italians tiring. Richard switched the power of his observation to those who might be leaving and those who might be arriving. Both were easy to spot, but the arrivals disturbed him with their anxious glances and expressions that seemed to

4

long for some space so that they could unpack their personalities with their suitcases and claim a patch of a foreign hotel for themselves. The departures fascinated him too. There was an ease and confidence in the way they operated in their surroundings, in the way they wore their clothes and looked towards the taxi stand while frisking themselves to check for passports and money. Richard almost frisked himself in sympathy. He wished he was going with them.

He was halfway down the staircase, low enough to note his reflection in the mirrors, when he saw the man sitting under the stairwell. He was flowing and swirling robes, his feet tucked unseen beneath him, and his hands folded in his lap. Each man simultaneously caught sight of the other in the mirror. It was not the stark whiteness of the robes that made Richard flinch, and nor was it his own natural reticence that made him turn his head away as if from a jabbing hand. It was the eyes, staring out from between the folds of the man's headdress, which intruded like a fist into Richard's world. The eyes brought the tremor back into his breathing and racing thoughts into his head. It had to be the British Council driver, he told himself. But this man did not rise to his feet with a smile of welcome and announce himself. Richard wondered if the driver was annoyed that his pick-up was a few minutes late. Perhaps he was hungry and wanted to be at home with his family.

Two more downward steps and the hotel's marbled shopping arcade came within the arc of his vision. It glittered and preened itself in its own wall mirrors while the chandeliers, the shop fronts and the pillars were reflected in the arcade floor and lay like an identical but separate underground world. The stream of refugees from the sandstorm was increasing, and a large knot of them had formed in the arcade. Many were looking through the glass frontage at the peculiar orange glow in the sky. The expression in their eyes suggested that what they saw was an omen, the arrival of the second coming or an imagined harbinger of doom rather than a simple sign that the sun was descending through the dust.

He looked again at the big man in the white robes. He was not imagining the scorn that burned in his eyes. What was more, the man was making no attempt to hide it. He appeared to be challenging Richard to respond, to do something. Richard bit his bottom lip and ignored the voice in his head telling him he was powerless and vulnerable. Perhaps it was a case of mistaken identity. Richard decided to confront him.

He hurried down the remaining stairs and into the shifting, swelling crowd. At ground level, the man was out of sight, and Richard pushed through the people and towards the seat under the stairwell with an urgency that bordered the unacceptable. Someone tapped him on the shoulder. The tapping hand stunned him. While life went on around him, Richard was rooted to the floor, and a cold sweat broke out on his forehead. With an irritable movement of the shoulders, he came back to life and span round, fists clenched. His eyes were angled upwards to meet those of the big man in the swirling white robes but he found himself glaring over the top of the crowd and into emptiness.

"Mr Shampers, please, Mr Shampers?"

Richard lowered his head in the manner of a man about to say grace. The obliging, obsequious hotel receptionist was standing in front of him and looking up into Richard's face with an expression of fake concern. Cascading from his head was a splendid red and white chequered *kuffieh*, its many knots carefully placed to decorate the shoulders. A hand emerged from the folds of his *jalabiyah* and a finger was raised in a gesture that said he wanted one minute of Richard's time.

Richard was immobile, impassive, a man in mild shock. His name, that foundation stone of his identity, was perceived, interpreted and pronounced so differently that he felt himself dislocate. The voice he wanted to hear was that of his wife, Nicole. That would ground him in something safe and sound.

"It's Chambers," Richard said, "Chambers - with a tsch."

The receptionist smiled.

"Your driver is waiting outside," he said, "in the blue BMW."

"Thank you."

But the man did not move. He stood and stared at Richard as though he were carrying a death sentence branded on his forehead.

"Is there anything else, Mr Shampers?"

Richard was rocked by a moment of anxiety. He wanted to shout out that he needed help. He wanted to say that there was a big man in the hotel and that the man was threatening him.

"No, nothing," Richard said.

He turned, pushed through the crowd towards the exit. His strained smile and muttered apologies suggested an expectation of understanding from people who had also been late for planes or meetings. He did not stop to wonder if any of them had ever felt his growing sense of danger, his need to put as much space as possible between him and the big man in the flowing white robes.

Disoriented, he emerged by the revolving glass doors. They were spinning so fast that the patterns of people behind him were reflected as a dizzy and flickering blur of light and colour. He waited for the doors to slow, hoping to catch the big man's image, to see him talking, and convince himself the man had been waiting for someone else. The notion flashed into his consciousness that if he turned and scanned the lobby, he would be admitting to himself that something was amiss, that he was being followed and that he was afraid.

Richard pushed at the doors and reeled into a sand-laden headwind. A rush of air funnelled down the road with a rumbling sound that reminded Richard of the bed sheets flapping in a gale in his garden at home. The British Council BMW was waiting at the kerbside. Richard strode towards it and grabbed for the door handle. He glimpsed another car parked nearby. There was a man in white at the wheel and someone with a white shawl pulled around the face and tied beneath the chin. The way the face jutted from the head covering surprised him. But most unexpected was the realisation that the eyes staring into his were those of a middle-aged woman. Richard did not try to account for the feelings of relief and comfort the idea of femininity brought to him, but he refused to make eye contact with either of them, pulled open the door of his car and dived inside.

"Let's go." There was a long pause between his command and the sound of the engine turning. Richard leaned forward and caught a glimpse of his face in the rear-view mirror. His jaw muscles were tense, his cheeks were taut, and his eyes were wide open and staring - already communicating what he now verbalised. "Better make it quick."

The driver pulled away and joined the traffic on *Jebel Abweh's* main thoroughfare. Richard's heart was pumping hard against his ribs as his driver put his foot down, and the BMW surged forward, its tyres crackling over the layer of sand that covered the road. Passing the guards outside the row of Embassies, Richard leaned forward, rested his hand on the passenger seat, the order to stop the car on the tip of his tongue. In a flash, the guards were behind them and the BMW was heading into no-man's-land.

Richard found a morsel of comfort in the car's power and its familiar Western interior but he somehow knew that the other car was behind them. He did not want to turn round and confirm it. He did not dare look at the man in white or his female companion. To do so would be to acknowledge their presence or form a relationship with them. If he did not see them, perhaps they were not there. Perhaps he had been imagining everything.

A car sped past them. Richard told himself that it was just another example of poor Middle East driving, but the car swerved to a halt across the road in front of them, the door flew open, and a man with a pistol stepped out. Another man was approaching Richard's side of the car. There was a blur of movement. The car door flew open; a violent tug at his hair, and he was out in the street. Sand was jumping in spurts on the pavement, and the air was alive with bits of rubbish, broken plants and spiralling grit that turned and twirled before sweeping downwards to smack him in the face. There was the frightened face of a passer-by, and in a second Richard was in the other car. A man's voice snapped out a command in Arabic, and the car roared away. Something cold and metallic was pressed hard against Richard's forehead and forcing the back of his head onto the thigh of another man. The man's skin exuded the sweet odour of cheap aftershave, and he was holding a rifle. Fumbling fingers were in Richard's pockets.

"Let me go." Breathless panic filled his voice, raised its pitch until the words cracked and broke while his heart rate soared. "Take the money and I won't tell anybody. Please, please...." Before he had finished, someone laughed and pulled a wad of local currency from his pocket. "Please you have my word...." There was a vicious laugh, angry eyes above him and a voice screaming into his ear:

"Shut up the fuck, you fuck."

A sensation like an electric shock hit Richard's jaw and shot into his neck and shoulders before running back into his face. A bright white light exploded in front of his eyes. He felt his head roll and he thought he was going to vomit. In his peripheral vision he saw the fist drawing back to strike again. The woman in the front seat span round and issued a shrill but commanding order. The man with the rifle responded to it by pushing his weapon forward like a sentry standing easy and he barked a command of his own. The tone and pitch of the voice was barely out of adolescence but it and the rifle blocked the swing of the fist. The moment of severe beating passed, but cheated of the pleasure of causing pain, the man with the angry eyes let out a cry of rage and pushed the pistol harder against Richard's forehead.

"You just shut up the fuck."

Richard was now awake to his predicament. Escape was impossible. There were at least three men and one woman in the car, and the rifle stood sentinel by his head. He tasted the blood in his mouth and heard the car engine roaring in his ears as they sped along the road. Through the driver's window he could see outside. The sandstorm had reduced the world to shadows, and the edges of things were invisible and merged into a wrapping of orange paper. He saw that they were heading for the poorer part of town. He watched the sun suffocating in the dust that hung between the shadows of the high rises, the minarets and the television aerials, and its light flashed and flickered into the car and died on the unknown man's thigh. Nobody spoke, but Richard felt the energy of the violent man's presence. He found comfort watching the back of the woman's head. It was angled towards the window, her interest grabbed by the outside world. She could have been travelling home on a bus after a shopping expedition in town.

The sun had disappeared by the time the car swerved off the road and skidded into a garage. A strip of rough material was pulled over Richard's eyes and tied behind his head. Dusk descended into night, and he entered another sensory world. Callous hands fumbled for his; bodies, stale with sweat, overwhelmed him and prevented him from moving. Cold steel ringed his wrists.

They had spread-eagled him on the back seat, removed his watch and cuffed him. He felt his shoulders click when they jerked him from the car, heard his breath heaving from his lungs when they pushed him forwards. One of the men kicked open a door, and he was manhandled through. The door thumped shut. He was shoved again. His shoulders bounced off walls on either side of him, and he fell headlong to the floor, mouthing a silent cry as the cuffs rode up his forearms and bit into the flesh. A door closed on the old world behind him.

To relieve the pressure on his arms, he rolled over and raised himself to his haunches. Pushing up his blindfold, he brought his clasped hands to his jaw and moved it from side to side. Reassured that the jaw was not broken, Richard looked up. White tiles covered the walls from top to bottom and there was a plastic chair and a mattress on the floor. His eyes returned to the tiles. His stomach seized when he realised he might be sitting in an abattoir. Perhaps he had but seconds to live before they cut up his body and hosed down the walls to wash away the evidence. He heard the click of an opening door and spun round. He was expecting to see a trolley with the executioners' tools on it: scalpels for the skin, an axe for his limbs and saws for the bones.

An ethereal figure in white filled the doorway. It could have been a manifestation of the second coming, or something that had materialised from the tiles themselves, but Richard heard reverential and whispering voices trailing through the door behind him. The man looked down at Richard before gliding across the room and settling himself on the plastic chair. Only his eyes were visible, and neither they nor his body made the slightest movement when he said:

"Dicky Chambers? We know everything about you."

This simple statement with no explanations, apologies or introductions plunged Richard into confusion. His mouth rounded on vowels, and his lips fused to spit out consonants but not a breath emerged to express his inner turmoil. He was struggling with the residue of emotion he thought he had discarded with the nickname "Dicky" but it was calling him back to when he was very young, to his mother's warmth, to Little Bo-peep and to Little Boy Blue. He needed that warmth now, the human contact, the knowledge that he was not alone.

"Yes," said the Second Coming, "we know why you are here now. We know why you were here before and we know why you left here in disgrace."

"But what do you want with me? Why have you taken me?"

The Second Coming turned his head towards the open door and raised his eyebrows as if to say, "I told you so," to the whispering voices at the door.

"We also know that you are now a well-respected expert on Middle-East history, and a man whose opinions are sought by the British Government."

"You know a lot about me," Richard said. "So you must know why I have been taken from my work and my family."

Neither his words nor his sarcastic tone appeared to find their mark. The Second Coming bulldozed his remark to one side without giving it a moment's thought.

"You may not be killed. You may not be tortured. One day you might write a book about us. You may remove your blindfold when you are alone. When you hear a knock on the door, you must pull it on. If you don't do this, you may be punished. Understand?"

The high-pitched squeal of a telephone burst into the room and caused Richard to jump as if he had woken from a deep sleep. The Second Coming barely moved.

"How long will I be here?" Richard asked.

"No questions are allowed."

"Why me?"

The Second Coming rose to his feet and drew himself up to his great height. He stared at Richard for several seconds before sweeping out of the room and into the whispering tones of deference. A hand reached into the room and grabbed at the door handle. The hand was followed by a woman's head. Her gaze met Richard's head on. An expression of concern flickered across her eyes before she pulled the door shut.

Richard stared at the closed door. Nicole had warned him of the dangers in the region but he ignored her. He groped for something to hold on to, something that might prevent the slide into the world of regret, of self-pity or self-recrimination. At that moment there was nothing to latch on to except the sound of a carpet being beaten somewhere in the city. It was an echoing and regular thumping against a background of eternity.

CHAPTER 2

He awoke with a spasm, floundered on the mattress, his breath coming in gasps. He turned to his left but swung his face away to stare into space. He closed his eyes, stilled his breathing and daydreamed of slipping out of bed, tiptoeing into the kitchen and making coffee for Nicole. He saw himself at the curtains, feeling their softness between his fingertips, pulling them back and letting the daylight break over him.

He raised his cuffed wrists and rubbed at his jaw. A wedge of light, the same light he had let in with indifference at home, cut through a tiny window under the ceiling and spilled into his cell. But there was no pitter-patter of small feet crossing the corridor to his room, no soft, morning bed-turnings to stir the silence. The enormity of his captivity surged through him. How dare these people snatch him from his family? There was no question that they had taken the wrong person. Surely it was only a matter of time, and they would release him unharmed, throw him out of the car in some anonymous quarter of the city, and he would have to make his own way back to the hotel and safety.

But what if there had been no mistake? The Second Coming had known his name even if the version he had used was obsolete. "Dicky" Chambers had been rebranded as "Richard" Chambers some twenty years previously in an attempt to upgrade his image in the academic world. Perhaps, then, in the short time he had been in the city, he had committed an intercultural faux pas and insulted someone or offended some institution, and now they were teaching him a lesson he would never forget. He sent his mind out to scan the previous forty-eight hours, to pinpoint some event that might explain this terrible mistake.

He had arrived after a flight from Manchester, a long wait in Nicosia, and an MEA flight to his destination. A taxi had met him and brought him to the Intercontinental Hotel. It was true that the driver had raced through the squalid suburbs, scattering goats and people alike from his path and shouting abuse at anyone who dared challenge him. Perhaps someone had taken offence and now wanted revenge. Richard doubted it. He had been huddled in the back seat, immersing himself in eucalyptus and other scents, losing himself in the silhouettes of the minarets and the promise of the orient against the lightening sky. Nobody could have recognised him.

He had spent the rest of the first day resting in his room and going through his presentation. The long flights had brought his body but his mind and spirit were still in transit. The body in the hotel room was dislocated and lonely. He tried to deal with his dream-like state by conversing with his wife and young son on the telephone and telling them how happy he was to be back in the city where his academic career had started some thirty-five years previously. He did not tell them about his sense of estrangement. Nor did he tell them of the memories and feelings that had already flooded in with the eucalyptus, the call from the minaret and the warm air playing at his nostrils. But each intake of scent-filled air brought a fragment of past love: the cheeky grin, the crackling blue of the eyes; the arm, languid and naked over the back of the armchair, the jealousy and the guilt unchanging. One memory sparked of another so that he recalled a number of gestures, of snatches of conversation and other moments he was unwilling to face.

Later that first day, the novelty of these memories wore off, and Richard reflected that it was no surprise that they had been waiting for him. The songs from that year still haunted him. "Brandy" would send him into extended daydreams, and he always walked away from "Jealous Guy" when he heard it on the radio. Nonetheless, Richard had relished the idea of returning to the region, even if his first visit had ended in ignominious dismissal. Nicole had been more circumspect. There was nothing to be gained from going back, she said, but pain and disappointment. Her husband would do nothing other than walk around in his own memories, make comparisons with the past and see everyone as trespassers on his terrain. Anyway, she said in a more pragmatic and down-to-earth tone, the place was now politically unstable and dangerous.

The Foreign Office assured Richard that the danger to British nationals wishing to travel to the region was minimal, and Richard had looked forward to the trip despite Nicole's warnings. He had even decided to go two days earlier in order to reacquaint himself with the place where "Dicky" Chambers had trod, lived and worked as a volunteer teacher at the boy's school.

After lunch on the second day, Richard went back to his room intending to go through his presentation for the last time and to deal with a backlog of emails. He was anticipating a mail from a colleague in New Zealand and his report on a four-year study into suicide attacks in the Middle-East. Of particular interest to Richard was what these attacks revealed about the nature and characteristics of the bombers themselves. He clicked on to the internet and then to his email provider. While waiting for a connection he looked through the window, let his gaze dance over the house tops and the minarets to the low, parched hills on the horizon where he found an irresistible desire to revisit the school where his teaching career had begun. He was still staring through the window when the login box appeared on his screen. Richard's hand hovered over the keyboard. While he logged off and got to his feet he was aware that the delicious anticipation of the visit was spoiled by ill-defined feelings of guilt. Making his way to the door of his room he eased his concerns by telling himself that in this faraway place, the events from that faraway time were somehow disconnected from him. Revisiting the past would be a secret pleasure, his own private cinema show.

It was the middle of the afternoon when he pushed at the doors and reeled out into the street to revisit his past. The warmth was as tangible but as untouchable as the women in black who shuffled beside the battered yellow taxis and the moth-eaten buildings. The women seemed to turn a disdainful ear to the car horns, the *muezzin's* call, and the shouts of *jihad*, the shouts against Western imperialism, and the shouts about the rising price of vegetables. Mingling with it all and clinging to his clothes were rich and honeyed odours, heavy with suggestions of the orient and ready to carry it across the world.

While he strolled to the first circle, memories emerged, followed him down the main street and competed for his attention. From the tiny roundabout the school entrance was visible as lush and heavy oleander twisting up and around a black, iron gateway. There was no movement of any kind except the flower petals bobbing to the faraway sound of the city dwellers on their way home for a late lunch.

With memories now snapping close at his heels, Richard stepped under the oleander and followed his shadow until it broke over the low wall that separated the accommodation block from the play area. There was only the faint plop of his shoes, the sound of cicadas clicking, and the sun burning the back of his neck. A quickening of the air made him turn. Far away in the desert a huge brown wall, stretching from horizon to horizon and reaching high into the sky, was shutting out the sun in an orange glow. A sandstorm was coming.

Richard turned his head towards the shaded passage that joined the play area to the cloistered courtyard circling the classrooms. His eyes lingered in its darkness, and a wistful expression came to his face as though he were moved by a long musical note of great sadness or beauty. He was remembering the idea of his young self and the mixture of laughter, shouts of surprise and excitement that would rise up from the playground at the end of the school day. In his mind, the sounds faded to empty and distant

13

shouts and the leathery thwack of a bouncing ball while from beyond the school gates and from all the seven surrounding hills came the settling sound of a breathing city preparing itself for lunch and an afternoon nap.

The sound of the ball was still present in Richard's memory. He even walked in time to its bouncing rhythm towards the narrow passageway. Before he reached its entrance, the sound stopped, and all that remained was a vague pulse in his temple.

Richard gazed into the silence. Just inside the shade of the passageway, and framed in a vaulted recess, a memory was waiting for him. Khalid is lying on his back, and his feet are drawn up, the skin on his legs soft and pale. One arm curls upwards so that the boy's head rests on the palm of its hand while the other arm circles a football, which lies on his chest. The boy is staring at the wall, his lips moving to some repetitive learning exercise or prayer while warm breaths of wind flirt with the hair over his forehead. Dicky embraces him with a look, his eyes caressing the curve of the boy's legs where they enter his shorts.

Lying on the mattress in his cell, Richard fidgeted at this memory and the residue of feeling that accompanied it. He lay for some time, staring at the damp marks on the ceiling and tried to come to terms with the fact that Khalid was still dancing in his life, still talking and living in his dreams. As unacceptable as that was to him, it was not a crime, and it did not explain why anyone would want to imprison him. The only living person he had met in the play area was the school caretaker and the man had challenged Richard's presence there.

While Richard had begun with muttered words of apology, the man's eyes, glaring out from between half-closed lids, never left Richard's face. The expression was not without interest but it was empty of emotion. He could have been looking at some television programme which neither excited nor bored him.

"What you want? Private land here, private land."

"I used to work here," Richard said, "back in 1973."

The expression in the man's eyes remained one of indifference.

"Private land," he said, "leave, please."

Richard held his body still, but he gazed around him with eyes full of reclaimed youthful wonder, experiencing everything for a second magical time: the lengthening shadows, the heat of the sun and the breeze running over the flowers at the school entrance. Under these flowers, another fragment of memory was waiting for him and it began with Sandra calling his name. The call had an upward inflection and it contained a command that even after thirty-six years could not be ignored.

Dicky squints across the baking play area and into the sunlight. In the afternoon heat, Sandra is a shimmer of red and white hanging beneath the oleander, but she seems to rise out of the ground like the birth of Venus, a genie setting off towards him. As she nears, the genie becomes a tangible young woman with heavy, bouncing breasts under a red T-shirt, and with hair, parted in the middle and dropping like silky-straight black curtains to her shoulders. When she is within touching distance, her hand reaches out, its fingers clenching and unclenching, and it plucks at Dicky's shirt. Her voice, betraying her upper middle-class upbringing in Sussex, follows.

"Good Lord. Aren't we safe? Has someone started a war?"

There is a thump as Khalid boots a football high into the air, and Dicky watches it while it reaches its zenith and then returns to earth with a resounding thwack. Khalid traps the ball with one foot and, flicking it upwards, catches it on his chest and then volleys it to Omar Khoury, who is standing at the assembly room door.

"Well done that boy. What'll we do if they invade?" The hand that has mangled his shirt now unfolds and caresses his shoulder while her voice whispers into his ear: "Will you take care of me? Will I be able to find you if I need you?" She draws closer, her breasts pressing into his arm; and she adds with playful remonstration, "Or will you be a naughty boy and run away like you did before?"

Dicky says nothing. The expression in his eyes suggests that he is not really in that place, in that time and with that young woman. He is far away with a dream and he is following that dream with a look that wishes and wishes in vain. Khalid is running away from him, and Dicky is staring at his flying heels.

Through an open window, a wave of excitement rolls out of the assembly hall and gathers them both in its power. The final dress rehearsal for the school play is about to take place and Dicky rises to it as a man might rise to the call to arms. He sets off towards the hall with the confidence of one who knows that his duty calls, that England expects. Sandra draws back her shoulders and pulls her heels together, her feet pointing outwards at ten minutes to two.

"Tonight at 19.30. Alright then?"

She rattles off her words with the authority of the Gatling gun which says *we have it and you don't*, to all dissenters, and she watches her rounds follow Dicky to the door. Her expression turns to one of mild distaste when he fails to reply or fall to the floor like a spear-waving native. She sets off in pursuit and disappears from view.

"Leave now," said the caretaker. "Private land, private land."

Richard stared back at the man with an expectant twist to his brow but neither of them said a word. Everything around them was hushed, and nothing seemed to move except a memory and the oleander bobbing in the school gateway. As the caretaker continued to scan Richard's face, a new expression took hold of his eyes. He lifted his arm and pointed at the sky behind him.

"Storm coming," he said. "Good you leave now."

Richard followed the direction of the man's persistent and outstretched arm and walked across the play area, under the oleander and into the street.

Sitting in his white-tiled cell, Richard wondered whether the man had thought he was dealing with a paedophile. Perhaps he had followed him to the hotel and called the police to warn them. He doubted it. By the time he had made his way back to the hotel, tins, cans, and corrugated sheeting were blowing and rattling with an erratic wind. And there was nothing to stop it - no skyscrapers, no forest, nothing - just barren land. The people he passed in the street were faint forms of varying shapes and sizes and they seemed unsure of themselves, disoriented ghosts who guessed that they might be haunting the wrong time and the wrong place. Nobody could have followed him in such conditions. The storm had enveloped the city and choked it.

Richard pushed at his mattress and brought himself to a sitting position. The desire to speak to Nicole was so strong, he spoke to her across the void:

"I've been…"

He held his breath and scanned the room, searching for something he could focus on, something that might take his mind off the notion that was forming in his head, something that would divert his emotions and prevent them from falling into a pit. He could already feel himself sliding down and assuming the position of pathetic victim with no dignity and unworthy of love or appreciation.

A rapping of knuckles on the door prompted him to fumble at the blindfold, to pull it over his eyes. The door creaked open.

"You awake, yes? Toilet. You want toilet?"

The voice, barely past adolescent breakage, held hints of care and respect but it also reminded Richard of his undergraduate students and a thinly disguised contempt which said, "The world and all its promise belongs to us. You have had your chance. You are on the way out." Maybe they were right. At fifty-seven years old, he was no longer connected to his students. Until he reached his forties, they and he had somehow all lived within the boundaries of the same house. At some point, possibly when he took the chair of Professor of Islamic history, he found himself evicted.

"Yes, I want toilet."

Shoes, probably backless slippers, flopped over the floor towards him. In a second, he was enveloped in the smell of cheap aftershave and the young man's warmth. It was a dewy morning warmth, laced with toothpaste and soap, alive with a mother's remonstrations and heavy with the promise of happiness from the day ahead. He wrapped a hand around Richard's wrists and removed the cuffs. The hands were warm, the fingers delicate.

"Come with me, please." His voice carried the soothing authority of the geriatric nurse. "Let me take you down."

He put one hand under Richard's elbow, the other in the small of his back and led him through the door. The hand was open, the flat of the palm pressing on his spine, the fingers crooked, and their gentle pressure guiding him through the darkness in an awkward silence. Richard sensed that the boy wanted to say something and that he was having difficulty articulating it. Eventually he blurted out:

"Manchester United. You like?"

Richard guessed this was a conversational gambit – the global topic of football thrown like a grappling iron over a huge cultural gap. Richard was not the least bit interested in football but he decided to take this opportunity and grab it.

"Manchester United? Good team. Ryan Giggs."

He said the player's name in a way that suggested the words themselves had a hundred associations which both understood and shared in the silence that followed.

"Ryan Giggs, yeah. The boy's a bit special."

"Great pace."

"Yeah, great pace. He's so good at finishing."

Their feet crackled over the concrete floor, and their arms and shoulders rubbed up against the walls of the unlit corridor. Richard heard the guard's breathing quicken like a child about to articulate, eager to please his parents.

"Ryan Giggs is fast, skilful and sharp," he said. "With Luis Figo, he is the most fantastic winger I have ever seen in my life."

"Absolutely. What more can you say."

"How could I appraise him? Fantasy star? Yeah that's Ryan Giggs."

"Your English is very good," Richard said.

"Thank you, thank you. I learn from football. I learn from music, yeah? I listen and I write what I hear and then learn words. My father have all record and CD." The guard stopped, swung his arms outwards and brushed Richard's arm before making noises which Richard interpreted as indicators of enormity or of excitement. "Big number records, yeah? From Elvis to Madonna. I listen, I write and I learn. You like music?"

"I love music."

"Music is my life."

"Cool," Richard said.

He was delighting in this comfort of human contact. It gave him hope and brought life back to his spirit. Richard imagined this boy scribbling down and learning the football commentaries he heard on global television, memorising the content of football web sites and learning songs by heart. But without the contact with native-speakers he would never develop an understanding of the language patterns he needed in order to put together his own sentences and develop his own voice. Nonetheless, he was happy the boy spoke some English. There were other voices, distant and muted as though the ground was covered in snow but Richard was unable to discern the language. He supposed it was some kind of local dialect and so different from his own area of expertise, classical written Arabic, that it constituted a different language altogether.

The guard had become silent, and the hand which had guided him grabbed at his wrist.

"Stop please."

Richard did as he was told. Deprived of sight, he could feel the boy's nervousness. It was in the air and crackling around them both.

"Beatles. You like? I'd like to be under the sea with you. You like, yeah?"

"Very good," said Richard. "Good day, sunshine."

"You say go and I say go…"

"Go, go, go," said Richard as the guard led him into a smell of disinfectant, oil and excrement.

"What does your father do," Richard said.

"Do?"

"Yes, do – what is his job?"

"He sell records downtown. The lights are brighter there…"

There was a wistful quality in the boy's tone that suggested Richard had lost him. He sent out another line from the old song to get him back.

"You can leave all your troubles there…"

But it was too late. He and the young guard had disconnected.

"Don't hang around, yeah?"

The boy's shoved him in the back with the palm of his hand, and Richard took a couple of steps forward. A door closed behind him, and he removed the blindfold. In a second, he took in the electric cables looping the shower, the sockets hanging from the walls, the peeling paint, the damp and stained linoleum floor. He looked at his reflection in a shaving mirror. The thinning hair was still a dishevelled dark brown with scatterings of grey, and hung down over the nape of his neck in an attempt, perhaps, to reinstate himself at the student house. But there were cracks through the centre of the mirror so that the hair, the bruised and swollen jaw seemed to belong to someone else. The blood on his shirt belonged to him. He rubbed at his eyes and said:

"Kidnapped."

An urgent knocking at the door brought him back to himself, left his emotional reaction to the word hanging in the air before it had time to settle.

"Hurry, yeah?" said the young guard.

Richard fumbled at his belt and dropped his trousers. There was a streak of dark brown on his underpants, evidence of fear, of embarrassment, of punishment.

"Please come out. Hurry. It's cool, yeah?"

Richard grinned at his reflection. He had already heard this use of informal youth language from his foreign students at the university. It represented an attempt to connect, to show that student and teacher were on intimate terms. Although Richard knew in his head that his students intended no offence, his stomach responded indignantly to their attempt at closeness. In this stinking hole, he found this inappropriate language use charming. It reinforced his hope that a mistake had been made and that his captors might release him.

"Come out now. Come out."

The boy's tone now had an edge - a suggestion of panic. If he was as young as he sounded, Richard guessed, he was probably under orders, unpredictable and dangerous. "Okay, okay," he said. He wobbled to his feet and hauled up his trousers to hide the accident from his guard.

The door clicked open, and he was tugged out of the bathroom.

"Don't let me in trouble, yeah?"

The boy guided him down the corridor with the barely concealed irritation and urgency of the nurse who knew his patient had dirtied his underpants. Richard had seen a report that identified the elderly as an abuse category. He had read about the maltreatment, negligence, the abandonment, the lack of respect and the verbal and physical aggression against the lost voices of the elderly. He did not consider himself old, but then, he did not yet see himself as kidnapped either.

"No long in toilet please. Hurry every times. Yes?" He led Richard through the door and into his room and another sort of life.

"Yes, yes, okay."

"Get in now - get in to where you belong…"

The door clanged shut and, for several minutes, Richard stood still in the room. He did not turn. He did not remove the blindfold. He wanted the security of darkness, the security of his own thoughts and memories. Between the memories, he glimpsed a number of questions lining up to be answered. He snatched at the blindfold and pushed it up to his forehead, but the first question appeared on his lips before he could stop it.

"Why me?"

He removed his jacket and tie, and flung them on the floor. Why would anyone want to kidnap an academic from the North of England University? Academics were supposed to be objective champions in the quest for degrees of truth. It was true that he was a leading authority on the development of Arab nationalism in independent Muslim countries. His advice and opinions were often sought by policy makers. For ten years, the main thrust of his research had been of great interest to those engaged in the fight against terrorism. The focus of this research centred on whether or not Arab nationalism was following the Western pattern and rooting itself in the political and economic organisation of the nation state. Of great interest to Richard was how Islam would respond to the development of nationhood. If religion was removed as the supreme authority, would it develop into a private matter, left to the conscience of individuals or would it lead to extreme forms of theocracy that might prove a threat to Western powers?

A single knock on the door interrupted him. The doorknob squeaked, and Richard fumbled for the blindfold. A cloud of scent billowed through the door.

"You want eat?"

Richard shook his head.

"You must eat, yeah?"

"No, thank you."

"You not eat, you die. I just don't understand. That's uncool, man."

"No really," Richard said, rubbing his tummy and shaking his head, "not hungry."

"I bring something, yeah?"

"No, not 'yeah,' OK? Now listen - I told you I'm not…"

The door slammed shut and blasted his objections away. Richard fell to his knees and pushed up the blindfold. Falling sideways to the floor, he drew his knees up to his chest and lay in the foetal position.

Never had he felt so low. He could not even change his underpants. He looked up at the window, his only link with the real world, and with a surge of optimism, he got to his feet and grabbed the plastic chair. He dragged it to the wall and, gingerly, he placed one foot on it and pulled himself to a standing position. On tiptoe he was able to raise his eyes to the window and peer out.

The chair rocked forwards and backwards. He cracked his jaw against the wall, and a flash like an exploding star shot into his head, his neck and ended in his knees, which buckled beneath him. He clawed at the tiles to brake his fall, but found himself kneeling on the chair with his hands and forehead resting against the wall in a gesture of surrender. The crack on the jaw had impaired his vision. He closed his eyes and, breathing slowly, he searched his mind for the normal life he had lost.

He thought of his son and his wife and all those things that made up that normal life: watching Ben while he slept, his nine-year-old body sprawled in a careless fling of arms and legs; planning the next walk over the hills with him, or taking him to school, watching him leave the car, turn his head to wave at his father before mingling with the other children. Recently Richard had noticed that those turns of the head were diminishing. Soon he would be too big; too big to go school with his dad, too big for cuddles and laughter, too big for walks on the fells, and the time would have gone and the memories of the little boy just a song.

He and Nicole had been married for ten years. For him, and he liked to think for her also, the marriage had been an unqualified success. It had brought him an emotional stability he would not have imagined possible as a younger man. He thought that for Nicole, the marriage brought security and a man she loved to love. He had never asked her what she treasured in their union, but he did not need to. They no longer embraced or kissed when they met but the light in his eye was always reflected in hers. He had been hoping to catch a glimpse of that light through the window, to see a normal street with normal people like Nicole going about their mundane business. There was just a wall and a dank hole, a mere strip of sky visible above it. Richard raised his head and closed his eyes. He imagined himself to be in the strip of blue and sucked in drafts of air from some place far away, a place where his family lived, breathed and moved in freedom.

Another knock on the door. Onto his feet. Blindfold on. The sound of slippers flopping on the floor.

"You no want eat?"

"No."

"You want tea?"

"Yes please."

"Take."

Something light and round was placed against his hand. He grasped it and heard liquid being poured. The cup warmed in his hands. "How long will I be here?" His question sounded to him like an attempt to open a conversation in a dentist's waiting room, an attempt to reach out for human contact in the face of something unpleasant.

"Tell me what you see, yeah?"

"See?"

"Yeah. How you feeling?"

Richard breathed out through his nostrils. "Angry." He said it quietly so that the word sounded weak. "Confused."

"Confused?"

"Yes, confused." He raised one hand to his ear and made rapid circular movements with a finger. "You know, confused. I don't understand why this is happening. Why me?"

"Well - no speak good English."

"What do you want from me?"

"You want I have problem? No speak. Cover eyes, yeah?"

"They are covered. Why have you taken me?"

There was a silence. Richard had not been expecting an answer and he did not get one. The boy had been using the tactics he was familiar with at the university. Irrelevant information combined with pauses meant evasion – probably in any language.

21

"Drink the tea, yeah?"

The young guard's voice was now edged with fear. Perhaps he was feeling uneasy himself, uncomfortable carrying out his orders. The slippers made towards the door.

"Will you give me my watch?"

The door clanged shut.

"Please tell me the time. Please…the time, tell me the time."

Silence.

Richard slipped off the blindfold and sat down on the chair. Sipping at the tea, he watched his hands. They were flickering like the hands of a clock blocked by their own cogs as the battery ran dead. He was not ready to live timelessly, to have no perception of time's passage, to loiter unattached to both the immediate past and to the future. The absence of some regular and repetitive action to mark off equal increments of time would mean the end of his story.

He placed the tea on the floor, stood up, and sat down again while groping for some past experience he could draw on which might guide his reaction to his present situation. He found nothing but names and associations. There were pirates with wooden legs, parrots and hidden treasure. There was Patty Hearst, Natascha Kampusch, Aldo Moro and John Paul Getty.

He was on his feet, looking wildly around him. His heart was thumping. He needed to be in the strip of blue freedom outside the window, to feel the spaces and fresh air on his face, to relish the choice of going anywhere he chose. He threw himself against the door.

"Hey. Are you there?"

No answer. He banged harder.

"Are you there? I need my watch. Are you there?"

He raised both arms and hurled them at the metal frame.

"Hey. Toilet. Toilet again. Open door. Toilet…"

The key grated in its lock. The door opened. Angry eyes peered at him through a red and white chequered headscarf. A hand swung. A flash of light blinded him, and darkness descended. The slap in the face had caught him of balance, and he was on his back and holding his temple. The angry man coiled over and into his darkness. There was no flopping of sandals or smell of scent with its promise of happiness. This man was hissing his words and spitting garlic.

"Door open, blindfold on, you fuck. No forget. Blindfold fucking on. Understand?"

"Yes, yes, I get it."

Richard lay on his back like an upturned beetle. When the door slammed shut, he rolled over and got to his feet, telling himself to keep calm. Activity was the answer – release the adrenalin with repetitive movement. He took several steps forward and stopped at the wall. He spun round and walked to the opposite wall – three paces. He repeated the process between the other two walls – seven paces. Then he paced around the room in the largest possible circle without brushing the tiles – seventeen paces. That meant just over one hundred circuits to the mile.

He put one foot in front of the other and started walking. He decided to track the distance by counting the circuits but the questions that demanded answers presented themselves again.

"One, two."

What time of day was it? How long had he been there already?

"Eighteen, nineteen."

Why were they keeping him? How long would they keep him for?

"Thirty-one, thirty-two."

Was anyone looking for him?

"Forty, forty-one."

Had they told his wife?

Round and round he walked and after a time, his body went at its own rhythm. At a conscious level he counted the circuits. Underneath, he descended into extended daydreams. How long could he tolerate being alone?

"One hundred and fifty, one hundred and fifty-one."

He knew of people around the world who had survived years of solitary confinement.

"One hundred and sixty-nine, one hundred and seventy."

What was he afraid of? He sat down on the chair and whispered:

"The unknown? Have I not yet got over that hurdle?"

And yet Richard guessed that it was the unknown that disturbed him. He did not know the time of day. He did not know what the future held. He did not know who his captors were or what they wanted. Worse, he did not know who he was any more. All those hooks upon which he hung his identity – relationship, nationality, career and class - had been removed. With nowhere else to go and nothing else to do, Richard turned his eyes and ears inwards and drifted backwards to his childhood.

He was visited by several confused fragments of memory. Firstly came the memories of very early childhood: a beach and the warm sun, black planes flying low over him, and sand between his toes, the odour of the vomit blanket before it was soiled. Even now, fifty years or so later, the smell of car leather brought on nausea. Then there was the swinging of the hammock in the garden, the drone of bees and the smell of the flowers, and his mother carrying him into the kitchen in the washing basket. He recalled lying in his cot and watching the green tree swaying outside his room, the sound of his father's voice booming through the morning light: "Awake for the sun has scattered into flight, the stars before him from the field of night."

Richard knew that these fragments belonged to him but the precise points in time at which they had occurred collapsed into other and similar memories of very early childhood. Later, when his mind could make connections, his memories had taken their place in time. There was a house called Ashwood, a little boy alone, the heat of a coal fire on his face and a musty smell from the pages of the book on his lap. Richard was unsure who it was that memory brought to mind. Was it giving him an image of the boy he had been then or a picture of the 57-year-old man he was now? And the memory was changing with the turning pages of the boy's book. There was now an older man there, and there was a sense that both boy and man were floating above the carpet and a suggestion that the man had said something unpleasant because the little boy was crying. The image of the boy disappeared but the older man remained and he seemed to catch a stronger light. It was his own father he was remembering, and the day he told Richard that his mother had died.

The memories faded, and Richard was left hanging in the present. Most images of his childhood were shrouded in the dark wood and parquet floors of Ashwood and the feelings the name evoked. Since that time, Victorian houses had been associated with being alone, with the BBC Home Service, a sense of loss and with books, hundreds of books stacked dustily and unreachable on high shelves.

But did any of that matter now? Did his roots matter? His father's values had been crafted in another time. It had been a time of empire, of respect for king and country and of fair play, of doing the right thing and keeping a stiff upper lip. Richard had grown away from those values a long time ago. He had developed his own leaves, his own idea of where he was going, and to go there with imagination and curiosity. Being alive, Richard thought, was to be curious, getting ideas from the world around him and through the channels of his own intelligent mind. The world around him was the university and the discussions with fellow scholars about contemporary terrorism. He loved the cut and thrust of intellectual debate. There were those of his colleagues who thought the 9/11 attacks and the two Gulf Wars represented a new phenomenon in the Middle East that could only be understood in their 21st century context. Richard disagreed. For him, the sources, processes and issues that determined the course of the region could only be understood against the background of Middle Eastern history and civilisation.

A knock at the door brought him back to his present plight. Richard covered his eyes. The door clicked, and someone entered the room. Richard stood up, his head twisting from side to side like a deer that has caught the scent of the hunter. Light clothing rustled as if billowing in a breeze. The door closed, and the ensuing stillness revealed the delicate and shallow breathing of an unseen individual. Richard lifted his arm. He had a strong desire to reach out and touch the person, to replace the lost world of vision with one of touch and smell. He recoiled, struck by a need to retreat into his own world of darkness, to be invisible and on equal terms with the rustling presence.

"Who is there? What do you want?" There was a strained desperation in his tone so he repeated his questions on the breath of a sigh, "Please, what do you want? Who are you?"

Richard crossed his arms over his chest and waited for a response.

"Cigarette?"

Richard shook his head. There was a sound of a lighter scraping – once, twice, and Richard found himself wondering why, after all the years of their existence, lighters never lit at the first attempt. He found this useless speculation calming, gave him some control in a hopeless situation. There was a noise – a hiss like that of gas escaping or a snake threatening and a cloud of smoke drifting into his dark world. He had no idea what was to come and into the dark he repeated:

"Please – what do you want and who are…?"

"You," the voice said, "and you already know who we are."

CHAPTER 3

"All I know is that you've taken me against my will." Richard spoke in the familiar monotonous tone, without irritation or accusation, which he used when remonstrating a student for producing sub-standard work. The tone had been well practised, was designed to develop perceived objectivity when dealing with students and to separate the problem from the person. "You've forced me to miss an important lecture. You're keeping me from my wife, my child and my work. What is going on?"

Having put a slight questioning lilt to the word, "on", he took two steps backwards and leaned his shoulders against the tiles. Richard heard the man's hand alight on the chair back. The chair legs screeched as they were dragged over the floor and they settled with a wobble in the centre of the room. There was a creak, an exhalation of breath and the static crackle of cloth rubbing against cloth. Richard guessed that the newcomer had sat down and crossed his legs. The man seemed afraid of breaking the silence, and Richard was unwilling to intrude upon its quality of peace and contentment. He turned his blindfolded eyes to the light coming through the window, and his dark world became shades of red and yellow.

Richard folded his arms and waited. Only small sounds reached out to him: the slight kissing of lips as the man pulled a cigarette from them, the hiss of smoke exhaled from between the teeth, the stub hitting the floor. The man's heel ground the stub into the concrete, and a loud intake of breath suggested that a decision had been made.

"We are," the voice said, "the People's Democratic Party. But you know of our existence, I think." His voice was resonant and warm, and his words flowed and lingered in Richard's ear with vibrations of friendliness. "You have written about us in articles and books. If my information is correct, you intended to talk about us at the conference here. In many ways you're responsible for people like us."

Richard leaned towards the presence and thrust his neck forwards in a way that suggested his nose might identify the exact location of the speaker. Despite his blindness, Richard was developing a picture of the man. The source of this picture, this brightness, this intelligence, this approachable energy was contained and encoded in the voice.

"So, what do you want?" Richard said. "Why have you taken me from my family?"

His own voice sounded strange to him. Its pitch and tone had abandoned its cool detachment and found the unfamiliar territory of anguish, of desperation. Against the blindfold, he felt his eyeballs rolling and looking for answers in the dark. But the friendly presence sidestepped his questions by not responding, and Richard's words evaporated in the air between them. When they had vanished the voice continued with its own thoughts.

"Yes, you're partly responsible for us, you know? How are you responsible?" His pause was long enough for Richard to formulate an answer but too short for him to verbalise it. The voice seemed anxious to move on. "Because of what you taught in the past? Maybe because of what you wrote in the past? Perhaps because of the things you are doing now? You wouldn't remember. I'm sure you have forgotten…"

"You have lost me. What use can I be to you? I'm just an academic and…"

"And you are a teacher." The emphasis and tone on the final word contained an almost reverential respect that coloured the words that followed. "Have you ever wondered what influence you have had on your students? There may be many people out there whose lives have been touched and influenced by you – by a gesture, a look, a word or an action that you have long forgotten."

"So have you brought me here to discuss memory?"

"No, teacher, no, *ustazz*. But every action has a reaction…." The remark came with a hint of sadness and seemed to trail away into a daydream. Then he slapped his thigh and began speaking in a tone as jaunty as the one Richard used to adopt when reading "Mr Friendly" to his son Ben. "But you are right, *ustazz*. We have better things to do than discuss memories and responsibilities. You can help us in much more effective ways."

Richard wanted to smile at the man's tone and, despite his imprisonment, he found he had dubbed him, "Mr Friendly." But he managed only a flicker of the lips before realising that friendly expressions needed a visible reinforcement. Without that, he thought, you might as well smile into the darkness. The desire to retire still further into himself strengthened, and into the darkness he said:

"But what can I do for you?"

Beads of sweat were rolling down his forehead and temples. Absently, he wondered how long it would be before the sweat poured over the blindfold to soak his shirt. It was stifling in the room and his breathing, the remnants of his free life and identity, was loud enough to overlay everything except the two voices. Despite the heat he shivered. He was vulnerable, wanted to wrap himself round his life like a protective blanket.

"You are Richard Chambers, a well-respected authority on the Middle-East. You're a teacher and an academic and, I'm told, a sympathiser and not an apologist for Arabism. You might be a person who could make a contribution to our cause."

The words stung Richard back to life. He recognised his own voice stirring, the voice of the academic, the critical thinker.

"That depends."

"On?"

"On the cause and the contribution. The end does not necessarily justify the means."

He waited for a reaction but he was unable to interpret the silence which followed. Sweat was now running down his neck, and a pool was forming between his sternum and stomach. He straightened his back and pulled his stomach in. Mr Friendly said:

"On the cause? You know the cause. I've told you, have I not, that you predicted all this."

"So what?" Richard tried to keep the emotion from his voice but the last word flew from his mouth and emerged between the two men tipped with impatience. He wanted to sound the cool and calculating person he believed he was. In a more reasonable tone he said, "Why on earth can I help you?"

"Because…"

The voice withdrew into uncertainty, faltered and then vanished into the air. Not even a rustle of clothes disturbed the perfect stillness of the other's pause. Richard insisted.

"Because?"

He leaned forward, searching for the face, needing to observe the effect of his words. But darkness and silence rendered his words ineffective. He was the boxer in the dark, throwing his wild punches. He waited for his opponent to respond while sweat rolled down his stomach to the top of his trousers.

"I tell you what," said Mr Friendly. "You tell me why we've taken you. Perhaps it'd help if you gave me the last part of your talk."

The voice had come out of the thin air. No smack of the lips or clearing of the throat preceded it, but it was there, flowing in the air around him.

"You came to give a talk at the British Council, did you not? What a pity to come all that way from England with a prepared speech and not to give it."

Richard wiped away the sweat that was now forming a pool at his belt.

In the free world, he had rehearsed the plenary presentation until he knew most of it by heart. But the lecture belonged to a part of him he could no longer reach, and he had left his heart on the road somewhere between this place and his hotel. He could barely remember a word.

"Then we can do a deal," Richard said. "You tell me why I'm here and then I'll recite what I can remember."

"You can't recall your lines?"

"Stuff's happened," Richard said. "Other things are on my mind."

"Let me help you then," said Mr Friendly.

"The conclusion?"

"The conclusion."

"Then you'll tell me what you want and why you have taken me?"

"I will tell you."

Richard searched his memory for the lecture that events had so effectively erased from his mind. The British Council had announced their conference a year previously. The conference topic had come as a series of questions.

What are the root causes of Arab nationalism? How do these causes influence the direction and destination of any Arab nationalist sentiments? Are there similarities between Arabism and Western nationalism? If there are similarities, have these been adequately examined? In view of its Islamist connections, how secular is Arabism and can it be described as nationalistic at all or is it a spent force that can be disregarded?

In view of his work and expertise in this area, The British Council had invited Richard to come to the Middle East in order to give the opening plenary, and he had accepted. He decided to talk about the Gulf Wars and how they had influenced nationalist sentiment in the Middle East. Six months later, he had sent an extended synopsis of the lecture to the Council, and they had announced it in the conference programme.

Trying to remember his presentation now, however, was a bit like waking up in a dark and unfamiliar room and groping for his glasses. He decided to improvise, but the words faltered on his lips, had no fluency or rhythm.

"If Sadam had been allowed to succeed in his gamble, the UN would've followed the League of Nations into defeat and humiliation. And the end result would have been unacceptable. That is to say, the world would've belonged to the violent and the ruthless."

He paused. He had been trying to fix his eyes on those of the listener in order to gauge the effect of his words. The desire had been automatic. In taking up the pose of the lecturer, he had forgotten, for just a moment, that he was unable to see his audience. He turned his eyes towards his own feet.

"What's the matter?" said the voice from the air. "Have you forgotten your words?"

The pitch and tone of the voice contained a paternal concern that

29

grabbed for Richard's attention. He raised his head. In this place, in his darkness, the listener was taking control of the conversation. Unsure of himself, Richard allowed the other to prompt him.

"So tell us whether Sadam succeeded or not."

"No, he was not allowed to succeed, and a powerful coalition, an international force, was mobilised to remove him from Kuwait. But this force was revealing of a new and…"

"Dangerous?"

"Yes, a new and dangerous era."

"So Sadam was…?"

"So, after the war, Sadam was given permission to resume and continue with his distinctive style of government. In the last part of the twentieth century, the message was clear for all to read. The outside powers would act to defend their own interests. What were these interests? The most important were oil and markets, and the interests of the international community…"

"That is to say," interrupted Mr Friendly, "a respect for the rules of the US, is it not? But go on, you have not finished."

"Apart from this message, the people of the Middle-East had, in 2000, the power to make and shape their own destiny."

"So what happened next?"

Richard was reluctant. His words, so alone, seemed distant - even dishonest. The verbal expression lacked the conviction with which a look or expression could colour them. With no vision he was unable to see or even feel the impact of his words. And yet Richard knew that by finishing his sentences for him, the man was properly with him, was even able to read the shadows of his thoughts.

"Go on," said the voice. "Tell me what happened next."

"At the turn of the millenium, the governments and people in the Middle East had the opportunity to go the way of fragmentation; like Yugoslavia for example. At this time there were a variety of movements and many individuals who made it clear they would choose this rather than compromise on their religious duty or national rights. What happened in Lebanon could have become the blueprint for the whole region. Was there an alternative to this picture? One alternative was that governments and people could have united and urged for something more sinister and more powerful and more threatening for the West. That something was *jihad*."

Richard paused, expecting to be interrupted again. Or perhaps he was disgusted at his own rather hollow words. *Jihad* now had a new meaning. *Jihad* was not a combination of letters on the page and nor was it some interesting concept that could be examined at will like a piece of meat in a supermarket. *Jihad* was the presence in this room. It meant the sound of beating carpets, the smell of a filthy toilet, and the interminable, unbearable silence. Mr Friendly seemed to pick up Richard's thoughts and run with them.

"Urging for *jihad*, if I am not mistaken, had its own dangers, am I right?"

"Yes. The threat of *jihad* was enough. It was the threat itself that provoked the response of a new crusade..."

"That is to say the second Gulf War, if I am not mistaken."

"That is correct. Until the second Gulf War, the people of the Middle East could have decided their own fate. That is now a dream. The nightmare is that since the invasion and occupation of Iraq..."

"The western powers are now facing a *jihad* of their own making."

"Exactly."

Mr Friendly slapped his hand on his thigh.

"You see?" he said. "I told you that you predicted the rise of groups like ours. That is to say, groups engaged in *jihad* against the Western powers, those insidious whisperers who whisper in the hearts of men."

"We're not all devils," Richard said. "What do you want from me?"

"Have you finished your lecture? Have you nothing to add?"

Richard shook his head.

"You've missed a most important point," Mr Friendly said. "*Jihad* has always been interpreted in the West as holy war, an unlimited and religious obligation that continues until the entire world has adopted Islam. But we take a different view. The term '*jihad*' has the literal meaning of striving, more specifically, 'striving in the path of God' and we interpret this in a spiritual and moral sense."

"Or nonsense. What do you want me to do about it?"

"You can help us."

"I can?"

"You're famous and well respected. What would you do if you were in our shoes?"

"You can't win a war against those insidious whisperers as you call them. You can only talk."

"Really? And do you think that the US will listen?" His voice was animated, charged with a desperation of his own. "Do you think the US will tolerate anything other than a liberal democracy created in its own image?" The chair creaked. Richard guessed that Mr Friendly had moved, was now leaning forward in the chair. "There's no doubt that the US will try and create societies in this region that reflect their own. And we know that, for the US, democracy is good as long as it produces governments that the US deems to be acceptable. Creating their style of liberal democracy here will be difficult for them, but destroying it will be even more difficult for us."

At this point, Richard faltered. He was getting a glimpse of this man's impossible world, a world in which men might be prepared to give everything to achieve a dream. His own work was appropriate and scholarly, politically correct and backed up with evidence. Somehow it now seemed detached and distant, lacked the conviction of personal belief – was even redundant. Feeling under pressure, he retreated into familiar territory – the world-renowned academic questioning his students.

"And what do you suggest as an alternative? You call yourselves the People's Democratic Party. What is your brand of democracy? Tell me what it would look like?"

Richard stepped backwards and leaned against the wall. The tiles were cool against his back. He folded his arms and began formulating objections to Mr Friendly's explanations before he had uttered a sound.

"We need to regain control of law and order, throw out the foreign invaders and take control of our assets." The chair creaked again, clattered lightly as it tipped too far forwards. "When that is achieved, we'll set about developing our programme."

"Which is?"

"First, good governance, and then a democracy that'll emerge from the people. We want real and workable democracies, not shoddy imitations of the Western ideal."

Richard pushed himself from the wall and straightened his back. He had often wondered how it was that some people in history were so sure about what they wanted, where they were going and how they intended to get there. Trapped in his blindness, Richard lifted an arm and then let it drop. An arm's length represented his known world, and Mr Friendly was a long way beyond his reach. He was still animated, his voice full of energy, passion and self-belief.

"We've no interest in democracy operated by the few or by US puppets. Nor do we want democracy as a brand, a simple idea that people can be persuaded to die for as easily as they can be persuaded to buy a particular brand of washing powder. We want democracies which embrace every level of public life from the village to the presidency."

"Fine ideals." Richard's criticism was present in his emphasis on the second word. "But are they enough? I mean, what about religion? What part will it play?"

"We aim to reduce the role played by all religions in a way that you've done in the West. But we don't aim to destroy them. Islam has shaped our traditions…our identity even, and it underpins our culture. But we wish to develop a movement that embraces all religions, a movement that encourages love of country and local pride, an identity based as much on nationality as on faith. We feel and we hope that this notion of a separation between religion and state will be supported in the West."

Richard was suspicious of any talk of an ideal social order but he found himself admiring his adversary – even liking him. Or was it the fact that his almost perfect English made it possible for him to be himself and to feel at home?

"And the means? How will the end justify the means?"

"At the moment we've few alternatives. *Jihad* is a means to an end. We care nothing for personal survival. The material and human costs are insignificant. But don't think we care nothing for human life. What would you do? At the moment there's no other way than death – paradise in the shadow of the sword."

There was a long pause as if both men were gathering their thoughts for the next round. The door creaked open. Richard's stomach lurched when he heard the cold clink of metal on metal coiling across the floor in his direction. A cloud of garlic enveloped him and rough hands pushed down on his shoulders, forced him onto the mattress.

"No speak, you fuck. No move."

Something cold was fastened to Richard's ankles and wrists. Drawn up into a foetal position, he heard the man say:

"A day, a week, maybe two weeks. No move."

The Chain Man tightened the blindfold, removed Richard's shoes and socks and left the room. With his arms and legs chained together, Richard struggled to sit upright. He breathed a sigh of relief when he found that the chain was long enough for him to stretch his legs and lift his hands to his face. He sniffed at the air. There had been such a long silence that Richard wondered whether Mr Friendly had left with the Chain Man. He doubted it. His presence was there, a static of electricity crackling all around him, and then his voice, now mournful and resigned.

"So many of us have become desperate," he said. "But we're not all fanatics. We're not even all Muslims. It's a simple fact that whatever our faith, many of us came home one day to find our families killed in an air strike. No paradise awaits them, my friend. We're filled with rage and grief. There's no other way than death."

There was a rustle of clothes, and the sound of shoes clipping across the floor to the door. It swung open. The voice said:

"Welcome back, teacher. Welcome back, *ustazz.*"

The door closed.

Silence.

Invisible darkness, the voice of the insidious whisperer in his heart and Richard was unable to stop a succession of pictures and sounds from appearing in his head. It was the word, *"ustazz,"* which had ignited the touchpaper and thrown a light on these events from the past. Richard struggled with a sensorial storm. He plugged his ears with his fingers to smother the sounds and covered his eyes to blind them to unwanted images. One memory refused to budge. He was back in a place of dreams, back in the classroom and listening to another sound from long before.

"Ustazz, ustazz, ustazz, me ustazz…"

The boys have been simmering on the edge since the lesson began. It is Ramadan, and they are hungry and tired. With a frenzy of excitement, their bubbling restlessness has overflowed.

"Me *ustazz*, me, me, me…"

The disparate voices find each other through a magical tuning mechanism and rejoice for an explosive moment. From the relative safety of his cell Richard recalled the eyes glowing through hours of teachers' chalk dust. The dust is suspended in a wide shaft of midday sunlight that blazes through the open window and warps the air, shifts raised hands from their supporting arms and leaves them fluttering over the boys' heads like illusory birds in the desert.

Omar Khoury jumps to his feet and encourages his classmates to join him in a chant.

"*Uuu…stazz, uuu…stazz…*"

Omar is twelve but nobody dares challenge the leadership qualities bestowed on him by his great height and a warbling, croaking voice that suggests an early entry into the world of adolescence. The class rallies behind their leader and erupts. The chalk dust vibrates to the sound of their chant, a resonant and unceasing roar that rattles the blackboard and echoes through the door and into the cloistered courtyard.

"*Ustazz, ustazz, ustazz.*"

At the front of the class, Dicky is arched over the teacher's desk, his white knuckles kneading its surface while his eyes flicker and blink at the unfolding chaos in front of him. His appeals for silence are swallowed up in the din, and his face drains of colour and petrifies as he loses control. He looks between his feet and at the floor, searching for a weapon or a way out. From the cool shade of the courtyard, Abu Haida, the school caretaker, turns his drooping moustaches and hawkish nose to the noise, and sidles over to the open window. Framed like a puppet on stage, he bends his nose into the heat of the classroom and pecks at the scene in front of him.

"*Ustazz, ustazz, ustazz…*"

Dicky squints into the chalk dust and finds the eyes of a fair-haired boy in the front row. The boy has been watching events in silence and with eyes that hold suggestions of sorrow and pain. He has responded to his teacher's distress by crossing his arms over his shoulders and pulling his closed knees towards his stomach. The eyes of boy and man meet and immediately glance away but their brief encounter somehow revives Dicky. He steps round the desk to confront Omar Khoury. These two protagonists, wrapped in a hot and consuming sunlight, are standing nose to nose when the rest of the class falls silent.

Richard allowed his thoughts to drift along with the silence until they found their natural resting place in his cell. He was struck by confusion, doubtful whether this event had occurred at all or whether it was an amalgamation of several memories from that period in his life and distilled into one. He thought he recalled several class rebellions like that one, and most of them had been prompted by his youth and lack of expertise. He picked up his memory again and followed it back into the silence of the classroom. Some things had already changed. The boys seemed to have disappeared in a haze. The only thing Richard saw was the aggressive stare of Omar Khoury's eyes. The only thing he heard was the whispering but daring voice hidden in the serried ranks: "It's Owl Man."

A faint but rhythmic crack of cane on wood accompanies this pronouncement and the boys peer with frightened eyes at the spot by the door where the sunlight strikes the floor. A well-polished shoe, picking up the rays of the sun, announces the arrival of the deputy head. The end of his cane rattles against the door frame and sounds like a racing clock.

Half in and half out of the classroom, Mr Khoury's black suit is barely visible. A mantel of darkness, it drifts off his shoulders and back into the courtyard shadows. He takes a step forward so that the bright sunlight touches one side of his face, and his round head hangs in Richard's memory like a partially eclipsed moon in the night sky. The light side of the moon is glistening and pale, and is broken by a wing of black hair sweeping from the temple and coming to an abrupt and pointed halt behind the ears. A chubby cheek is punctuated with a dimple and gives the impression that he is smiling.

The class remains still, but the absence of noise is soon broken by coughs, creaking chairs and rumbling tummies. The eyes of the brave shift around the room, seeking to catch the eyes of the timid with expressions that dare them break the silence. Perhaps sensing this change of mood, Khoury strides into the room. His back and arms round over the black cane, which he clasps between both hands. Standing in the full glare of the sunlight, he leans forwards as though to balance himself against a strong wind and lifts the cane to one ear. His shouts are accompanied by movements of the cane arm which rises and falls with the pitch of his voice. Khoury is conducting his own words.

Both cane and pitch pause on an upward note, and Khoury freezes with his arms crooked over his head and with his words hanging in the air. The boys hold their collective breath and wait for the crescendo. Khoury's eyes sparkle while he raises his arms higher and then pounces on his prey. He steps forward and, grabbing the fair-haired boy by one ear, pulls him to the front of the class. The boy wriggles and struggles and appeals to his classmates. Khoury raises his cane further and shouts, "Khalid?"

The rising pitch on the final syllable suggests that the boy has broken his word or stepped over some previously agreed boundary. The expectation that hangs over the room also confirms that everyone knows the penalties for breaking the rules. While the chalk dust still vibrates to the sound of

Khoury's voice, Khalid lowers his eyelids, raises both hands and holds them palm upwards in front of his heart. Khoury lifts the cane and lets it hover at his ear. With a flick of his wrist, Khoury brings the cane whistling down through the air. The other boys collectively pull their heads into their shoulders as the cane cracks against the flesh of the upturned palms. Khalid snatches his hands away and slides them both under their opposite armpit, holding them against the vice formed by arm and body.

Khoury raises the cane again, and Khalid's hands follow. His eyes are now closed, and his bottom lip is pushing outwards like that of a water jug. The cane cuts down through the air. There is a whooshing sound, a flash and a crack as the cane finds its mark. A spasm runs through the boy's body but he keeps his hands in front of him while raising his head towards Khoury's with deliberate care. The class gasp when Khalid's eyes reveal themselves. They contain an expression of pained humiliation that promises tears and an insolence that promises to spill over into words of anger. The boys are holding their breath, waiting for Khalid to respond. The bell rings. Silent and cowed, the boys rise as one and file past the victim, through the chalk dust and the sunlight and through the door. Without a word, Khalid follows them into the shaded courtyard.

Thirty-five years on, Richard still heard the cane thwacking against Khalid's palm and it prompted a light film of sweat to collect under his hairline. While he chased the tail of the memory, Richard was aware of the residue of feelings of injustice. The boy's pain and humiliation still hurt him as it had hurt him then. At the time, he had hidden from this realisation by attacking the person who had carried out the punishment.

"That was very unfair," Dicky says, "you should be ashamed."

Both Dicky and Khoury are silent for several moments, their eyes locked together like the antlers of fighting deer. Then Khoury opens his round eyes wide, nods and begins chuckling in a way that says: *Yes, I was young and inexperienced once. Don't worry. I understand you. Let me help.*

Instantly, a look of doubt passes across Dicky's face. Perhaps it is the lowering of his jaw, or the widening of the eyelids that Khoury sees, but at that moment, he pounces.

"Let me remind you, Mr Chambers. I'm the deputy head. You are a volunteer teacher here and a guest in our country for one year, I'm told." He lifts the cane and lets it dance in the air to the rhythm of his words. "You must never speak to me in that tone again. I will not tolerate it. Do you hear me?"

Dicky opens his mouth, breathes deeply and then closes his lips over clenched teeth. Khoury lowers the cane and holds it against his thigh.

"Good. Now I happen to like you, Mr Chambers. Let me explain something to you. Mr Khoury says that punishing one punishes them all. What does it matter who you choose?"

Through the chalk dust and the window, in the world outside, Abu Haida is hovering nearby, and a group of children are examining the wields that are appearing on Khalid's palms.

"Mr Chambers, please look at me while I am taking to you. Thank you. Now, Khalid was as responsible as all the other boys for what has happened here. Moreover, Mr Khoury saw you needed help, you know. The war's excited them and don't forget that it's Ramadan. You must understand that you're a Westerner, and Westerners mean America, and America means Israel to them. Mr Khoury's not surprised they make trouble for you. But you are new here and you have a lot to learn. And you will change the world?" Khoury interrupts himself with a barely suppressed laugh. "Please, don't try and lecture me on your English rules about fair play, Mr Chambers. They are out of place in our society. The boys are used to hard discipline. It starts at home, is reinforced at school and continues into the work environment. To take anything less than hard and decisive action would be seen as weakness, you understand? I repeat; there is no place here for you notions of fair play."

Khoury allows his face to darken. He takes a few steps forward and points a thick finger into the folds of Dicky's shirt.

"And you know, Mr Chambers, you mustn't let your personal feelings influence your judgement. You are sweating."

Khoury reaches into the top pocket of his jacket and pulls out a handkerchief.

"There," he says in a paternalistic tone, and Dicky takes the handkerchief and holds it to his ear like a flag of surrender.

"Why do you look so uncomfortable, Mr Chambers? Such things don't go unnoticed. What things I hear you say. I mean relationships between young boys and the teachers who care for them. Yes, such things as closeness are tolerated as long as you stay on the right side of the line. You must not cross the line. You must stay away from Khalid. Don't let him pull you down with him."

Khoury's eyes sparkle with delight. He begins chuckling again, and his dimples depress still further to give the impression that he is having a thoroughly good time.

"Yes, yes, of course you don't know what I mean, do you? Well let me tell you, shall I? I mean the boy and his family are bad. They are mongrels – part Palestinian and part Armenian - and they don't belong here. You'd do well to remember that before you get involved."

Khoury raises his hand to silence any possible objections and then reaches out to snatch the handkerchief from Dicky's hand.

"Have you finished?" His voice was still paternal and caring. "Yes? Good. I see you are in distress and disappointed, Mr Chambers. Well, you have reason to be. The boy will let you down in the same way that Mr

Rifkin has let you down. Our esteemed head master has already shown poor judgement by choosing Khalid to play Androcles. But what do you expect from such a man as David Rifkin? Not a person known to be able to separate work from pleasure, as I'm sure you are aware. He's ill again I hear. Such a pity, don't you think? Our school play has become quite an event in the educational calendar. We must make every effort to make sure the play is a success."

Khoury bends his knees, raises both arms and shrugs his shoulders.

"Rifkin has made a big error of judgement. His choice of play is wrong, don't you see? The Arabs are at war. They are fighting and dying now on the Golan Heights and in Sinai. It may be that we will also join the fight. You have seen out planes protecting us, haven't you, Mr Chambers? I tell you this. The people are not ready to be sympathetic to Androcles, his lion and any notions of Christian goodwill."

He lowers his arms and accompanies his words by beating the cane against his shoe.

"And tell me Mr Chambers, has the boy learned his lines for you?"

He pauses, watching the cracks of uncertainty appear in Dicky's face.

"No, there's no need to answer. I can do that for you. He spends all his time on the football field, doesn't he? He is idle and good for nothing. Discipline is the only thing he understands. You will regret your choice. Mr Khoury can't answer for the consequences. He has washed his hands of the whole thing."

In order to emphasise his words, he swings the cane under his arm and wrings his hands together.

"Mark my words. The performance will end in disaster."

He lowers his bottom jaw and moves it from side to side, grinding something real or imaginary between his teeth.

"Take this as a friendly warning, Mr Chambers."

He turns sharply, slips the cane out from under his arm and steps through the door and into the courtyard.

In the twinkling of an eye, these fragments of memory were gone but chained in his prison cell, Richard saw Khoury as he halted in the shadows. His cane was still twitching in his hands while he searched for new victims.

Richard lay back on his mattress, crossed his chained arms over his chest and wondered at the freshness of memory. The memories themselves were not unexpected. After all, he had willingly come back to the place where it had happened. Until then, those events had lain, fading images, at the extreme edge of his peripheral memory. He had believed he was disconnected from it all, had long since cut the umbilical cord. But he had not.

Richard screwed up his eyes, pressed the lids together in an attempt to crush the unexpected. The memories, so freshly revitalised by the sights and sounds of the city, had come with associated feelings. He thought he had buried them. They had not gone away. It seemed that they had been waiting in this prison cell for him to come and collect them. And now they were under his skin, vibrating like an old wound deep inside him.

BBC News Online

Fears for British academic

The Foreign Office says it is concerned for the safety of a British national who has gone missing in the Middle East. British Council and Embassy officials have been unable to contact Richard Chambers but did not comment on Palestinian reports that he had been kidnapped. Chambers' chauffeur-driven car was found abandoned shortly after he left his hotel to drive to the British Council offices. Several journalists and aid workers have recently been kidnapped in Gaza and the West Bank. All have been released unharmed.

Chambers, 57, has held the chair of Islamic History at the North of England University for the past three years and was in the region to attend a conference at the British Council.

"We are currently unable to contact him and are concerned for his safety," a spokesman for the British embassy said in a statement.

A Foreign Office spokesman in Jerusalem says all the main Palestinian militant groups have called for Chambers' release.

Details of what happened are sketchy. Police said four gunmen were seen in the vicinity of where Chambers' car was found. Security forces have set up checkpoints and are searching for the academic.

CHAPTER 4

Richard lost count of the number of days he lay chained on his mattress. The passing hours of one day merged into the passing hours of the next. Day and night were marked by the changing temperatures and by the moon's light which gave the tiles in his cell an iridescent quality. Sometimes, in the dead of night, Richard thought he heard the sound of waves cascading over rocks somewhere in the city. The unbearable solitude was broken only by the appearance of his guard when he needed the toilet and at meal times when the guard brought a water bottle and flat bread filled with pieces of cheese. One day, Richard said:

"Please, it's too hot. I've got a headache. Do you have a fan?"

"No understand. No speak." He sounded sullen, but Richard was learning to accept the boy's moods by now. He might be having girlfriend problems or perhaps it was his hormones tormenting him. But later, the guard brought a fan and placed it on the floor by the entrance. He even laughed.

"Cool, yeah?"

The fan was whirring and the air was deliciously cool to Richard's face.

"Oh-Lo-Oh, Oh-Lo-Oh," said Richard, his pleasure at receiving the fan riding his words.

"Life is good."

"Happily ever after in the sunshine..."

Richard was sick of these old hits, and tired of his own thoughts. He was desperate for human contact, even if that meant connecting with his kidnappers.

"You want family, too?"

As he said these words, Richard regretted them and, despite the blindfold, he thought a shadow fell across the room, and with it came the uncomfortable silence that can descend on a large group of conversing people. Eventually the guard said:

"Family?" He uttered the word as though it represented a concept beyond his reach. "What you do with family? You look to Man U. You listen Beatles. You go for walk with wife and kids in Abbey Road. You know what is family for me? We look to the rubble and we look to the checkpoints and the guns. How many rubble and how many checkpoints and guns must you walk through before you come to place where you feel nothing – nothing - not even for kids?"

Richard had never before heard his guard so talkative. He had been quick to anger too, and when the door clanged shut, Richard was left wondering whether the anger had been used as a smoke screen to cover some other emotion. He lay back on the mattress. For the rest of the afternoon, he drifted in and out of sleep. Whether awake or half-awake he was in a troubled place where random thoughts and dreams merged and moved in his head while the fan hummed in his ear. It was an image of Khalid that haunted this half asleep dream.

He and the boy are sitting in silence in his room. The powerful sunlight is filtering through the mosquito nets and peppering their faces in pinpricks of light and shadow. Khalid is rubbing his damaged palms with his fingertips. The boy's fingers are delicate and slender like the rest of his body, and like his slender face with its arched eyebrows and the cheeky grin, the shock of fair hair. Dicky is allowing his gaze to dance around his room, to touch on its practical furniture, the oil stove that would barely penetrate the cold in winter, and then to brush the boy's arms, the football he was holding, and his legs. Dicky's face is crowded with random movements that never quite settle into expression: a flicker of eyelids, his brow creasing and uncreasing to passing thoughts and feelings, his eyes finding the boy, embracing him, glancing away. Khalid is reclining in the chair, feet together, knees drawn up and with the football in his lap. His head is resting in his hand while the other arm, soft, pale and delicate is hanging over the back of the chair. Dicky is beyond the boy's peripheral vision, making rash promises of support while allowing his eyes to linger on the skin of the boy's arms, the curve of the shoulder and the elegant neck.

When he woke up and away from this dream, Richard was struck by a momentary but shattering glimpse of how he must have appeared to the boy – the yawning gulf of age, culture and experience that separated them.

One day, the young guard returned to check the fan, which was making unhealthy noises. Without a word, he ripped the plug from the wall and took the fan with him out of the room. Richard lay back on the mattress, his face breaking out in pinpricks of perspiration. City sounds drifted in through the window: klaxons blared, voices shouted and there was the screeching of an ambulance siren, which brought him the comforting thought that someone needed help more than he did.

He closed his eyes to sleep. Once, he woke up from a dream and thought he heard Sandra again. Maybe it was a shrill voice from the world outside but he was sure he heard her question, felt her doubts.

"Are you queer, Dicky?"

Richard stared at the ceiling of his cell. Had he been queer or had his love for Khalid been a one-off experience? At the time, doubts as to his sexual identity tormented him and they had certainly accounted for his awkwardness with Sandra. Richard took a long breath of resignation while powerful memories of that evening came back to him. He saw Dicky in his room. He was glancing at his watch, peeping through the adhesive tape and mosquito netting at the play area below and waiting for Sandra to come and seduce him. Pressing his right cheek hard against the window, he looks at the edge of Abu Haida's private pleasure. The caretaker's oleander is a blossomed blessing for each boy who passes through.

Behind him the radio has already crackled and hissed its way to life, and Dicky plays with the tuner, chasing the stations with the dial as they dance in and out of earshot. There is a boom as he traps a voice. It is a full, rich, brown voice that resonates from the mahogany case of the radio itself, and its vowels are silky and smooth like chocolate melting in the mouth.

This is the BBC World Service. Here is the news at 17.30 hours GMT. Heavy fighting has erupted again between Arab and Israeli forces along two fronts.... The entrapped speaker begins to break loose, and makes burping noises before apparently ducking his head into a bucket of water. *To the south, Egyptian...forces...broken the Israeli line...of the Suez Canal...*, and the voice retreats and hides behind a spluttering hiss.

Dicky pours another glass of *arak*, tops it up with water and watches the combination rise in the glass like billowing clouds. He raises the glass to his nose, closes his eyes and breathes in the licorice odour. He then tosses the contents into his mouth before replacing the glass on the chest of drawers. The vibration kick-starts the radio back to life. It reacts to news of the war by setting up a howling lament, singing for a while before fading away to a monotonous hum. Dicky stares at it, refills his glass and floats over to the taped windows on a cloud of licorice.

Recently disturbed oleander petals are lying like blood spots on the sand beneath the school gateway. Someone has passed through, but there is no sound of footsteps on the staircase, nothing to suggest that it is Sandra who has arrived and that she is on her way up to see him.

The sun, serene and splendid, hangs low over the city, and Dicky follows its dying rays as they surge red through the window and reach the most hidden corners of his room. The unmade bed, its sheets upturned and crumpled, is crimson-warm and sexy as silk.

The radio tinkles back into life, before retiring to a lingering and singing buzz. There is a rat-a-tat-tat of knuckles, an extended SOS signal, beating out on his door.

"Dicky? Dicky? Are you there?"

Sandra's tone is conspiratorial and it hits Dicky like Midas' touch.

"Dicky?" The door knob turns while her knuckles rap on the door, and Dicky mouths Sandra's name. It comes and goes on an irritable sigh.

The door opens, and an odour of rich-sweet perfume billows into the room like a gas attack. Dicky flounders in the face of this testimony to her efforts, this threat of her intentions, but before he has the chance to put on protective clothing, Sandra charges. Her bangles and bracelets rattle, her bosoms bounce and vibrate, their nipples straining through a blue T-shirt and pointing at him like accusing fingers.

"I thought you might have forgotten our date." She places her arms akimbo, flings one leg outwards and wags her head. "I see you've locked yourself in your own little world again."

The use of the word "again" contains a suggestion that Dicky owes her something, and that she has come to collect her dues. Although this suggestion is buffered by half-closed eyes, which twinkle with an expression of mock suspicion, Sandra is not taking any prisoners. She steps towards him to take him by the shoulders and kiss him. With his back to an imaginary wall, Dicky sidesteps, matador-fashion, and grabs at the *arak* bottle.

The mahogany voice booms and soars, dips and falls to a deep-toned but watery buzz. Her offensive thwarted, Sandra retreats into the chair at the coffee table. She shifts her position several times while the muted radio voice gurgles its way to an extended silence. In that moment of reprieve, Dicky strides over to the window and looks at the free world outside. The sky is closing in, the slanting rays of the sun have paled but there are deep-red clouds pressed one against the other.

Sandra fingers the top button of her T-shirt, unfastens it and then flicks back the collars. Noting that Dicky is still preoccupied with the outside world, she forces her chin into her breast bone and surveys the wide expanse of flesh beneath her eyes. Apparently satisfied, she leans forward and talks quickly. Her words overtake those of the radio announcer in a race to capture Dicky's attention. Her fingertips run like a spider from one breast to the other - faster and faster they move to the rhythm of her voice while her eyes, concentrated and focused, are those of the boxer waiting for an opening.

"Don't you like to be touched? You seem to be one of those people who dislike physical contact. I can tell what you're like, you know. It's the way you move and the way you remain motionless – the way you hold your head." She watches his face change as a number of thoughts pass through his head. He glances at her and then looks away and back at the clouds. Very low he whispers:

"There's a difference between touch and invasion of privacy."

"What was that, Dicky?"

He half-turns towards her, lets his gaze brush hers before turning it away to look towards the floor. He shakes his head. It is a signal to her that his remark is not to be taken seriously. The expression in his eyes is dark and contemplative, but Sandra is not looking at his eyes. She is leaning so far forward that she is almost resting on the balls of her feet and getting ready to spring.

"Human beings were made to touch each other, Dicky. You must know that." She lets her fingertips move across the surface of the table rather like a blind person interpreting Braille. She lifts one of her arms and searches for his eyes with hers. "Put your hand around here, just above the wrist. Your hand will curl around the shape – like a duck to water. It won't bite you know. Try it, Dicky."

Dusk has come and gone in a moment, and both are now wrapped in a veil of warm and perfumed night. He looks up and their eyes lock. "Try it, Dicky. Touch me."

Dicky remains motionless but Sandra refuses to call off her attack or allow him to break eye contact.

"Some people might say that there's no difference between touch and impact. Are you one of those, Dicky? You're wrong you know. There's touching and there's being touched. That is what matters and that is what I want you to do. Don't you want that too?"

Sandra looks for a movement or a sign that her words are finding an opening in his reserve and hitting home. The mahogany voice is still spluttering through the news bulletin. The voice becomes hoarse then crackles away to settle on a rising whine. At first, its low pitch whispers like the wind, is warm like a blanket and then it squeals in a way that resembles a pig about to have its throat cut. A few seconds go by – moments in which speech is prevented – moments which absolve him from further comment.

The radio dies, and a curtain of silence falls between them. Dicky steps over to the coffee table and sits down with a care that suggests he does not want the curtain to stir. He presses his shoulders hard against the chair back, stretches his legs under the coffee table, and circles the glass in his lap with his hands. Sandra is following his every movement with eyes that assess and judge.

"Don't you like women, Dicky?"

In response, he raises the glass to his lips and tosses half its contents into his mouth. He appears to throw the *arak* around his mouth, let it find every taste bud on his tongue before swallowing it on a breath.

"Of course I…"

"Only there are so many queers about. You never can tell these days. Are you queer, Dicky?"

45

Sandra never removes her eyes from his face. One eye watches him with an expression that suggests she has found him guilty and issued a sentence. The other eye is awash with tenderness. Before she can verbalise her conflicting feelings, the radio voice finds itself again.

Sandra straightens her long black hair with her hand. She lets it come to rest on her bosom.

"No? Then prove it and touch me, Dicky – please?"

He gets to his feet, rolls around the chair and treads purposefully to the chest of drawers. He switches on a wall light and refills his glass. Some of the *arak* splashes onto the wooden surface near his sleeve but he appears not to notice. He navigates his way back to the coffee table and drops into his chair. He leans forwards. He places his elbows on his bent knees and runs his hand through his hair, not looking at her.

Suddenly, he is staring towards the darkened windows and peering into the darkness over the city. A sound is penetrating his room, an animal sound of terror that gets louder and louder until it becomes a metallic wail that pierces the stillness of the night. A window rattles, someone screams, and the fear that is vocalised finds its place in the eyes of the two of them. The wall light in Dicky's room flickers and dies. Both he and Sandra jump to their feet and look for comfort in the eyes of the other.

"Air raid," Sandra shouts and she rounds the coffee table and throws her body against his. They stand clinging to each other and both look through the window and into the darkness and dangers outside. She has an expression of triumph in her eyes. He has no expression at all – just a stare into the darkness.

Richard's guard returned when the room began to darken, and the day turned to evening. He unlocked the padlocks on Richard's feet and hands and helped him to his feet. The guard guided him down the corridor and ushered him into the toilet and locked the door. No sooner had Richard finished washing than the guard was banging on the door.

"Hurry. Not too long in toilet, yeah?"

Richard replaced his blindfold and tapped on the door. A key was turned, his arm was taken.

"Don't you have any brothers and sisters?"

"Two sisters, yeah?" His voice was full of joy. "Two very beautiful sisters. Asma she gonna be doctor, yeah? She want save life. Ayah she is teacher. They take care of the little brother."

"Like you take care of me?"

"Yeah – they teach me. Love is everything, yeah?"

"That's what they say."

"We are very…how you say…?" He put the palms of both hands round Richard's forearm, intertwined his fingers and squeezed.

"Close?"

"Yeah, we close."

The next question came out before Richard had the time to consider it.

"They know what you do here?"

There was a tug at his arm and the boy pulled him down the corridor towards his room.

"Do they know what…?"

The last words were smothered in an explosion of breath as the boy pulled at Richard's arm.

"No speak now. No speak."

And Richard returned to his chains, the edge of eternity and the darkness of reflection. During these sleepless nights he found that it was much easier for him to remember his childhood and adolescent development than the events leading up to his capture. He guessed that in looking back over his life, he found the security that he did not have in the present, something sure that he could hold on to. Surveying his early life, he was gripped by a confused series of memories. These were as bright and as alive as hilltop beacons, but like beacons they were surrounded by a vast darkness of lost time.

One such beacon of memory is that hot summer day in the garden at Ashwood. He is standing at the end of the driveway and peering down the road that runs under the railway bridge. The road is full of silence and the sorrow of emptiness. The little boy tells himself that his father's car will arrive before the next Pullman steams over the bridge. By nightfall, when the Pullmans have all passed by, he gives up hope. By that time, his birthday is nearly over. Maybe his father will come next day.

Now, curled up in the foetal position, Richard reflected that the death of his mother had broken his father's heart. As a coping mechanism, he had thrown himself into his work. An acknowledged authority on language acquisition, Lionel Chambers had been an early convert to the notion that children were equipped from birth with the neural prerequisites for acquiring and using language. In an attempt to reject previous theories that tried to explain how children acquired adult language, Lionel first turned his attention to the imitation theory. His early studies proved that even when children tried to imitate what they heard, they were unable to produce sentences that did not conform to some inner grammatical pattern. Nor did he hold with the reinforcement theory and he showed that attempts to correct a child's language were doomed to failure. He demonstrated that children did not know what they were doing wrong and were unable to make corrections. In his later years, he devoted himself to the study of deaf children and how they acquired communicative ability. His research on sign language was crucial in the attempt to understand the biological foundation of human language acquisition and use. His conclusions were that these were not dependent on the ability to produce and hear sounds but on a more abstract cognitive ability which accounted for the similarities between spoken language and sign language.

The success of this groundbreaking work brought Lionel modest fame. He was in great demand at conferences. He was also in demand at home, but Richard's earliest memories of his father were reduced to vague moments that had lost their place in time. As Dicky grew older, his father's greatest influence on his son was that of absence: absence of demonstrative love, absence of apparent interest, absence of someone to look up to.

A man of few words, Lionel never read the books that other fathers read to their sons. His mother had done that. Richard retained only dim memories of his mother: the softness of her bosom, the warmth of her lap, and the rhythm of a poem spoken on sibilant breaths of tobacco smoke. He suspected that the poem had been one of hers, one that she had never committed to paper. His father once told him that poetry had always been her passion, but it was in her later years that she began to write down what had already developed in her head.

In the morning, his guard returned. Richard said:

"It's cold at night. Do you have a blanket?"

The boy was sulky and uncommunicative.

"No speak."

He accompanied Richard to the toilet. On the way Richard said:

"I like what you say about sisters. Maybe one day I will meet them."

"No speak, yeah?"

"So, what you do with your life?"

"I wanna go Manchester – see Rooney play before he go to Real Madrid."

"You think he go to Real Madrid?"

The guard guided Richard into the bathroom in silence. A few minutes later, when they were on their way back to his room, the guard began speaking – fast and nervous like a presenter anxious to get the words out before they were forgotten.

"There's always speculation and when other big teams are talking about you it's nice that you're talked about. But as he said many times before, he a United player and he very happy here."

"You read that?"

"Yeah - on United website. We want to create history."

At the door to his cell Richard rubbed his stomach and said:

"Tummy bad. Need fruit."

A minute later he was back in chains. The door closed. The key turned, and Richard faced the featureless desert that was the day ahead.

Random memories and reflections passed through his head. Both his mother and his father had made a living out of words but they had chosen different ways of running with them. His father had taken the academic route but his mother had found ways of using language in the most creative of ways. She had been a pioneer in broadcasting at a time when broadcasting was virtually closed to women. Her articles and political commentaries were in great demand, but in her late thirties she began to lose interest in journalism and began writing the poems she had always wanted to write. Nonetheless, by the time of her death in a car crash in 1959, she had become a role model for newswomen everywhere. A volume of her verse had been published posthumously, but Richard's father said he had never been able to read them.

When Dicky was deemed old enough to understand, his father had opened himself to reveal his feelings about his wife. It was a once-in-a-lifetime event. In a matter-of-fact tone, his father said that he and his wife fitted together like two pieces of a jigsaw puzzle and that separately, their lives were unintelligible and pointless. Both professionally and emotionally they complemented one another, and when she died, half of him went with her. He would never recover from his wife's death and he did not want to. At one time, he had considered suicide.

A knock at the door. Blindfold on. A few seconds later the door opened and the guard entered.

"I need toilet," Richard said.

"Not now. Eat."

"Yes now. It's urgent."

"Later."

"It's urgent."

The guard knelt down beside him and unlocked the padlocks.

"We must be quick," he said and helped Richard to his feet. Richard felt the man's hand guide him through the door and into the corridor. It seemed to him that the boy's touch was full of compassion and love, and in a burst of gratitude he half turned, grabbed the hand and squeezed it. There was a sharp intake of breath, and the hand twisted itself free.

"Be quick in toilet," he said.

A few minutes later the guard took him back to his chains but when Richard pulled up his blindfold, he saw a blanket and some slices of orange on the plate with the cheese and bread. There was also a new fan purring by the door.

The hours passed and for most of that time Richard was lost in space and reflecting on his past. The absence of a mother through death and a father through career had left Dicky with a sense of abandonment. This was reinforced by a series of nannies who were always fussing around but who never encouraged any emotional development in their young charge. The discovery of books was a turning point. He idolised William Brown, and swaggered with him to the woods and made hideaways, fished for minnows and climbed trees to collect birds' eggs. He even took William, his outlaws and his disappointment with adults to junior school. With his imaginary pals he played the fool until he received the punishment and rejection he was expecting. With no guidance from home, he felt that in this way he was in control of his world.

The adult Richard had long since forgiven his father and although the little boy was still disappointed, Richard had him under his arm and occasionally told him: *It'll be alright. Look at me. This is what you have become. Don't you like what you see?*

As the light began to dim, the young guard came and took Richard to the toilet.

"Can you bring me a book?"

"No book allowed, yeah?"

"A newspaper then, a magazine, a…"

"No read. No read."

"Then bring me a pen and a piece of paper so I can write, yeah?"

"You want write?"

"Yes, please."

"I ask, yeah?"

And then he was back in the room and facing another night of reflection. When it was dark, he heard someone moving outside his room. There was a knock on the door and a voice asked:

"You cold? You need more blanket?"

"No, thank you."

"You hungry?"

"I'm not hungry."

"You turn off fan?"

"I turn off fan."

There were no more sounds or voices, and Richard lay back again on his mattress remembering the dawn of his self. Allowing his mind the freedom that his body was denied, he collected all those fragments of memory that remained for him to savour.

As a teenager, he progressed to the absolute certainties contained in the books of G.A. Henty, Rider-Haggard and John Buchan and devoured their tales of right and wrong, and the belief that good always prevailed over evil. This belief was tarnished when prejudice came knocking on his door one evening in the shape of irate local parents. There had been a spate of vandalism in the area. Someone had been slashing bicycle tyres, and Dicky, who was innocent of the crime, was the chief suspect. There was no evidence, they said, but Dicky was a loner, someone who sloped around the neighbourhood with a penknife hanging from his belt. Dicky, they pointed out, had no mother and his father was often absent. Clearly, the boy was being raised with no discipline and no sense of right and wrong. He was found guilty without trial because there had been nobody there to defend him.

He had returned to his books but found that the certainties they contained were no longer so certain. It was only later, when he was studying at postgraduate level that he moved away from the position which saw knowledge and human values as somehow indisputable, timeless and objective. Instead, he made a seismic shift. Knowledge was a matter of opinion, a social construction, and everything was relative and nothing was certain.

Thirty-four years later, lying on a mattress in his cell, Richard was struck by confusion and doubt. His current situation created an emotional need for something sure and eternal to hold on to. In this time of trial, relativity was not enough.

One morning, he awoke to the sound of urgent knocking. He fumbled for his blindfold. Several people walked in.

"Sit up."

He struggled to obey the command, struggled to come to terms with the present again. He guessed that three, perhaps four men had entered the room. Their whispered voices were fast and low and urgent like the remnants of a bad dream. Someone grabbed at his hands. He heard a key slide into the padlocks and his hands and legs were free. Fingers fumbled and tightened the blindfold.

"Need toilet. Quick," Richard said.

Soft footfalls disappeared from the room. The door closed but Richard knew that someone was there, a presence filling the room like the Holy Spirit. Into the darkness Richard said:

"Need toilet. Please – quick."

The unseen presence began to speak, and his words reached Richard like hammer blows to his bladder.

"We have decided," Mr Friendly said, "we have decided on your fate. When all is said and done, we must all die some day."

It had occurred to Richard him that they might take his life but now as the warm urine soaked through his trousers and trickled into the mattress, he felt the essence of his being quivering on a thread.

BBC News Online

Fears grow for missing Briton

It is now more than two weeks since the academic, Richard Chambers, disappeared on his way to a conference. It is feared that he has been abducted, but there is still no clear picture of who might be holding him, where or why.

Chambers was taken hostage by masked gunmen as he was driving to deliver a lecture at a conference. Kidnappers have abducted dozens of foreigners in Gaza and the West Bank but none has been held so long as Chambers.

A Foreign Office spokesman said: "The longer it goes on, the more concerned that we become. He is incarcerated, and what that must be doing to his mental state and his general health, we have no idea."

CHAPTER 5

Richard plucked at his blanket, wrapped it beneath his buttocks and around his lap and lay back on the mattress while the urine dried cold against his leg. Mr Friendly signalled his stubborn presence by humming a tune, and Richard struggled to come to terms with his fate. Until now, he had somehow managed to accept his situation. The word "kidnapped" explained everything and somehow it acted as a barrier to further thinking. Imminent death was another matter. At a stroke, his future had been removed. There would be no more time to put of till tomorrow those things he could do today. With no more time to waste and no more time to kill, it seemed to him that time itself was now a vast cloud swirling over him, and he was waiting for it to disperse.

How would his captors deal with a man with a death sentence hanging over him? Were they going to let him eke out his last hours in peace? Would they try and make it pleasant by offering him a last meal, his favourite food as the thing to look forward to, an edible barrier to everlasting darkness? He could not even say what his favourite food was and doubted his ability to stomach anything in his last hours. Would it have time to digest before they cut his head off? Was a plate of pasta or shepherd's pie adequate in the face of the eternity of nothingness that surrounded it? Perhaps he should ask for a return to his first food, a simple glass of milk. That might round things off nicely.

With his future denied to him, Richard tried in vain to force his mind back into the safety of endless memory, but he found that the hanging cloud prevented him from connecting with those beacons of his personal history. Nor did his present have much meaning. What was the use of experiencing these endless days of squalor and despair if he would never be able to look back on them? What was the purpose of living in this bleak room, in these silences, in this time when night and day had no real meaning if he would never be able to recall it or talk about it to Ben and, perhaps, his grandchildren?

He had an overwhelming and recognisable need to take his questions to some higher being, throw them at his feet and say, "Deal with those and then get back to me." This need had been an ever-present companion in his earlier life, something he had befriended soon after his mother's death when his father insisted that he attend Sunday school.

Dicky had been attracted by the idea that God cared for him and wanted to hear his prayers and understand what was on his mind. So Dicky prayed and unburdened himself of feelings that he barely understood: grief at his mother's death, guilt that he was responsible for his father's absence. Dicky also learned how to praise God in prayer and to thank Him for all the wonderful things he had given to him, especially the succession of nannies who took care of his everyday needs. He learned to tell God how sorry he was for the bad things he had done and he learned how to ask God to take care of his father, whom he loved.

By the time he became an adolescent, Dicky had grafted God onto his life and he called himself a Christian. The graft had not outlasted his mid teens and the rediscovery of his father, and although remnants of Christian belief still moved inside him, he had long since given up on higher beings.

If God had been the first to go, the next was a belief in absolutes of any kind: absolute truth, absolute right and wrong, and absolute good and bad. This process had begun during his A-levels, continued during his university years and took off when he embarked on the slow process of making a name for himself in his chosen profession. In the beginning, Richard had always sought out the opinions of eminent others in an attempt to win their blessing before submitting articles or giving important lectures at conferences. At some point, and he could not recall when, there were no others whose opinion mattered. He became the authority. He was that higher being to whom others sent their work to seek his blessing.

Richard pushed himself up to a sitting position. Mr Friendly had stopped humming his tune. He was holding something and turning it in his hands.

"Yes, we must all die one day, *ustazz*." Mr Friendly's tone was light, almost jaunty. "We try to kill time but time ends up killing us, does it not? But your day has not come yet."

A tremor ran through Richard's body and it was followed by a feeling of gratitude towards the man who had delivered the message of salvation. At the same time, the cloud lifted from his head, and his world flooded back with all its particles of no limits, of infinite distances and choices, of desires and memories that made life both meaningful and beautiful. Breathless, as though he had just arrived on a mountain top, he said:

"You are not going to condemn me to death then." He was nodding as he spoke, but his mind was elsewhere – on a place bathed in sunlight, on happy futures, on him, his wife and Ben, and on his sore ankles and the newly found movement in his arms and legs.

"Perhaps," Mr Friendly said, "you've just experienced something more significant than death. After all, the moment of our passing is one experience nobody can have."

"Sorry?"

"You've experienced despair. The prospect of death forced you to live through moments without hope, a meaningless existence with no past, no present and nothing to live for. I wanted you to experience this in order for you to understand it."

Richard nodded along with Mr Friendly's tone but his were not movements of agreement. He was far too happy to be alive and free from his chains to pay much attention to what his captor was saying. He allowed the man's words to pass in and out of his mind without interpretation but the gist of what was said remained in the air like the smell of stale urine on his leg.

"What can it matter to you what I have or haven't experienced?" Richard asked. "And why would you go to such lengths for me to experience despair?"

"Because telling is never enough. Unless you have experienced despair you can never understand it, grasp its implications."

Richard wondered how his captors saw him. Was he, to them, just a middle-aged academic with his head in the clouds and divorced from all reality? His joy at being alive was laced with slight irritation. Knowledge was knowledge whether it came from books or from direct experience. But direct experience, he admitted, had one insoluble problem. It came with the built-in distortions of memory.

"And why," he said, "do you want me to experience despair?"

From outside came a now familiar thump. Someone was beating a carpet. As if in response, there was another thump and then another and each synchronised with the others to set up a succession of regularly spaced beats.

"Because only then can you know what it feels like to be a refugee. The despair you experienced is the same despair felt by many of our people after the destruction of Palestinian society in 1948."

"At least they were alive. Can you turn the fan on please?" Richard's voice was edged with a mockery that the other chose to ignore. Richard heard a movement and a second later, the fan sprang into life.

"But think about the life they were living," Mr Friendly said. "You have read that 700,000 people were exiled from their homes and homeland. You have read that most of these were driven out by direct military action by Israeli troops. And you know that even today, Israel refuses to allow

Palestinian refugees to return to their homes. And Israel refuses to pay them compensation even though this is required by international law. Yes, you have read this but you can only imagine what it feels like to live a life in exile."

Outside the air was now alive with the sound of carpets being beaten, and they set up a sound like war drums.

"And all that happened sixty years ago." The mockery that had edged Richard's voice now turned into a derision that did not surprise him. As a historian he was suspicious of any attempt by individuals or groups of individuals to memorialise the past and use it as evidence in support of an idea or a theory. The past was absent by its very nature. Most memories were therefore accompanied by nostalgia or by nightmares; but they were sometimes useful for propaganda purposes. Eye-witness accounts of atrocities were very powerful. "Are you telling me that you are old enough to have seen and experienced all that?"

There was a slight pause, an intake of breath that hovered in the air and announced the departure of jauntiness from Mr Friendly's tone.

"It may have been sixty years ago," he said, "but my father never let me forget those who escaped the massacres, who left their homes and towns. It is a story of anguish, lament, anger and political demands for justice. But what haunted him until the end was the look of despair on the faces of the refugees."

Several seconds passed – seconds filled with the thumping carpet beaters and the purring of the fan. Richard felt it cool to his forehead and to his newly freed legs and arms. Then he heard light footsteps and felt the warmth of the other man's body bending over him. Mr Friendly touched his arm. "Listen, *ustazz*." The hand remained in place long enough to tell Richard that he should remain silent. "My father was fourteen when an Israeli unit entered the city he was working in. He'd gone there to sell fruit but he was rounded up with other young men and detained by the newly-formed Israeli Government. They were deemed a threat because, before falling, the city was one of the few Palestinian towns to resist the takeover. My father was separated from his brothers and family and sent to a place called Jalil. Every prisoner was interviewed, numbered and put in a pen. It was, essentially, a concentration camp. For two days they got no food and were forced to dig their own latrines. With forty men crammed into a tent, conditions were very bad. He spent nine months in detention and all the while having no contact with his family. My father was lucky in many ways. He had distant relatives over here. They came and took him and gave him shelter in the camp. But worse news was to follow."

Mr Friendly's pregnant pause prodded Richard's irritation, and the first symptoms of resentment declared themselves. The man had already tricked him into believing he was going to die – and all to prove a point. Now he was manipulating his feelings.

"Yeah, very interesting but…"

"Very interesting?" interrupted Mr Friendly. He was touching Richard's arm again in a way that suggested there was no malice in the words he was going to say. "Is it only interesting then that his family was massacred along with a hundred others in the village of Deir Yassin? Is it only interesting that at the age of fifteen, he was alone and living in a refugee camp in a foreign country that didn't want him. Is the word, "interesting" the best word you can find? If I were talking about a Jewish family in Germany in 1943 wouldn't you find it outrageous?"

Richard's resentment now invaded him, surged up from his stomach to stiffen his muscles and redden his face.

"Yeah, yeah - all very sad." Richard wondered at his tone, at its callous rejection of a human tragedy. He was sympathetic to the Palestinian situation, and the injustices against them did outrage him. But at that moment, in that place, in his darkness, he refused to be emotionally blackmailed. "Look. I've asked you before. What has this got to do with me?"

"Everything, *ustazz*." He spoke sharply, scolding Richard for his apparent indifference. Mr Friendly turned away and coolness descended on Richard as though a cloud had drifted over the sun. "You know our story, *ustazz*. You are a known as being sympathetic to the cause. We've decided to use your academic celebrity to help us fight our enemies. I have to tell you that this decision is not in my hands. There are those amongst us who have reached the point where hating is the norm, and fighting serves no purpose other than fighting itself. They had other options for you but for the moment I've convinced them. I'm also a pawn in the game, you see?"

"So what were these other options?"

Mr Friendly remained silent but Richard sensed his presence by the chair, felt his eyes watching his inner struggle. The thumping of the carpets had ceased and through the window came the distant roar of traffic. The city was settling itself into its routine. Eventually, there was a click and a scraping sound, and a few moments later an intake of breath followed by a long purposeful exhalation. Mr Friendly said:

"To use you as a human bomb and blow up a bus?" The questioning tone and the pause which followed suggested he was allowing Richard to develop an image of this option, to see it in its full horror before rushing in with other possibilities. "Behead you? Let you go? Have you denounce the West? Perhaps we could release you in exchange for the release of our brothers in prison. The possibilities are almost endless. Perhaps we could adopt a combination of all of these options."

Richard heard Mr Friendly's heel stubbing out his cigarette on the floor. He said:

"Your friends came up with interesting options. Do I have a say in the matter?"

"I wouldn't recommend interfering."

"So – you think you can use my modest academic celebrity to help your cause. And what do you hope to achieve?"

"A point made against Western methods, but not against the West itself."

"So where's the point of conflict?"

"It's a conflict of ideologies. I've told you before – a differing view of what it means to be free and democratic."

"So why do you intend to use me?"

"Because at the moment, the enemy commands the most effective weapon against us. You know what that weapon is? It is control of the world media. We have been demonised as sub-human and brain-washed terrorists. And through the media they can provoke and organise the herd instinct of its peoples to defend their way of life from a bunch of fanatics who threaten their life-style. You write books. You're a sympathiser to our cause."

"But not to terrorism."

"Which is what exactly?"

"The indiscriminate killing of innocent men, women and children."

"Like the bombing of Dresden?"

"No," Richard said, his tone brimming over with intolerance. "That was a war situation."

"Nonetheless, in order to defeat a terrorist state, the allies were forced to resort to terrorist methods."

"No, it was a question of survival."

"Or of the ends justifying the means, perhaps. Since we have no state of our own, we don't have the luxury of being able to declare war on our enemies and fight them. We can snipe at them, wear them down and make life uncomfortable and dangerous for them."

"You mean you can murder them with a clean conscience."

Richard was astonished. Given the precariousness of his situation, his words were provocative and his tone was daring. They also contained Christian convictions he thought he had left behind him. Perhaps those convictions were part and parcel of his cultural value system and woven into his very fabric. And yet, he no longer feared for his life, at least not from this man. The vibrations of friendliness he had noticed in the man's voice still lingered and now deepened into an intimacy born from a partnership in the search for truth. Each was trying to enable the other to see the world through his eyes, and this involved neither submission nor dominance.

"Doesn't it depend a bit on what you mean by murder?" Mr Friendly said. "Take the *Belgrano*, for example. You know that war was never declared against Argentina but it didn't stop your submarine commander from killing several hundred sailors, did it?"

"And Thatcher got the criticism she deserved for that. That's the point isn't it? We were free enough to voice our disquiet and…"

"But murder," interrupted Mr Friendly, "was still committed, was it not?"

"So what do you want from me? We can talk about this for hours and go round in circles."

"You are right, *ustazz*. This is why we need you. In the end, right and wrong depend on the effectiveness of propaganda. Once an enemy is identified, propaganda offers proof of his depravity in order to persuade normal young men to kill. And that persuasion is frighteningly effective. Why else would a loving family man drop napalm on other people's children?"

His tone was flat, the question rhetorical but in the pause that followed, Richard felt the pathos in the thoughts that were producing the words. He decided to let Mr Friendly deal with his own question.

"And the propaganda outlives the purpose to which it was put. Take the Kamikaze pilots, for example. It's likely that they were brave young men doing their duty to save their way of life, but even sixty years later, I hear the propaganda machine saying that they were not free men. They were brain-washed products of the Japanese war effort, and their lives were not freely given. And this is how our suicide bombers are portrayed, is it not? You can help us, *ustazz*. You can help us because in time, right and wrong depend on those who write the history books - on people like you, my friend."

"You expect me to sacrifice my work…to be a martyr for your cause?"

Richard heard a sound and felt the man's warm shadow break over him.

"The truth needs no martyrs, *ustazz*," he said, fumbling at Richard's blindfold and removing it.

The first thing Richard saw was the fan by the door. Then he saw a man beside it. Richard had been expecting to see a representative of global *jihad* standing over him. Instead he saw a man in a pair of shorts and T-shirt. A cigarette was angled in the corner of his mouth like a Hitler salute but his head was wrapped in a *kuffieh* so that only the central part of his face was visible.

Mr Friendly leaned sideways and turned the fan down. Then he sat on the chair and took up the pose of the talker – one leg thrown over his knee, the body leaning backwards and sideways, the eyes crackling with amusement and with the excitement of discussion.

"Can you think of a better idea that that – a better way of using your presence here? I've told you that I'm a pawn here almost as much as you are, but I do have some control. The West and its teachers have taught us the language of freedom and now you will see the results."

Mr Friendly rose from his chair and walked to the door. Half-turning towards Richard he said:

"You asked us who we are and I've told you. What we need from you first is a brief account of your life. We need details that can be proven but which only you and a few others would know. It is a sort of authentification – proof, if you like, that you are who you say you are."

"What if I refuse?"

Mr Friendly faced the door. His hands were clasped behind his back, and his head was lowered. Richard was certain there was no expression on his face, not even an expression of disagreement or disapproval. It was as if he had not heard his question or if he had, he had chosen not to listen. He said:

"You will then read a denunciation of the West and Western policies in this region. This will be for the world to see, you understand?"

"And if I refuse?"

Mr Friendly span round.

"If you refuse," he said, "then you'll be in the hands of the haters, those of us who put the blame for everything on the West and its people. For them, only wickedness can explain your actions. Satan is in you, and our duty is to hate you as we hate Satan. They have no interest in you as an individual. Their world is split into friends and enemies. Listen to me my friend. You are free to refuse my requests; but if you do, I can do nothing to help you. You will die."

CHAPTER 6

The matter-of-fact tone Mr Friendly had adopted sent a running shiver across Richard's shoulders. Burying his face in his hands, he closed his eyes to the impossible choice of cooperation or death. A few seconds – maybe a minute – passed. He was aware of Mr Friendly leaving the room but when the door closed with a clang, Richard lifted his head and rested his chin on the tips of his fingers. He raised his eyes to search for a higher being, a judge to whom he could make the case for each option. He almost heard the Almighty bellowing down from above: *Follow your conscience but don't forget that you have a wife and child. Your life is not your own.* Richard shook his head in a gesture of rejection.

He shuffled his buttocks and, pulling the blanket from under him, he flung it over the plastic chair to dry. Richard lay back on the mattress and cupped his hands behind his head. He decided to inspect his problem by looking at the strengths and weaknesses of each option. He soon found that attempting to consider either his own death or compliance with the demands of his kidnappers was like trying to imagine his parents having sex. There was a wall around the topic, and on the other side of the wall was a place called no-man's-land.

Richard closed his eyes. The morning heat had already dried his urine but its acrid smell persisted. Outside, a continuous and distant roar suggested that life in the city was in full swing. Inside, the hum of the fan was having a hypnotic effect, and Richard felt himself drift towards the peace of sleep.

He was suddenly awake and alert to the sensation that he was not alone. He had not heard the door open but he knew someone was in the cell. He groped for the blindfold.

"Leave it," commanded a woman's voice. "I want you to see the human being inside me."

Richard pushed himself into a sitting position. There was a black robe and a white head scarf at the door. Both were unremarkable and might have belonged to thousands of other women from the region. She was everywoman, a person at whom he would not look twice in the street had he not seen the face on the night he was kidnapped.

"How can you see the human being with a blindfold? There are enough blindfolds in the world. Look at me please."

Richard did as he was told. The shawl covering her head also hid those indicators of age – the neck and the hair – so his attention was drawn to the eyes. Both were partially hidden by the eyelids, which dropped downwards like teardrop-shaped curtains. One eye was shining outwards with passion and enthusiasm. The other was turned inwards as though deep in introspection.

"So have you come to offer words of advice or female pearls of wisdom?"

Richard heard the sneer in the tone of his voice, but the woman waited while its effect dissolved in the air. She barely moved, could have been a statue had not the hem of her robe picked up the breeze from the fan and stroked the floor. Her hands, clasped over her stomach, were invisible under the sleeves of her robe. When the moment was right for her, she said in an even and controlled voice:

"Women can offer many things. Above all we offer this. We know and understand the human need to have control over life and death. It is the women who control life through childbirth and motherhood. The closest men can get to this control is through killing."

Her English was faultless, and the words rode on a tone which encouraged reflection rather than debate. Then, in a more conversational voice, she went on:

"And I know what I am talking about. My husband is dead. I have had three children. Two girls are also dead." As she spoke, the introspective eye seemed to turn a half-circle while the other eye filled with light. "But the boy is alive. He is my life. He needs me now, and I am here to…"

Her last words faltered and were carried away in the hum of the fan.

"But I have another passion. I have the Hope and Flower School. My father founded it in 1984. He was one of Father Peter's pupils. I wanted to see you because they tell me you knew the priest."

It was the enthusiastic eye which now found his face. It glowed with a fearful but expectant light. Unsure as to what to say Richard was non-committal.

"Knew him? I met him a couple of times."

He shrugged his shoulders and shook his head. He did not want to contradict her but he needed her to know that he would be reticent on the topic. The woman nodded but said nothing for a long moment – sensitive, perhaps, to any need he might have to retrieve the priest from memory. Richard needed no such pause but he wondered at his reluctance to admit his admiration for a man whose integrity ran like a joyous peel of bells over the past. That integrity was out of place in the sordid surroundings of a prison cell but Father Peter's power of presence was such that he somehow permeated all of Richard's recollections of his stay in this country so many years earlier.

At that time, Father Peter had been setting up a school for the youngest victims of the region's conflicts. His main concern was the psychological mark the constant wars were having on the lives of children. Their right to survival and protection had long since vanished and, if nothing changed, they would take the same road as their parents. Father Peter faced a huge financial problem due to the *Yom Kippur* war in particular and the economic instability of the country in general. High levels of unemployment were making it difficult to raise funds, and the sustainability of his work was under constant threat. Without the support of the ex-pats, it would have been difficult to run the school at all. His positive spirit was unrelenting. Even Sandra had been almost impressed by him. "You might think you were in the presence of someone holy," she had once said, "until you knew he was queer."

The tail end of a shout from the world outside drifted through the window and into his cell. The woman was still silent - aware of the noise and clamour of memory that she supposed filled Richard's head. When enough time had passed for her, she nodded her head.

"My father always said that we Palestinians are the victims of the victims – he meant the holocaust victims. But we work towards his ideal that children must be educated in the philosophy of peace rather than in the mentality of killing, retaliation and war. We integrate the laws of peace and democracy and empowerment of women programmes for older children. My mission is to continue the work of Father Peter. My father learned a lot of things from the priest. In turn my father passed on the guiding principles of the man's life to me."

"You've lost me. What guiding principles?"

"To be strong; to go ahead; not to surrender, and to know what you want and don't want, what you need and don't need; and to be frank with oneself. I would give anything to speak to Father Peter now."

"That makes two of us," Richard said. He reflected that only once, since releasing God from his life, had he sought advice from one of His representatives on earth and that man had been Father Peter. The need to lay his current dilemma before this same man was now urgent and compelling. "What would you ask him?"

"I would ask him for his support. Our school is near the wall – there are checkpoints and sniping towers. We are threatened with demolition. I would ask him to give me hope. Tell me about our inspirational father. What kind of man was he? Tell me what you can remember."

Richard shook his head and pursed his lips. It was his way of telling her not to expect too much.

"I sought his advice."

"About?"

"About feelings I had towards one of my students."

"A boy?"

Richard nodded. The ease with which this admission came out surprised him. For years he had conversed neither with others nor himself about his youthful infatuation. But in the presence of the introspective eye, his own embarrassment appeared trivial. In the face of death it was meaningless.

"Did you get the advice you wanted?"

"Yes I got it."

"Good advice?"

"Yes, but at the time, it went over my head. It was some years before I saw the value of his remarks and the truth of his insights. I think he shared with me the benefit of his own reflections."

"Reflections on?"

"On the inner conflict his own sexual orientation brought to him."

The reference to Father Peter's homosexuality was received by a lowering of the head and a moment of silent remembrance.

"An orientation which killed him?"

"I'm not sure," Richard said. But he knew that after relocating his school to Switzerland in 1985, Father Peter died of a pneumonia-like illness. A man ahead of his time, Richard guessed that he had died of AIDS before AIDS had a name.

"What type of man was he?"

Richard looked over her shoulder and into the past, focused on the afternoon he had sought the priest's advice. Dicky has tracked Father Peter down at the English Club. A relic of colonial splendour, the club squats on the edge of the Western quarter, and at a place where the energy of the city runs its course and trickles into the desert. Father Peter is standing under the portico, which extends along the wall as a colonnade. His arms are at full stretch, and his cassock falls in vertical folds from under them. He is swivelling his head from one side to the other, aiming his thick, plastic-rimmed glasses along his arms and to his fingertips, which brush the columns on either side of him. The black glasses appear as a natural extension to the priest's black hair, and both resemble carefully chosen accessories to the black of his cassock.

The priest is beside him. His eyes are flashing through the lenses of his glasses.

"About one metre eighty-five." The words are pronounced with deliberation. "If I am within five centimetres either way," he adds, "I tell myself I'll have a lucky day."

Pressing his hand into the small of Dicky's back, Father Peter whisks him up the steps towards the club's entrance. He weaves his way under the portico and across the marbled walkway in a manner that suggests he is avoiding obstacles. Just before the two men arrive at the entrance, the priest dances across Dicky's path, stretches out his arms and puts his hands on Dicky's shoulders.

"Today I step over the red bits. Tomorrow I step over the black bits. If I succeed I shall receive God's blessings. Life's a lottery, dear boy." His eyes, shining balls of intelligent light, scan Dicky's face. "Let's go inside. You look like you need to talk."

Richard blinked away the memory and hesitated. He reflected that, like most human beings, Father Peter was a mass of contradictions. Despite this awareness, Richard had a need to peel those complexities away until a few core words remained. He said:

"He was eccentric, perhaps superstitious."

Nothing changed in the woman's face. Richard guessed that something more was expected.

"He was sensitive."

The woman's passionate eye glowed with satisfaction. His comment seemed to hit the right spot and it pleased him.

"He was open to the needs of others. His personality invited you to pour out your troubles."

The woman said nothing but the expectant quality of her silence told Richard she required more of these positive remarks. He made a sound designed to suggest that he was thinking while he raised his eyes, scanned his memory until he saw himself struggling for words in front of Father Peter.

"I need your advice," Dicky says, "about Androcles and my feelings…"

"Yes, I can see something is troubling you."

"I've been following you all afternoon."

The priest steps backwards, lets his eyes flicker from Dicky's toes to his head.

"Have you been walking after me? In this heat and in those jeans, dear boy? For God's sake, get yourself a cassock."

Dicky is propelled through the door and into the heart of the club. The clubroom is dominated by three French windows, which are open and startlingly white against the lawn outside. The billowing net curtains, the polished floor and the photographs of royalty are bathed in a yellow-green mantel of light.

The lawn rushes down to a pool, surrounds it, and hurries on to skirt the tennis courts before halting at a high wall. Much of the grass has continued its momentum to form high tufts at the base of the wall but nothing prevents the wail of the *muezzin* from wafting over the wire-topped battlements. The sound drifts through the club windows to whisper in the ears of the flower arrangers, the dart players and those who send their post through the diplomatic bag that, *this land belongs to us. We belong here, and you do not.*

Inside the clubroom there are two groups of people as separate from each other as planets and both circled by an atmosphere that discourages outsiders. A number of individuals look on, gravitating first to one group and then the other but joining neither. The group under the chandelier consists of middle-aged men. They are leaning forward at the waist, and holding their glasses in front of them. In the centre of the circle stands the American ambassador, a large man in a red jacket. He is reaching the conclusion of his lecture on the war and its consequences for the region. His voice rises with his fist. He pauses when Father Peter appears, and the assembled crowd allow their heads to follow his and settle on the energy field that has arrived in their midst.

The other group is looser and consists of straw hats and dresses, all flowers and bosoms. One woman raises her eyebrows to greet the priest but her face collapses to a scowl when she sees Dicky.

"Whoops," says Father Peter and, pushing hard in Dicky's back, they swerve away and into the path of a waiter with a tray of drinks.

"Whoops again," says the priest steering Dicky towards the window. "Still persona non grata, dear boy? Well, if you're of the opinion that the ambassador's like a character from a Maugham novel and you decide to share it with the man's wife, what do you expect?" Father Peter glances at Dicky's profile and seems to assess his mental state. "Don't be surprised if you are removed from the embassy cocktail party list, dear boy, but do count yourself lucky. She doesn't want to cause another fuss after what happened today." Father Peter smiles at Dicky in a triumphant way. I know something you don't, the smile says, and I'm waiting for you to acknowledge that. "Dear boy, there was a most terrible scene…really most terrible."

"He had a childlike quality about him," Richard said. "And he loved gossip and scandal. He told his stories with the enthusiasm of a schoolboy trying to impress his peers. And although he was a very special person himself, he had the ability to make you feel special. When he asked for my help it was impossible to refuse. He made me feel that I was there to help him rather than the other way around. It was his essential humility, you see?"

"He asked you to help him?"

"Yes, he was worried about the headmaster of our school and asked me to intervene on his behalf."

"And you carried out his wishes?"

"I did my best at the time."

A smile lit up the woman's face but there was no further verbal response. Perhaps, Richard thought, she found great comfort in simply being with someone who had done a favour for the priest.

He scanned his memory again, found father Peter staring through the windows and at the struggle a sunshade was having with a gust of wind. The priest shakes his head in a way that suggests either disbelief at what the wind is doing or that the scene he is about to describe might be incomprehensible to reasonable people like Dicky.

"Your Reverend Rifkin was here. And we all thought he was ill. Ill? He was blotto, dear boy – as pissed as a fart. He drifted in here about lunchtime on a cloud of whisky fumes and went straight for the American ambassador - asked him why, given that the Nazi jackboot was now on the foot of the Jews, the Americans were supplying Israel with napalm. Didn't they know it was burning women and children to death? Dear boy, it was such a dreadful scene. Rifkin was taken away and packed off in a taxi. The man needs our help. So, what can we do?"

They pass through the nearest window and emerge on the terrace, which is separated from the pool area by a balustrade. Father Peter rests his hand on Dicky's forearm.

"There's one person I can trust." He squeezes Dicky's arm. "You must speak to Wilfred about it. He and Rifkin go back a long way. Will you do that for me?" The smile that follows contains the absolute belief that he knows Dicky will do what is asked of him. "Good. I knew I could count on you."

He sidesteps away and, in one swift movement, he corrects the angle of the chairs, flattens the tablecloth, and shifts the sunshade. Finishing with a flourish he raises his arms over his head, places his clasped hands on his hair and surveys his work.

"Sit here, dear boy. I'll get you a beer. I am most grateful to you."

A gust of wind swoops down and lifts the tablecloth before catching the priest's cassock, which rises like a black balloon.

"Oh, my word!" He lifts his chin and swivels his head, his nose sniffing at the air. "Chalk dust. That's what it reminds me of. Chalk dust. There's a sandstorm on its way and it's getting nearer." He floats away but Richard still heard his words as the priest disappeared into the heart of the club. "Just mark my words, dear boy."

Sitting on the mattress in his tiled cell, Richard reflected that both he and the woman needed to mark the priest's words now. They were both in need of a father confessor even if their requirements were different.

"And would you," the lady asked, "like Father Peter's advice now?"

Richard realised it was useless imagining the advice of a man who was more than twenty years dead but this lady needed confirmation of her belief in him. It seemed churlish to disappoint her.

"Of course."

Richard looked again over the lady's shoulder and into the past. Now that he had said these words he wondered how they influenced his memories of the man and the conversation they had engaged in that afternoon by the pool. Was he imagining it all – the judged advice given as impersonal musing? Was he now building a monument to a man who had never existed?

He saw himself sitting in the shade of the umbrella and surveying the pool area. The pool itself is disturbed by constant gusts of wind that stroke its surface. Along one edge of the pool, five young men are sitting in a row on sun beds. All five are competitively muscled, with the restless and careless limbs of the trained soldier. They are staring at the sky in the manner of superstitious people waiting for an omen when excitement animates them and they break ranks. Thighs are slapped, arms are raised, and fingers are pointed. The vapour trails over the distant mountains form Z-shaped patterns in the sky, and the exploding missiles that seek out the planes linger as star-like splashes of brown.

One of the soldiers holds a clenched fist in the air, contorts his face and yells, "Come on, c'mon, c'mon." He allows the final syllable to develop into a roar that is taken up by several of his mates.

Father Peter emerges from the sliding doors as the five soldiers fall back on their sun beds in one parade-ground movement and lift their beer bottles as one. The priest deposits two glasses and a bottle of Watneys on the table.

"A gift from home, dear boy."

He lifts his cassock in a feminine motion, sweeps it under him and sits down like a swan landing on the water. Father Peter allows his eyes to flicker to poolside, but he never lets Dicky escape from his peripheral vision. Even at rest, a part of the priest's body is constantly in movement and gives the impression that he is responding to some tune in his head. His chin rests on one fist and then the other, and he crosses and re-crosses his black leather shoes.

"How's the play going," he says. "An excellent choice if I may say so – but I wonder how well the notions of love and compassion will go down in time of war. You have a good boy playing Androcles, I hear."

He removes his glasses and stills his body in the manner of a diver about to leap into the water. He then searches Dicky's face for a movement that might give him a clue as to the emotional state of the listener.

"I'm all ears, dear boy."

"You work with children," Dicky says. "Have you ever had any…?"

Father Peter raises his hand and holds it, palm outwards, at the level of his heart. The gesture brings Dicky's question to an end before it has found the time to realise itself in words. A smile comes to Father Peter's lips, and he lowers his hand.

"Yes, dear boy, the number of pupils at the school is growing as the current war goes on. As you know, this is one of the most violent areas of the world. I need constant funding. Don't think I'm a saint. I'm just a fund raiser." His tone is light-conversational, but his concentration on Dicky is absolute. "And the chances of raising money are the same as missing the red bits on the marble or miscalculating the distance between the pillars. Sometimes you win and sometimes you lose. So much is out of my control. I can only do my best. Many of our boys are so traumatised they are unable to speak."

From poolside there is a roar, and the soldiers are on their feet and making some kind of war dance, pointing into the sky and cheering. One of them shouts, "Got him, ye-e-es," and they all punch the air as one and flex their shoulders. This performance misses the priest entirely. His head is now tilted to one side, and he is studying Dicky's face with the same attention that a person might give to a favourite book.

"The American ambassador has been most helpful, but…" A muttering waiter in a white jacket appears and circles the table at which they are sitting. His circuits of the table shorten. Eventually, he springs forward, plucks at the beer bottle and the glasses and closes the umbrella. Lifting it from its holder, he holds it like a spear at his ear. He prods his finger at the club wall.

"We close. We close. Sandstorm coming."

The priest does not move, and the waiter trots down the steps to poolside.

"But the school is always on the point of closing down. We need money and plenty of it. Love is not enough, dear boy."

A minor row is going on beside the pool. The soldiers have risen to some kind of threat, have formed a circle and are closing in on the unfortunate waiter, who is trying to close the umbrellas. The words "wog" and "Abdul" drift up to the terrace on gales of laughter.

"Hey *Ram Jam*," someone shouts, "bring us some more beer and some of those BFCs – you know, big fucking crisps. Now run off with you."

Other white jackets materialise from nowhere and converge at speed on the pool. Things are turning nasty, but Father Peter behaves as though he and Dicky matter, and the rest of the world and its troubles have ceased to exist.

"You know – love and the source of love fascinate me and keep me going. Love has many sources, don't you think? It can be sex, love of humanity, and sometimes of God? For a man of the cloth there's no doubt where love comes from."

At poolside, rough talk and bad language are flying about. The waiters now outnumber the soldiers and are waving their arms and gesticulating as they begin a circling manoeuvre of their own. Sensing defeat, the soldiers stand in a line, pectorals and trapezoids flexed but making sideways movements towards the clubhouse.

"As for sex being the source of love, it depends what you mean by the word 'sex.' If it means the desire to possess and enjoy another human being then that reduces love to combat and involves conquest. This will make lovers insecure and afraid of loss."

The soldiers are now marching up the steps to the terrace. Their paces are punctuated by bursts of laughter. One of them clenches his fists and makes to turn round and charge, but a companion puts out his arm to restrain him.

"There's a vast amount of sexual feeling which never finds sexual expression in terms of orgasm. For example, love of another person's wife, unrequited love and love of someone much, much younger than you and even love of children…"

The military men linger on the terrace and stare at the darkening sky in a way that suggests it has somehow disappointed them. Then, heads down they amble past the priest and the young man, skirt them at a distance like iron filings beside a magnet.

"But sex - the desire to possess, the concentration of efforts on orgasm - prevents love from being as creative as it could be. Is the need for sex always a part of love?" The look in the priest's eye suggests that the question is not rhetorical but requires an answer. Then he shrugs. "Only we can say that. Only we know what we think about when we masturbate."

The priest and Dicky exchange a look but before Dicky can utter a word, Father Peter has picked up the thread of his thoughts and is running with them.

"But I think — I really do believe - that love and sex can be kept separated. Passion is a yearning for the unattainable, isn't it? Then perhaps we are happiest when the object of our love is out of reach, when love and sex do, in fact, part company. Perhaps, if you can manage to love at a distance, you will remain as free as the wind."

To reinforce the priest's point, the wind strengthens still further, picks up particles of sand and gives the world a washed-out look. Father Peter grabs for his glasses, slides his face into them and clips them over his ears. "And now, dear boy, we must be leaving."

A waft of eucalyptus follows them into the club house. The members have left, and the room is full of waiters. Fresh from their victory over the soldiers, the waiters have thrown off their servility and are now sitting around in whispering groups. Dicky and Father Peter leave the building under a cloud of sullen stares and mutterings.

Richard said, "Essentially, Father Peter's advice was this. If you can love at a distance, you will never be weighed down by chains of jealousy, and nothing will prevent you from doing whatever you want to help the beloved and watch the person grow and develop. He said that with no concerns to tie you down you will be free to dance for joy under the stars."

"A great man," the lady said. "He must have made a big impression on you."

"He did. I never had to humiliate myself by putting my problem into words. He had learned to read people's eyes – learned to read the shadows of their thoughts. And when his advice came, it was given to 'you' but it was never clear whether the 'you' meant people in general or you in particular."

"A clever man, too."

"He was. I respect him now and I respected him then."

"So, naturally, you did the favour he asked of you?"

"To love at a distance? I found it impossible to..."

"No, I mean, did you speak to this man Wilf about his friend's drunkenness?"

"Yes, of course. I went to see him when I got back to the school that evening."

"So what happened?"

"At first I didn't want to speak to Wilf at all."

"Why not?"

Richard cast his mind back and waited until a picture of Wilf Steele developed in his head. Initially, he found that thirty-five years had reduced Wilf to a wheeze and a shuffle of slippers. Then, grey and bristling, Wilf emerged in Richard's mind. Wreathed in pipe smoke, he was a relic of wartime service in the Middle East, and a man who had never found his way home.

Struggling with the memory of that evening, Richard finds Dicky in the accommodation block. He is standing in the unlit corridor, brushing sand from his clothes at the door of Wilf's room. The smell of pipe smoke is emerging with a slice of light from the half-open door. He sees the shadow of the man with whom he is putting on the school play. It is the shadow of a person he barely knows: an ageing but dormant homosexual who lives for his boys, a man who has been intimate with Reverend Rifkin, and a man who loves to manipulate and to plot.

"I was afraid," Richard said.

"Afraid of Wilf?"

"No, I was afraid of myself. After what I had seen on my way home, I was afraid of the power of my own pain, of my own doubts and my own little jealous games. There was little room left to concern myself with Rifkin or my promise to the priest."

"But you did speak to him?"

Her voice was full of concern, and Richard sensed that his relationship with this woman was dependent on his relationship with Father Peter and whether or not he had carried out his wishes.

"Yes, I spoke to him."

Dicky is now over the threshold of Wilf's darkened room. Wilf is standing with his back to the door, bending over his desk. There is an open exercise book lying in the light of the table lamp. Wilf's careful and detailed corrections are visible. A pile of closed books lies on the corner of the desk. Wilf turns, stares at Dicky from head to foot and chuckles.

"Got caught in the sandstorm, did you? Have you seen a ghost?"

The blunter-than-usual Yorkshire vowels suggest that Wilf is deep in himself, in dreams of a faraway place called home where people are open and honest and speak their minds. In these moods, Wilf is rarely communicative. Dicky is making a movement to leave when Wilf says: "You had better come in." And as an afterthought he adds: "Close the door behind you."

"Did he say what he would do?"

"He did."

"So what did he promise?"

"Nothing."

"Nothing?"

"I told him Father Peter was concerned about Rifkin. I asked Wilf if he could help. His response was odd."

Wilf steps backwards into the shadows. Long moments pass while he studies his pipe with an expression that suggests disappointment at the pipe's behaviour. Then he worries over an apparent blockage in the mouthpiece. He removes the stem, thrusts a cleaner into it and then withdraws it with a powerful movement from the hip.

"The die is cast," Wilf says. "There is nothing I can do. It is like our school play. The lines are learned, the props are in place and the audience is waiting. There is nothing more to be done." Wilf then steps out of the shadows, takes a hard look at Dicky's eyes and says: "Unless the play is hijacked by someone with an axe to grind. And we know who that person might be, don't we?"

The Yorkshire vowels have blunted still further and suggest that Wilf has retreated still further from the younger man. Dicky is speechless, and his hand wanders to the pocket which contains his recently purchased powders.

"I thought for a terrible moment," Richard said, "that he had read my innermost thoughts, had seen in me what I could not accept myself."

"So you didn't pursue the matter?"

"As I was leaving, Wilf realised something more was expected of him.

He said he would have a word with Rifkin after the play."

His words appeared to pacify her, and her eyes revealed satisfaction.

"But," Richard added, "it turned out that Wilf was right. There was nothing anyone could do. Father Peter's concerns came too late. Like me, Wilf was playing games of his own."

"But at least you responded to his request."

Richard nodded. He said:

"Who told you I knew Father Peter?"

There was a slight movement of her head, an acknowledgement, perhaps, that she had heard the question. She muttered something under her breath before swirling round and making towards the door.

"What is your name?" Richard asked.

From the doorway a voice said:

"My father called me Jihadi."

"Strangle prescient, don't you think?"

"Not really. Given the conditions here, he knew that any thinking person would become one. That is our tragedy."

The door closed with a light click but the woman's quiet words were making him shiver again. This time the shivering refused to go away. It was as though he were gripped by a raging fever.

CHAPTER 7

Richard was woken by a tickling sensation on his head. Something large and crawling was in his hair. He ran his hand across his scalp, trapped an insect, which squirmed between his fingers. A cockroach. He flung it across the room and pushed himself up to a sitting position. Richard leaned against the wall, drew his knees up to his chest and watched the insect scuttle on the floor and disappear under the door. He had read somewhere that cockroaches could live for three months without food, thirty days without water and were able to survive for up to a week with no head. He was no match for this most hated of insects. In an environment like this, they would survive and he would die.

A few beams of light were coming through the window and into his cell. He rocked onto his haunches, but his thighs felt powerless, and he made the groan of the aged as he rose to his feet. He supported himself by resting his hand on the wall. The tiles were dewy-damp to the touch, and the air in the cell was warm to his face. He dragged the chair to the wall and, very carefully, he stepped onto it in order to get a view of the sky. It was early afternoon, and he strained his ears to catch a human sound from the free world outside.

Gingerly, he stepped down, and as his foot touched the floor, he realised his bladder was full. He walked around the room trying to control his need but nobody came. Feeling more and more uncomfortable, he slipped the blindfold over his eyes and tapped three times on the door. The door opened.

"Why make noise?"

It was his young guard, and his voice was edged with irritation.

"I need pee-pee."

"Please no make noise, understand?"

"I need go pee-pee."

"Later, please."

"Bring a bottle then."

"Not now. Later. Quiet."

The door closed, the key turned, and Richard unbuttoned his fly and urinated on the floor. He stepped over to the wall, leaned his back against it and slid to the ground. He drew up his legs and sat with his chin on his arms. He watched two streams of his own urine race towards him. He was wondering which stream would reach him first when one stream ran into the other like the closing of the Red Sea.

He saw himself as a man hanging from his fingernails and feeling the fingers unfurling. He knew that if he weakened and let go, he would fall into insanity. He considered saying his prayers but decided it might be more beneficial to both body and mind to get up and exercise. He started with a series of stretching movements – swirled his hips, bent his knees and touched his toes. Then he did some sit-ups and press-ups and he told himself to increase the number of repetitions daily until he felt his muscle tone returning.

One of the things his father had passed on to him was a belief that a healthy mind needed a strong body to live in, and so after the chest and stomach exercises, he decided to walk and he would do so without counting so that he could think. He moved in circles, and his mind wandered until a trance-like state came over him, and with it came the sensation of his father's presence. Richard half-expected to see him on the plastic chair with newspapers scattered at his feet, his head leaning sideways, the cigarette held at his ear. Richard saw his smiles and the gestures, heard those long utterances on Milton, Shakespeare, and Chaucer, the heated exchanges about revolutions, and the thoughtful silences that followed.

His father's opinions came as a shock to Dicky. The more he argued with him, the more Dicky came to see that however radical and revolutionary he thought himself to be, his father was several steps ahead of him. There was no doubt that behind the cold façade of the famous academic, lay a spiritual man with passionate feelings about politics, society and the individuals in it.

During these years of reconciliation, the linguist had done more for his son than discuss literature - he took him travelling. Dicky had just finished his O-level GCE exams when his father suggested that they drive through Germany and Austria. Dicky did not know it, but his father wanted to show him some of the places that had influenced him in his youth. Dicky was amazed to discover that this most stuffy of men had been young at all. More than this, there he was in the still bomb-damaged Frankfurt and asking awkward questions about Air Chief Marshall Harris and his bombing campaign.

The following summer, he had taken Dicky to the pre-Alpine region of

Northern Italy. Dicky had never known that his father was an accomplished climber, and their renewed relationship was played out against a backdrop of ledges, ropes and rocky crests. His first summit, *Cima Carega*, had been an inspiration. Never before had he felt such delicious breezes, experienced such blue skies or seen range after range of mountain rising from a haze and floating in space. Never before had he been so high, and with nothing to compare it to, he had been able to feel the mountains in their totality. But it was on their descent that something momentous occurred.

The mountains had been unsettling him, and he would turn at every sound expecting to see someone standing behind him. Only when his father told him they were on the Italian front line of 1916, did Dicky notice the trenches, the spirals of barbed wire and the memorial stones to the dead with their faded sepia prints of faces staring forever outwards at forgetful generations. Then he understood the source of his discomfort. He had sensed how the shape of the present was conceived in the shadow of the past. It had been a pivotal moment in Dicky's life. That day, the sense of historical significance had impressed itself on his consciousness and had forged his subsequent career as a historian.

Richard was happy that he and his father got closer in his teenage years. Theirs was a relationship that developed in the realm of the intellect and things external. But it was too late to get emotionally involved. The important things – feelings, guilt and memories - had remained unspoken and they would remain unspoken because his father was twenty years dead. It was peculiar then, that the presence in his cell, a presence unseen but felt in the air around him, emanated love and compassion.

Now, walking in circles, Richard had nowhere else to go but the place and people where his life had started. "Well, dad, come out, come out wherever you are, and we can…." And then words failed. He stopped walking and stared at the tiled walls while his mind groped in emptiness. But the presence remained in the room – comforting, strengthening and humbling. With his father by his side, Richard could use his imagination to escape to places they had both known. Trudge, trudge round the bleak room; trudge, trudge up Helvellyn; trudge, trudge up Scafell and Skiddaw, *Monte Grappa*, *Civetta* and the *Rubihorn*; stepping over the river of urine, the Rhine, the Po, the white tiles of his room, the white of the cherry blossom in Devon and a love that he had never talked about.

It was one of Richard's greatest regrets that he had not found the courage to tell his father about his love for Khalid, the jealousy and the revenge which had led to his dismissal and which had driven him into the arms of Sandra. He had no doubt that his father would have told him what Richard now knew. The object of his affections was, in fact, a mirror image of himself as a youngster and Dicky the elder was protecting him.

At the time, Dicky was unaware of any desire other than that to love and to be loved. There was no overt sexual attraction, and Dicky would have denied its existence. History was full of close but wholesome relationships between older men and young boys, and anyway, sexual advances would have destroyed the romantic illusion.

There was a knock on the door. Richard sat down on the mattress and pulled on the blindfold. Several people entered the room and walked around. They ignored him, and Richard stayed quiet, hoping to work out how many voices he could distinguish. The Chain Man's voice was harsh and pessimistic in tone. It grated in comparison to the pleasant and joyful behaviour of the young guard, who was humming; *I Want to Hold Your Hand.* Dominating all of them was the voice of the Second Coming. Everyone else deferred to him, waited until it was their turn to speak and doing so in respectful tones. Only Mr Friendly could match him in authority. Suddenly, the fan was switched off.

Richard was about to protest when there was a sound like that of a plug being inserted into an electrical socket. Someone switched on a drill. Richard dug his heels into the mattress and pushed himself backwards against the wall. He was shaking like a jelly, expecting to feel at any moment the drill head pounding into his body. Where would they start – at his knees, his ankles or his arms? The drill hammered on the concrete floor and continued for several minutes until the tools were collected and the people left the room.

Richard removed his blindfold. The fan had been put to one side and steel rings had been inserted in the floor near the door. They were going to chain him again. This would mean an end to his walks, the exercising and escapes into the past where everything was so secure. There was a knock at the door. Blindfold on. A man walked in.

"Shut up the fuck."

The Chain Man grabbed at his foot and put a chain around it.

"Sit the fuck still."

He fastened the chain to the link in the floor and left the room. Removing the blindfold, Richard saw that the chain was about six feet in length and long enough to allow him to continue some of his exercise regime. For the moment, his fingers held steady. He could hold on. Another knock on the door. Blindfold on. The door opened, and hope came into the room with an under-the-breath rendition of *Please, Please Me.*

"Take."

An exercise book and a pencil were pushed in to his hand.

"Lift blindfold," his young guard commanded, "and face the wall."

Richard did as he was told.

The young guard leaned over Richard's shoulder and tapped his finger on the exercise book.

"Write," he said.

"Write what?"

"Write the story of your life. Like a book – about you, yeah? You know – I wanna take you by the hand..." His words merged into the rhythm of the old song, and the boy's voice picked up the beat and ran with it to full song.

"Stop it," snapped Richard. "Why you want me to write book?"

"You say you want write. So - write. We want names. People you meet when you are here before."

"How do you know I was here before?"

The guard became silent. Richard heard him drawing the plastic chair across the floor. The guard sat down at his shoulder.

"You must to write," he said, "about you."

"I can't write. I don't have my glasses."

"OK you say me – I write, yeah?"

The book was snatched from his hands.

Richard was about to protest and to hit back with a laugh and stinging words about his guard's English. It was not feasible that he could copy down Richard's words at the first attempt. Richard was unsure whether it was self-preservation or an unwillingness to wound the boy that prompted him to remain silent. Sooner or later, the guard would discover the truth for himself.

"Where do I start?" Richard said.

"Start with trip here in 1973."

"Why?"

Richard sensed the youngster's face darken.

"Don't ask," he said. "Say."

For the first time there was real irritation in his voice – or perhaps it was fear.

"Please turn fan on," said Richard.

The guard got up, and Richard heard him move towards the door. A second later, the fan hummed into life. On his way back to the chair, the boy said:

"Please. I try take care of you. I follow orders. Just talk – please."

Richard had no answer to this. Although he was unwilling to hurt the boy, he was uncomfortable about having his words written down. The written word was permanent, spoke to people across geographical boundaries and time. The written word meant that the dead could speak. He decided to play a game.

"In 1973, after one year at university, I was given permission from my tutors to accept a one-year assignment as a volunteer teacher in the Middle-East." He spoke quickly, ran the words together and did not pause. "I lived in a rather squalid little room with..."

"Stop – too quick. I must write. Slow down baby, you move too fast.

Please – blindfold on."

Richard glanced at the scrapes and cracks in the tiles above the floor, and then towards the window and its connection to the outside world. The traffic noise had hushed but the heat in the cell would have been intolerable had it not been for the fan. It was probably time for the afternoon siesta. Richard pulled the blindfold back on and began again with his story. He span out endless and useless detail. He described his room and its view over the flat, city roofs. Then he described his excitement on seeing the minarets and on hearing the *muezzin's* call to prayers, which came to him on breaths of eucalyptus.

"Stop. Too quick. Too quick. Wait."

Richard heard the pen scraping on the page. The sound reminded him of Ben's first efforts; the way he curled his wrist round the pencil and followed every movement with his head as though willing the hand to get it right. He was reminded also of his paternal responsibilities, his need to be home again where things that mattered were passing him by.

"OK – say me, yeah?"

"The English headmaster, Reverend Rifkin, had the grandest flat because he socialised with foreign dignitaries. It was to his flat that I was sent on my first evening…"

"Go on. Go on."

But Richard had tapped into echoes of a terrible experience he had once chained down. The words "Rifkin" and "flat" loosened those chains and for several moments he brushed against moments of horror in Rifkin's flat on another evening thirty-five years previously. It was the evening before his own departure from the country and the last time he had seen Wilf Steele before the damp cold of Bradford finished him off in 1975. It was also the evening on which he had lost his virginity to Sandra, and he had begun the slow process of growing up and away from his childhood. Fragments of that evening, each with a different aura, filtered through into his consciousness, and he found it difficult to believe that they had occurred within the same time frame.

"Please, why you stop? Go on."

With an effort, Richard shifted the focus of his thoughts to the day of his arrival when Rifkin was still very much alive.

"Rifkin was tall, thin and gaunt," Richard said. "Draped in a *jalabiyah*, he was dancing around his flat and alarming his wife Stella with the movements of a small bird."

"Stop, stop. You speak too fast. You can't do that. Wait, wait a minute…"

Richard heard a sound as of a hand digging into a bag. There was a pause, and then a click. The guard was using a tape-recorder.

"Ok," he said, "just be naturally and talk, yeah?"

"Wilf Steele was also there on the evening of my arrival. He and Rifkin were old friends and had worked together in Jerusalem in the 1960s. Wilf and I put on a performance of *Androcles and the Lion*. It was after this performance that I was forced to leave."

"Forced to leave? Say me why leave?"

"Do you want to know a secret?"

"For me, yeah; for me. Say me what happen that night. You remember?"

"I don't need to remember. I have the photos."

"You make photos?"

"A friend make photos."

"Say me why leave. Say me, say you."

"OK."

Richard turned his thoughts inwards. Sandra had indeed captured the whole evening on her new instamatic. A few years ago he had scanned the photos and saved them to disc. They were islands of light surrounded by vast areas of lost time. To the eyes of a stranger, the photos showed an unremarkable audience in an anonymous Arab country watching an ordinary school play. To the eyes of the initiated, the photos were the key to the magic of a lost world. The lecturer in Richard honoured this magic by adopting a formal tone and a narrative style.

"There were a lot of people in the auditorium that night," he said. "Everyone who had connections to the school was there and segregated according to their social position and influence."

Sandra had taken several snapshots of the audience. She had started with those in the back rows – the school's non-teaching staff and their families. The caretaker, Abu Haida, is resplendent in his swirling *kuffieh* and waxed moustache. While his wife pecks at their six children, Abu Haida's hooked nose is angled to one side, his eyes surveying the scene around him as though it were a murder scene. The school driver, Mr Abweh, is sitting with his legs tucked under his chair, his hands crossed over his stomach. His face is immune to the turned heads and eyes that settle on his five pretty daughters and seem to ask, "Why no son?" The administrative staff, ladies with fans fluttering like butterflies at their faces, are keeping up conversation until the last possible moment, while the school cleaners, part of Abu Haida's network of informers, cluster round windows, now open to allow free passage to the scent-filled night air. The cleaners look guilty. Tired out by the toil required to rid the hall of sand from the storm, their heads are buried in their *kuffieh's* as if hiding from every grain that betrays their failed efforts by glittering like fireflies in the night.

Next came the shots of the performers' families. Intent on getting a glimpse of offspring or sibling, they allow their heads to bob and weave like boxers looking for an opening. Amongst the bobbing and weaving heads is the Buddha-like shape of Mr Sa'ad, the maths teacher, the black Western hat of local businessman Mr Megorian and the lace bonnet of his pretty French wife. The Megorian's seek the eyes of their son Gabi, who is playing the part of Ferrovius. Some way to the right of the Megorians' is a man conspicuous by his frayed brown suit, by his rigid dignity and by the fact that the seats on either side of him are empty. He seems aloof and oblivious to the occasional roving eye that settles on his open shirt, his gold teeth or his plastic shoes. He sits still; but his hands, which he keeps in the pockets of his trousers, are clenched as if to contain the furious beating of his heart.

Beyond the adoring parents are the teachers, their presence required by Khoury, their resentment apparent in expressionless faces and eyes that hold suggestions of running away.

Many of the seats in the front rows are occupied by the ballooning white *jalabiyehs* and ceremonial daggers of the local dignitaries. These men are too old to have anything but power and influence. Their too-old eyes are set in too-old faces, and each face is as expressionless as the others. Some British Embassy personnel are present in perfect manners, extravagant hats, and dark-suited and official indifference to the occasion. Amongst them all, often with his back to Sandra's camera, is Father Peter, anxious not to let such an opportunity for fund raising pass him by. His black cassock and black, plastic-rimmed glasses give him an element of authority which draws the people in the front rows towards him. Some people have risen to shake his hand and to exchange words with him while the eyes of those in the vicinity follow him like pointing fingers. The priest seems intimate with them all.

Father Peter was present in most of the shots of the front rows. One of them showed his profile before the pale round face of Mr Khoury. Khoury has removed his jacket and rolled up the sleeves of his shirt and he is running his hands over his wings of black hair. The priest appears to be looking Khoury in the eye, but the deputy headmaster is smiling at the old dignitaries around him, and his eyes sparkle with the knowledge that some of the priest's charisma has rubbed off on him.

"When the lights dimmed," Richard said, "a breath of nervous conversation rippled across the auditorium and the audience coughed and spluttered its way to an anticipatory silence. Then, Wilf broke through the stage curtain to address the audience."

Sandra had taken a snap of Wilf blinking in the limelight. His blue-grey cardigan is bristling with pipe cleaners, tobacco pouches, lighters, pens and pencils. Wilf is holding his pipe in the air in a futile attempt to stem the tide of twittering that is running over the audience again.

"Wilf thanked everyone in order of their importance," Richard said. "He thanked Mr Khoury for allowing him to remove the boys from the classroom; he thanked the Reverend Rifkin for his invaluable support, and he thanked the performers for their enthusiasm and commitment. This speech was his moment in the spotlight, a moment when he collected his dues and felt appreciated. It was also his swan song although he didn't know it. But what unfolded later that evening was a double tragedy. Both were the result of jealous and spiteful acts. One of these acts was of his making and the other of mine."

"Go on, go on," said the guard, "Why you stop? Please, please me."

"At the time," Richard said, "Wilf had other concerns. He guessed that his play would be sabotaged by the internal politics of the school. He thought he had appeased Khoury by having his eldest son play the emperor, and his youngest – Omar – the lion. But Khoury had bigger plans. He wanted the English out of his school and then he would assume the headship. With Rifkin on one of his drinking bouts, there was little we could do to stop him. Khoury planned to discredit Rifkin by showing that his choice of play was misguided and his choice of the boy to play Androcles was disastrous. This would give him the evidence he needed to demonstrate that Rifkin was an incompetent drunkard and bringing the school into disrepute. We had no idea how he was going to do this until the play started. It was during the first act that Khoury struck."

To the casual observer, Sandra's shot of Khoury showed a delighted spectator on his feet and applauding the efforts of the cast. Khoury has risen from the darkness of the auditorium, and his round and bald head catches the stage lights and appears like a bodiless spectre hanging unsupported in the torrid air. Khoury is clapping his hands but he is not applauding the actors. He is creating mayhem and throwing barbed taunts at the hapless Androcles: "Speak up, speak up, boy. We can't hear you. Stop your mumbling and speak up."

"Khoury was right about one thing," Richard said. "Poor Khalid had not learned his words. I prompted him as best I could and he hung on to my words like a lifeline. Those moments when he was dependent on me were amongst the happiest of my life."

"Don't let me down, yeah," said the guard, his voice thick with sleep.

"But Khoury was determined to disgrace Khalid and bring the whole English edifice tumbling with him. When Omar the lion limped onto the stage and held up his front paw, Khoury's round face shone, and he cheered. When the lion lay under the tree to sleep, Khoury made expansive movements with his arms in an attempt to encourage the dignitaries around him to join him in his excitement. In the back rows some of the parents stood up to see what the fuss was about, and the embassy staff fidgeted on their chairs and rolled their eyes towards the ceiling."

The sound of an even but broken whistle suggested that the young guard had dropped off to sleep. But the sights and sounds of memory were pulling Richard backwards in time. Sandra had snapped a number of pictures showing Wilf in the wings. He is standing as still as stone, a relic of Pompei, caught in the volcanic ash and staring motionless at the disaster unfolding in front of him. The only signs of change in the pictures have occurred on centre stage behind Wilf. In one, Androcles is pulling at the thorn. In another, the lion has fallen forward and collapsed on Androcles' chest. Androcles' eyes are filled with a concern that begs everyone else to share. In the last photo in the series, boy and lion are staggering around centre stage in a grotesque parody of a dance.

"At the end of this farce, the school's non-teaching staff marked time with their feet and cheered as the curtain came down on the first act. Some of them thought the play was over and applauded. Others waved their arms to stop them. Some of the British embassy staff headed towards the exit with Father Peter pecking at their shoulders.

There is no visual record of what went on back stage at this point. Sandra was busy with the audience and never saw, as I did, the prostrate form of the lion. Poor Omar's eyes were rolled back and white. His face was pale, and his features seemed somehow dislodged from their normal position and threw his face into an expression of confusion. 'Full of sand,' he was saying. 'So hot...so hot...can't breathe...no air...,' and I remember feeling nothing but excitement that my little plan would succeed."

Richard paused, expecting a response from his young guard, but the boy's even breathing suggested that he had not heard a word. Richard needed no photograph to recall those moments between acts and nor did he verbalise them for the sake of the recording. They had been private moments that produced images for his memory only. Khalid's hair is curling over the nape of his neck, and his neck is moving languidly in concerned circles over the prostrate lion. Khalid has removed the top half of the lion's outfit, and Omar's head is resting on Khalid's thighs. When Dicky approaches with fussy importance, Khalid shifts his body to shield the head he is now cradling in his arms. He bends forward to place a kiss on Omar's forehead. While Dicky watches, a hand emerges from his dying dream and brushes his forearm with its delicate fingers. Khalid says, "Thank you, *ustazz*. Thank you for helping me. You have saved me from disgrace. I will never forget you."

"It was during the third act," Richard continued, "that Khoury and his cronies made their final charge, and I played out the jealous act that led to my shame and dismissal."

Sandra's visual record showed that by the time the curtain rose on the final act, most of the embassy staff has gone, but Khoury has been joined by Abu Haida and Mr Abweh. They are standing up and pointing at the stage. The scenery now represents an area behind the emperor's box in the Coliseum. In the middle of the stage, a young boy is staring at the tormenting spectres below him and repeating Dicky's prompts like an automaton.

"If you arrange for me to sacrifice when nobody is looking I don't mind," Khalid says. "But I must to go in the arena with the rest. It's my honour you know?"

These lines bring howls of derision from the audience.

"You don't know what honour is," cries Abu Haida.

"Idiot," says Mr Abweh.

"And then it was time for Omar the lion to reappear on stage," Richard said, "and I knew that my moment had come. I helped Omar into the top half of his outfit and tied it at the back. Poor Omar made a weary gesture towards his mouth. I ignored the gesture, and placed the lion's head over his shoulders. I tightened the ties and, slipping two sachets from my pocket, I poured the contents into the lion's outfit. What was in the sachets? Itching powder was in one and sneezing powder in the other. It never occurred to me that these might harm him. I didn't know he suffered from acute asthma. I grabbed the lion by the shoulders and pushed him stagewards."

Sandra's pictures showed that Khoury and his cronies are on their feet, standing in the footlights, about to deliver their *coup de grace*. The man in the frayed brown suit has risen from his chair and stands in the aisle. His eyes, sparkling with indignation, are fixed on Khoury and he has extracted both hands from his trouser pockets and holds them in front of him, fists clenched.

"By now," Richard said, "the teaching staff were sitting with fixed smiles on their faces while the parents were muttering to one another and shaking their heads in wonder. When the emperor gave a signal, Omar the lion emerged from his cage. He bounded into the arena, and Androcles fell to his knees and prayed while the lion circled him. His first roar was unconvincing in its ferocity but it was followed by a sneeze so loud that it stunned the audience in general and Khoury in particular whose facial expression switched from one of pleasure to shocked horror. Androcles buried his face in his hands and threw them heavenwards. The lion arched his back and sneezed again before bumping into the boy and knocking him sideways. There was another sneeze and then a series. One of the lion's forepaws collapsed, the beast deflated and his head rolled until he let out a cry for help that reverberated around the assembly hall. Khoury jumped to his feet, shook his fists and shouted. The lion was now on his back, writhing and scratching himself and sneezing so violently that Androcles set about dismantling the animal by fumbling at the stays that kept the costume together. Seeing that something was wrong, the emperor emerged from his box eager to speak his lines: 'My friends, an incredible thing had happened. I can no longer doubt the truth....' But nobody was listening. Spectators turned to their neighbours. Their whispering questions became more demanding. Some people were on their feet. Mr Abweh was walking down the aisle to join his family. Abu Haida was looking through the window searching for someone to blame, and Father Peter was rushing towards the stage to offer assistance."

There was a rustle from the boy behind him. He yawned and made stretching noises. "OK - enough."

The tone of the voice told Richard the boy was tired and not a little bored.

"Go to sleep," he said and he picked up the recorder and left.

Alone with his thoughts Richard followed the series of Sandra's photos to their conclusion. The man in the frayed suit has resumed his seat and pose of quiet dignity and he smiles while Khoury bellows.

The last photos Sandra took that evening could not do justice to what happened and could never match the memories of those who were there. No photo could capture the shriek from the stairwell. It flattened all other noises in its path so that silence fell like an axe. No photo could capture the fear that hung in the air or the sound of feet hauling themselves up the stairs. The last picture showed Stella Rifkin through a forest of arms and legs. She has collapsed on the floor begging for help and claiming her husband is dying. Even in the half light, there is something about her dress that is causing a stir in those of the audience who are close to her. One man is kneeling beside her. It is Father Peter and he has rubbed her dress and has his fingers to his nose. The photo could not speak but Richard still heard the one word he spoke; "Blood."

There was a knock, and the door opened, and several people came in. They were talking amongst themselves, and Richard continued with the final threads of his own thoughts. He collected all those fragments of memory that remained from that night: the sound of their feet as they ran across the play area, father Peter's black cassock flapping round his ankles, the wedge of light shining through the half-open door to Rifkin's flat, and a light sound, nothing more than the drip of a tap or the light groan of a person turning in sleep and then the wet thumping as of a large fish thrashing for its life.

Someone approached and tightened his blindfold. Then, another man grabbed at Richard's feet and unlocked the padlock.

"Stand," said his guard.

Richard stood up. He was guided across the room.

"Sit."

He was pushed down onto the plastic chair. More whispering, and someone came and put his hand on Richard's shoulder.

"Stand," said his guard. "We leaving here, yeah?"

"Leaving? Where are we going?"

"No ask. Walk."

Feeling weak and light-headed, Richard allowed himself to be led across the room.

"Are you going to set me free?"

"Maybe. Do what we say. Maybe."

Richard staggered out of his cell. He had lost count of the number of days he had spent there. Maybe he would never see it again, and before he had taken three steps, the memory of it began to fade into obscurity. He might soon be a free man again.

BBC News Online

Brown pledge for missing university man

Gordon Brown has said the UK Government is doing everything it can to secure the release of abducted university academic Richard Chambers. The professor was seized at gunpoint over two weeks ago.

The prime minister told the Commons there was, "No conceivable reason for him to be kept - he was an academic attending a conference."

On Tuesday, the Palestinian Prime Minister said he was also working hard to secure Mr Chambers' release.

"There continues to be nothing more important than the Middle-East," Mr Brown said. "But until we know who we are dealing with, we can do very little. It is not Government policy to negotiate with terrorists."

There has been no direct information on Richard Chambers' fate since he was seized after leaving his hotel over two weeks ago.

CHAPTER 8

"Don't move your head."

Richard kept his head turned towards the front while his young guard guided him along a corridor and through another door. The guard placed his hands on Richard's shoulders and, squeezing them together, guided him downwards.

"Sit here."

Richard tensed his thigh muscles, put out a searching hand beneath his buttocks and lowered himself, relaxing when he felt the wooden chair, solid and unyielding beneath his weight. The warmth of the youngster's hands remained on his shoulders, secured him in his seat. The guard's fingers massaged his muscles. Richard wondered how they would feel to the touch. Stringy was the first word that came to mind, stringy and tough like a piece of old meat. Perhaps, Richard thought, that was what the guard was doing – softening up the muscle for the executioner's sword. Richard shrugged the hands away, rose to his feet and upended the chair, which clattered to the floor. It took the guard several moments to register what had happened. Richard heard him gasp and step backwards.

"What you do? What you do?"

Richard noted the harshness in his guard's tone and the briskness with which he picked up the chair and righted it.

"Sit," he said.

The young man was nervous, and the air was thick with tension and the guard's gasps. Richard extended his hand, felt for the chair and sat down again. He felt sorry for his young friend. No doubt he was anxious to impress his colleagues, to show them he was in control and worthy of their trust. Richard knew they were in the room. He could hear their whispers in the air around him. He identified the voice of Mr Friendly and the rough tones of the Chain Man. There was one other person present, and a bright light had been erected. Richard could not see it but he could feel its warmth on his face. Someone stepped towards him. It was Mr Friendly.

"Take the cover from your eyes."

Richard removed it and threw his head sideways as he was blinded for a moment by the glare. A video camera appeared through the yellow balls of light that bounced around in front of his eyes. It was placed on a stand in front of him. A studio light was behind it. The camera operator had wrapped his body in a white *jalabiya* and his head was hidden under a *kuffieh*, but Richard recognised the eyes immediately. He had seen them long ago in the lobby of the hotel on the evening he had been taken. Behind the operator there was a television. The sound was turned down, but a football game was taking place and it connected him reassuringly with things normal, safe and sound. Mr Friendly was standing at his back. He leaned forward and spoke quietly into Richard's ear.

"Tell everything to the video. Start when you see the red light."

Richard resisted the urge to twist from the waist and look into Mr Friendly's eyes. He simply turned his ear towards his voice and whispered:

"What do you mean? Everything I said before?"

Richard was surprised. Despite himself, he had echoed Mr Friendly's tone in a way that suggested complicity, a bond of loyalty that separated them from the others. It occurred to Richard that he might be forming an emotional attachment to the man. He had read research concluding that kidnap victims often latched on to the most approachable kidnapper in order to maximise the probability that this person would enable the survival of the victim. It could be a powerful attachment, like that between parent and child, and several cases of this syndrome had been recorded.

"No, not everything," said Mr Friendly, leaning further forward so that Richard felt his breath hot against his neck. "Just tell us what happened to Rifkin. We need to offer proof, if needed, that you are the person you say you are. The video is a sort of fingerprint. It's unique to you. Only you can say what happened to Rifkin that night. Most of the others will be dead by now."

Richard turned his head. The number of questions passing through his mind was matched by changes in facial expression. He took several moments to rearrange his features, set them into an expression of innocence before opening his mouth to ask his friend how he knew who was dead and who was alive. But the Second Coming cut him off with an impatient wave and pointed at the front of the camera.

"Start when you see the red light here."

Richard looked up while the Second Coming stepped over to the television, pressed a button and the world of normality and safety disappeared into a pinprick of light on the screen. Then the red light came on. For the second time that day, Richard reeled off his narrative curriculum vitae. But as the words rose to his mouth he doubted whether they reflected the memories which produced them. The more he narrated, the more he was aware of a gap between his actual words and the past they purported to describe. Had an event such as Stella's arrival in the school hall really been so dramatic or was he adding the bloody colour as an after-the-event-touch-up to give the images more power?

His memory had them all crossing the school play area at an uncoordinated trot, their legs moving to the rhythm of hearts bump-started by the insane pitch of Stella's screams. Father Peter swerves around the parked cars, his cassock trailing over their bumpers, but they all slow down to round Rifkin's old Fiat. Wilf eyes it with the suspicion reserved for black cats or the number 13, while Sandra casts a wary eye over the dust-covered bonnet, the windscreen and its wipers breaking like bleached bones through the accumulated sand.

"Father Peter was the first to enter the accommodation block," Richard said. "He lifted his cassock and rushed at the stairs, taking them two at a time before halting in the light that shone through Rifkin's door. The rest of us followed grasping the banisters as if they were saintly relics. The priest entered the apartment to the shock of an ambulance siren and the roar of a motor cutting through Abu Haida's oleander and into the courtyard below. Doors thumped. Feet scrambled. Urgent voices rose into the night air."

With his mind's eye, Richard scrutinises the splashes of red running down the sitting-room walls. The drops are feeding the dark and heavy pools that are spreading towards the centre of the floor.

Father Peter breaks ranks and rushes forwards. He drops to his haunches. He lets one hand hover over the spreading pools while he studies them with the concentrated expression of the scientist observing some rare natural phenomenon. The hovering hand drops, skims the surface of the pools and swoops up to stop under the priest's nose. His head recoils, and he whispers something that sounds like the last rites. With his free hand, he crosses himself, but his renewed mutterings are overlaid by a medley of sounds from the play area and the wail of Stella's voice rising from the doorway below.

"Two ambulance men carrying a stretcher arrived in the doorway," Richard said. "They were asking about the cadaver when Rifkin let out a cry for help."

Richard took a deep breath but he was unable to verbalise the nightmare sounds and images that appeared in his head. A loud thump is followed by a muted howl. Father Peter straightens his cassock with his palms and, crossing himself again, he begins a faint and breathy murmur, a prayer of salvation perhaps, for him and the others. Sandra is standing petrified and staring with sleepwalker eyes at some unidentifiable point in the middle of the room. Wilf is rolling his pipe in his mouth and staring at the toilet door.

It is slowly opening.

Rifkin appears just as the audience emerges *en masse* from the assembly hall. He is greeted by the sound of loud conversations, raucous jeers and laughter, and all of it punctuated by the sound of car horns. He arrives in the living area at a reptilian crawl, his stomach sliding on the jam-like substance beneath him. His cheeks are sunken, his eyes straining at their sockets.

"I remember that he was whispering," Richard said in a monotone. "Then he seemed to gather his strength and called for help. His flanks were pulsating to his shallow breathing, like a cat about to vomit. Sandra was still staring into nothingness. Father Peter was wiping his fingers on his cassock again. I allowed my attention to be diverted by the scene in the courtyard. So I missed what happened next."

But Richard was lying. In his peripheral vision he sees Rifkin raise himself to all fours. His flanks contract, and a stream of liquid with the colour and consistency of blackcurrant jam fountains from his mouth and splashes on the skirting boards. His head droops, and red vomit drips from his bottom lip while tremors run up and down his body in tiny flickers. He raises one hand towards Wilf and holds it palm outwards. For a few seconds he remains balanced on one hand while the other pushes away at some unseen terror. Rifkin's straightened arm trembles and cracks like a matchstick at the elbow, and he falls forwards into his own bloody mess. The blood somehow resembles the afterbirth, but this is the before-death; dark red and sticky at birth and at death. Sandra hurls out a silent scream at some real or imaginary danger. Father Peter crouches down and grabs for Rifkin's hand while the medical men move in for the kill. Rifkin somehow finds the strength to roll on to their stretcher. Someone says:

"For God's sake, what's that sticky stuff?"

"I hate to have to say this, dear boy. It's his liver."

"Then Wilf crumpled and fell to his knees beside the priest," Richard said. "His pipe slipped from his mouth and dropped to the floor. What struck me was the notion that someone else had taken possession of his body. I hardly recognised the crying and broken man in front of me. But there was no time to reflect. Stella rushed into the flat. She was the centre of a human storm, her hands flapping around her head in an attempt to push away what her eyes were telling her. She span off into the kitchen. There was the sound of running water, uncoordinated movements and careless banging, and she returned, bucket and rags in hand, and scrubbed at the floor. And all the time, a tremendous racket was coming from the courtyard. The spectators had gathered in groups to discuss what had gone on in the assembly hall. Some were starting their motors and hitting their horns. Then Khoury strode in."

Khoury's arrival is preceded by his footsteps flying up the stairwell. He starts to speak before he reaches the top of the stairs and his voice penetrates the room before he does.

"Mr Khoury says that you'll be glad to hear that my son is alright but someone will…"

He stands blinking on the threshold.

"Shut up, shut up, up, up, up…." Stella covers her ears with the rags. Blood-red water oozes into her hair, overflows and streams down her cheeks and neck. She picks a lump of human material from her hair and holds it up for the people to see. She looks at Wilf, screws up her eyes and crouches like a cat.

"He is responsible for this. It was him. It was him."

The lights then flicker and die. There is a roar of disapproval from the people below.

"Tell them," Stella said, her words rising from the top of a scream. "Go on – tell them."

And emerging from her scream comes another sound. It is the wail of the air-raid siren, and from somewhere on adjacent hills, beams of light dance into the night sky. The roar from below disintegrates into a mumble of fear and isolated sounds of farewell. The crowd disperses, and in a few minutes, there is dead silence from the courtyard below. But above, in the realms of night, the sirens continue to cut through the sky as if the city itself is throwing up a prayer to the Gods or a lament to the dead souls.

"The medical people took Rifkin away while they could," Richard said. "Stella ran off with them. Her hands were still flapping around her head. I remember looking for the nearest chair, sitting down and staring through the window towards the searching lights."

A warm wind gusts through the room. The world is baking. Only the full moon, shimmering under a layer of frost, offers any suggestion of relief. The lights flicker again, come on and then die. Night breaches the walls and surges into the room. For a minute there is a hush, a moment of tension while Father Peter finds a candle, lights it, and places it at Wilf's feet. Wilf is cross-legged and bolt upright. His eyes slant towards the floor. His pipe is idle in one hand. The upward light from the candle remodels his face so that he looks like a stranger. There is a smile and an eye-twinkle on one side of his face. The other side is as dark as the dark side of the moon. Sounds are emerging from his shadow. Most of them are incoherent, smothered by the city's sirens, but the words "loved you" and "no other way" suggest he is making a confession to person or persons unknown. He is untouchable. Surrounded in a vacuum; he is a cocoon of eternal loneliness.

"It was then that Wilf opened up and told us his story," Richard said.

But nobody else in the room seemed interested in Wilf's story. Richard hesitated for a few seconds and decided to say no more about it. But a few seconds were enough for him to hear Wilf's voice coming in a monotone from a place far away.

"I want to tell you something before I go."

His eyes sparkle and darken as the searchlights come and go against the night sky.

"Alan has been ill for a long time. We were together in Jerusalem when he started to get sick. I loved him, you see. We knew it was his drinking. He cut down for the sake of our relationship. Then the war came. It was the summer of 1967. We went through it together. Our relationship seemed stronger than ever. Then, something terrible happened."

The pitch and volume of his voice rise on the final word so that it sounds like a question, a plea for understanding from those who surround him.

"Alan started staying away. You know, working late, that sort of thing. One evening I came home, and he told me he was leaving me. He had fallen in love with a woman and he wanted to be with her. And, as you know, that other woman was Stella. I struggled at first. But what can you do? They really loved each other."

The sirens reach a crescendo and die. There is a sob from the floor and the sound of Wilf's voice.

"We stayed friends...a threesome.... Alan's health improved and he stopped drinking completely. But the lack of him became more important than the people around me. I was his friend, a ghost from his past. He now sat next to Stella, his present and his future. It was too much. Imagine how it feels to sit opposite those fragments of yourself that you gave to another man. I was no longer his business. The future was where his dreams lay, and I had no part in them. Stella and Alan went back to England, and I came here when I was able."

Wilf hesitates, allows expressionless eyes to seek out those of the priest and Sandra. Father Peter is cross-legged on the floor and presiding over the proceedings like a slightly disapproving Buddha. Sandra appears to have woken up, and her cheeks are pulled upwards in an expression of mild distaste.

"Please understand," Wilf is saying, "I had no part in his dreams but I longed to take those dreams from him. Two years ago I got my chance. Alan was in trouble, unemployed, drinking, and getting sick again. There was a vacancy here. I have connections in the church. I recommended him. This is no place for a sick man - no place for a recovering alcoholic – just one push might drop him over the edge."

Wilf intertwines his fingers. Squeezing them together, he renews his determination and recharges his will. "So, I persuaded Alan to accept the offer. I knew he and Stella needed the money, so they came. I reckoned that in a place like this he might need about six months to drink himself to death."

"And when he had finished," Richard said, "Wilf asked a question. He said, 'Am I responsible for what has happened here? Did I take his life?' Before any of us could answer, a window crashed shut with the noise of a rifle shot, and the candle at Wilf's feet snapped out. Then, his dark shape rose from the floor, loomed over the room and, with a rustle, he was gone.

Khoury then took charge. He told us that Wilf would be on indefinite leave until they knew what had happened. He told me to come and see him the following morning. He was holding the two sachets in the palm of his hand. His faithful servant, Abu Haida, found them. I could not deny what I had done."

Richard hesitated. Now was the moment of his great shame. Every second of it was visible and audible to him but he had never put those seconds into words in order to communicate them to others – not even to his wife. Nobody in the room seemed interested in hearing those words now. But then Mr Friendly had made it clear to him. This was his narrative curriculum vitae - not a confession. And yet, as Richard reflected, he still felt the warm gust of wind that blew through the window and touched Dicky's hair and face. Dicky puts out both hands in a way that says he wants to reject the uncompromising evidence. He opens his mouth and shakes his head. He looks like a man about to begin the horrible process of explaining away the facts but Khoury pre-empts him.

"You recognise these, don't you, Mr Chambers? Sneezing powder and itching powder, if Mr Khoury is not mistaken." He raises his hand and wags a finger in Dicky's face. "Don't even think of teaching on Sunday or any other day until we have got to the bottom of all this. My son is asthmatic, didn't you know? He's lucky that he too has not ended up in hospital or worse. Now, get out."

Something vanishes from Dicky's features, and he makes towards the door without uttering a sound. His eyes wander around the room but the forlorn look says that he is taking in nothing but an acceptance of his own guilt and it snatches the essential ingredients from his personality. Sandra watches his back disappearing into the black hole that is the stairwell and pulls a face that looks right through the sense of helplessness that pervades the room. She charges down the stairs behind him.

"Wait, Dicky. Wait please. I need you."

She harries him down into the entrance hall, makes a lunge and grabs at his shirt. They stop for a second between upstairs and downstairs, and he glances at her before dragging his feet up the steps with Sandra now at his elbow. He opens the door of his room and moves through the darkness to his desk. Behind him, the door clicks shut, and the key turns in its lock. For a moment, both Dicky and Sandra contemplate each other in silence. Her black hair, flowing over both shoulders, shines blue in the moonlight that streams through the windows.

"Dicky…"

He hesitates.

"Hold me, Dicky."

He turns away from her and looks through the moonlight to the world outside. There is just the sound of the cicadas and the breath of the city on the verge of sleep. Finding no escape he turns to face the inevitable.

"Please, Dicky, shut up and just hold me."

His eyes settle on the woman in front of him and then he jumps.

"Just hold me tight. Yes like that. Yes you can kiss me if you like. And you can touch me here. That's right. There."

They tumble on to the bed and he is fumbling at her dress.

Her moans of delight at first bring a look of shocked alarm to Dicky's face but as her groans rise to shouts another expression takes control of his features. It is a look of triumph and it suggests that her cries are his and they are cries of victory. It does not seem to matter to him that the sounds disappear through the open window and evaporate in the darkness.

"It was a night to remember," Richard said. "It was the night I lost my job and my virginity. But I'll never forget what I saw in the flat. It haunts me to this day."

Mr Friendly placed the palm of his hand on Richard's shoulder.

"OK, I think that is proof enough that you are who you say you are. Very good."

"Good? Is that all you can say? Do you know what effort it took to…?"

"We have something else for you," Mr Friendly said. The downward inflection on the final word was paternalistic, tender – a tone that suggested he was giving something rather than making a command. The red light had gone out. The Second Coming had taken the video recorder in his hands, was caressing it with his eyes and holding it with the care and attention one might give to a rare diamond. A piece of paper crackled in Richard's ear.

"Now," said Mr Friendly, "we'd like you to read this."

The paper appeared in Richard's peripheral vision. He raised his hand and took it between his fingers.

"Read it to yourself first," Mr Friendly said.

"But I can't read it," Richard protested. "I don't have…"

"Your glasses?"

They appeared in front of his eyes, lowered from behind his head. Mr Friendly had slipped his fingers under the earpieces so as not to touch the lenses. To Richard it was a warm, personal and human gesture, one that was sensitive to him as an individual in a place where his individuality and humanity had been stripped from him.

"Thank you."

"Read it."

Richard scanned the first few lines, took in the gist of their content while his kidnappers looked on. He felt the intensity of their stare and with it came the power of the past pumping through his consciousness. He is a little boy again, five years old and sitting in the school dining-room while several teachers crowd over him. They are forcing him to eat. He can't leave, they say, until he has eaten every scrap. He is the last boy in the room. He can hear his friends playing football in the playground, but distressed and traumatised by his mother's death, gagging at the smell of the food in front of him, he is unable to touch it.

Dicky had complained to his nanny about this injustice, but she had merely shrugged her shoulders, muttering something about a cruel world. Richard now knew that it was not a cruel world. The world could no more have human emotions than the chair under his buttocks. It was the people in the world that could be cruel. But they could also be good and humane, and they could be misguided, like his teachers; like Mr Friendly.

Richard muttered a string of oaths and looked at the people crowding around him. He was disgusted with himself, with this rush of feeling that had broken through his defences. He wanted to turn round, to hold Mr Friendly's hand, to get a grip and prevent unpleasant memories from taking hold and absorbing his emotional energy. Instead, he shook his head to rid it of an unwanted residue of images.

"The English is not good," he said to Mr Friendly. "Shall I correct it as I speak?"

"No, no," Mr Friendly said. "Read it as it is."

Richard waited while the Second Coming played with the camera. He wondered how he could make it clear to Western audiences that he was faking it. When the red light came on he would read the first sentence on a breath.

"I urge our nations to resist those persistent and cunning enemies led by the United Stated and Israel."

He paused while he allowed the breath to escape from his lungs. He had sounded like an airline pilot: masterful, masculine, but bored by the routine proceedings. He then stretched his cheeks to imitate a smile.

"The main threat to security in the Middle-East is not Islamic, Arabic or nationalistic. It is the poisonous breath of the United States and its presence in the Persian Gulf and in other places that now rely for their security on American protection or who have established close bonds with Washington."

Richard scanned the next couple of sentences. He decided to change tactic. His father had once shown him lists of the characteristics of formal and informal language. If he recalled, informal language was signalled by such devices as running words together, grammatical simplicity and abbreviations. He decided to insert the language of the informal and private dialogue into this public and formal message and make it sound ridiculous.

He would start with a hesitation and continue with empty modifiers and adjectives.

"Umm…well now, our traditions are under attack. And, er…global arrogance gains hope and strength through creating discord and disunity." He emphasised his words by drawing his eyebrows together and by enthusiastically nodding his head. "It is time for us to strengthen ourselves against the Zionists, the notorious Zionist media and the agents of arrogance, in particular the Americans." Richard cleared his throat. "Anyway, Western materialistic civilisation is directing everyone towards materialism while money, gluttony and carnal desire are made the greatest aspirations. And I hardly like to say this but even their religious festivals are days when people are encouraged to spend their money to oil the wheels of capitalism. Yes, it is difficult to believe but I can tell you that our civil society and its Western counterparts are not necessarily in conflict and contradiction in all their manifestations and consequences. This is why I tell you we should never be oblivious to judicious acquisition of the positive accomplishments of the Western civil society. This should be obvious to you, I think. But I condemn the nations of the Middle East who have commercial and diplomatic ties with Israel. All right? And I condemn American-backed efforts to broker a broader peace between Israel and the Palestinians. As if you didn't know it, these efforts are unjust, arrogant, contemptuous and, finally illogical. They are a losing transaction for the Palestinians, aren't they? And all the time, the political designers of arrogance are breathing their poisonous breath to make the world fearful of the People's Democratic Party and other organisations who hope to free the region from Western imperialism. That is a fact. Yet it is they who hold the banner of unity and brotherhood and freedom. OK then. I call on the countries of the Middle East to band together for self-protection, to create their own democracies and to reject the poison of the United States and its allies."

The Second Coming pressed a button and the red light went out. He then raised his hands and held them at chest height, palms upwards like an icon of Christ. Richard watched him and wondered whether he had managed to communicate his real feelings through visual and verbal means. It was a risky strategy. He turned his head towards Mr Friendly.

"How was it? Did you like it?"

He looked up as Mr Friendly swept past his shoulder and joined the Second Coming at the camera. The cassette was lying in the Second Coming's hands, and both he and Mr Friendly worried over it for several seconds before leaving the room.

No sooner had the door closed behind them than the Chain Man broke into a tirade.

"I fuck the West. I fuck the British and the French to fuck. Fuck the

Americans, fuck you…"

Richard listened in horror. The words were muffled by the *kuffieh* wrapped round his mouth, and this gave them an eerie and distant quality. But what made Richard's hair stand on end was that the *kuffieh* prevented Richard from seeing any movement of the Chain Man's mouth. His words of hate were disembodied so that it seemed that he was the dummy, and the dead were airing their grievances through him. Richard was bludgeoned into silence. He had heard and seen prejudice before, prejudice against blacks, against whites, against immigrants, but never like this. Something inside him rebelled against this world of absolute rights and wrongs and of hard and clear objective truth.

"How can you hate whole nations and all their people? How many Europeans have you met?"

There was a short silence. The Chain Man appeared in front of him. He was holding a rifle in one hand and a grenade in the other.

"Jews are pigs and apes," he screamed. "We kill Jews. Our path is *jihad*…death for the sake of *Allah*."

The man was staring at Richard but his eyes were blank and unseeing. Richard knew the man had worked himself up to a point where he was beyond the reach of normal communication. His words were somehow detached from human reason and emerging as dead things – pustulating and septic.

"Israel must be wiped out. *Allah*, take hold of the Americans and Jews and count them. *Allah*, take hold of the Jews and kill them. *Allah*, take hold of the Jews. *Allah*, butcher them and kill them to the last one…"

Richard reeled as though under a blast of foul air. He refused to be beaten into submission but the gun and the grenade made him jumpy.

"Think," he said in as conciliatory a tone as he could muster, "and put your case before the world. If you use violence against the innocent, you turn people against you."

Mr Friendly reappeared in the doorway and signalled to the Chain Man with an abrupt wave of the hand. Passively, he put down the rifle and the grenade and left the room. Mr Friendly sought Richard's eyes with his and apologised with a slight grimace and a shake of the head.

"It is not a question of violence and nor is it a question of hate," he said. "It is a question of what the world sees. And what the world sees depends on hearing what it wants to hear from its politicians – that God and right are always on their side. Let me give you an example. Listen to this and tell me who said it."

He strode into the centre of the room and stopped in front of Richard. He lifted his hands to his *kuffieh*, fussed with it for a moment before crossing his hands in front of him and taking up the pose of the actor. "I follow the path assigned to me by Providence with the instinctive sureness of a sleepwalker. But there is something else I believe, and that is that there is a God. And this God again has blessed our efforts during the past years." He relaxed, shifted his weight. "So do you know which recent leader said that?"

Richard pursed his lips and wondered when the West last had a leader so obsessed with God and claiming God was on his side. He realised he did not care. He wanted to be back in his room and in the safety of his own thoughts. He shrugged an answer.

"Tony Blair?"

"No."

"George Bush?"

"No, my friend. It was neither of these. But it could have been them, couldn't it?"

The question was a vacuum into which all of Richard's patience was drawn.

"Please. Aren't you going to take me back to my room?"

The door flew open, crashed against the wall, and the Second Coming burst into the room like an enraged bull. A shock wave of stale air rushed through the spaces around them, and Richard's thought processes were shattered by a cry of rage.

"You lie."

Richard guessed what was coming. Even as he raised his arms and lowered his head in protection from a beating, he was telling himself he should have read the declaration in a serious tone. He heard the Second Coming shouldering Mr Friendly aside and felt him arrive in his space. He was unable to see the expression on his face but in his mind he saw him mouthing hugely, while spittle sprayed his face and his ears rang to the sound of the man's wrath.

"You lie. Blindfold on. Stand up. Face the wall. There...by the mattress."

Richard did as he was told. A sudden boom was followed by a crackle as the television bounced back to life. He heard what sounded like a football crowd shouting, "Chelsea, Chelsea," and the quieter tones of an English commentary overlaid by one in Arabic. Every now and then the English voice came through - a whispering from a half-forgotten existence.

"Wayne Rooney is worse than an annoying wasp," the commentator said. "He just won't go away, buzzing all around the opposition's defence and penalty box. You'd kill a wasp but you just can't get rid of Rooney."

"Kneel."

Richard dropped to his knees.

"We have looked at the video." The Second Coming was breathing hard. He coughed and what came next was said on a strangled breath. "It is useless. You are joking with us."

"No, I…"

He was interrupted by a cry of anger – a screaming howl as of a seagull in pain.

"You lie."

Expecting a blow to the head, Richard ducked.

"I do not lie," he said. "I have told you what I think. The video does not lie."

"You dare make fools of us." The Second Coming was now speaking in the whispers Richard associated with the confessional, but he did not expect forgiveness. He prepared himself for the beating, the punishment he knew was coming. It was there in the Second Coming's voice, that tone of the judge summing up before passing sentence. "Do you think we cannot hear the lies in your voice? Do you? So if you won't freely give us your voice I will show you how I can make your voice my own. I'll make it speak my words, make it cry out when I want it to cry out, turn it on and off when I want it to. Down, you dog. On the mattress."

Richard lay down on the floor, and the volume of the television was increased. The English commentator was droning on.

"What makes him so difficult to play against is that he is a very determined player, very strong and driven. You have to dominate him or otherwise he'll punish you."

A pillow was put over his head. He heard the roars of the football crowd while he struggled to move his head and to breathe. A sudden pain shot through the soles of his feet, convulsed his whole body, forced his breath into the pillow. There was something wrong with the volume on the TV. The roar from the football crowd reached a pitch of frenzied chanting every time the cane cut into his sole. Then the beating stopped. The volume of the chanting decreased.

"The first thing to do," the commentator was saying, "is keep him with his back to the goal and force him in the other direction, away from that central area. Also, if the gap between the midfield and the defence becomes too big, then he's going to punish you."

A finger was run up and down the sole of his foot. Richard curled his toes, and the beating began again. He clenched his fists, his body tensed, and the crowd's roar reached a pitch of almost insane intensity. Richard sobbed into his pillow, and the words of the English commentator persisted.

"That's the other thing about him – he has great technical ability to go with the rest of the package. He is playing a more central role now and you can't just give him a couple of kicks to rile him. You won't get any change from him now there's been this tightening up of his mentality…"

The beating stopped. Richard lay curled up and quivering. He found his trousers were wet. He supposed he had urinated in them. The Second

Coming knelt down at Richard's head. He said:

"Now tell us how that felt. Can you tell us?"

Richard turned his eyes upwards and through a veil of tears, he scanned the Second Coming's face. There was a movement, a nervous tic under the eye which spread down his cheek, rippled over his top lip and up the other side of his face. It settled there for a second, and then began its return journey.

"What was that? Did you say something? No?"

The tic under the eye now moved up to his forehead, pulled erratically at his eyebrows while the eyes beneath watched Richard struggle for words. The Second Coming leaned forward, turned his ear to Richard's mouth.

"Sorry, did I hear a sound?"

He shook his head and rose to his feet.

"No, I thought not. I told you I would control your voice. There is no language that can describe the pain you have experienced. Speech is useless, is it not, in providing insights into the nature of pain? Do not ever lie to us again. Understand?"

Richard nodded but he was unable to force the words from his mouth.

"Understand? Speak now, dog."

Richard nodded vigorously.

"I didn't cry out," he whispered, "I didn't cry out."

"Oh yes, you cried out." The tic that had started under the man's eye spread to other parts of his face. Quick jerky movements were pulling at his cheeks and top lip, sweat was running down his forehead. "Do you want to cry out again?"

Richard heard the cane cut through the air like a helicopter blade. At last he found his voice.

"Yes, yes, I understand."

"Now take the dog back to its cell."

The young guard and Mr Friendly came and helped Richard to his feet. It was impossible to stand unaided.

"You will stay there until we have decided what to do with you," the Second Coming said. "Now, get out."

Richard allowed his arms to be taken, and he was carried through the door and into the corridor.

"You see the game, *ustazz*? You see the game? Man U versus Chelsea. Great play from Rooney, great play. He's very focused."

They carried him through to the toilet.

"One day, *ustazz*. One day you and me, we go to Olt Traffet, yeah?"

The mispronunciation of that famous stadium was too much for Richard. He was violently sick. Somehow the two men got Richard back into his room. He lay down on the concrete floor and curled up.

"February 1940," Mr Friendly said before leaving the room. "Adolf

Hitler. That's who said it."

Richard closed his eyes and fell asleep.

There was a knock on the door.

No please not another beating. What was the time? Was it night? Quick – on with the blindfold.

People entered the room. He recognised the voice of the Second Coming.

"Sit – face the wall. You have three hours to dawn. Three hours to live."

"Three hours?" Richard asked. "Why three?"

"You have lied to us. Lied. You are of no use to us. In three hours you die."

BBC News Online

Demands issued on Chambers' tape

The al-Jazeera Arabic news channel has received a tape purportedly from the kidnappers of the university professor Richard Chambers. It contains no new pictures of Mr Chambers, but shows a picture of his university ID card. The tape includes a demand for the immediate withdrawal of foreign soldiers from Arab lands in the Middle-East.

Mr Chambers was seized more than two weeks ago. He had been on his way to a conference when he was taken at gunpoint.

The tape was delivered to al-Jazeera in Jerusalem and was made by a group calling itself the People's Democratic Party.

A Foreign Office spokesman said that they remained concerned for Mr Chambers' safety.

"Our sole concern is for Mr Chambers' welfare, and for that of his family. What we and they want more than anything else is Richard's safe return," he said. "We of course welcome any sign that Richard may be alive and well. We hope that today's news may be a sign that Richard will soon be released."

The tape does include one specific demand, the withdrawal of foreign soldiers from Arab countries. Until now, the kidnappers have not made their demands public or made any contact with the media.

The BBC's World Affairs correspondent Neil Gladstone says that the People's Democratic Party is a known Palestinian group and operates out of a number of countries.

"It is a small armed group with suspected links to Al Quaeda. They are seeking liberation of all Arab lands from foreign invaders and claim they wish to establish democratic governments."

Mr Gladstone adds that if the tape is authentic, then it does represent a development in the lengthiest kidnapping of a Westerner to take place in the Middle-East for years.

News of the tape emerged hours after a senior UK diplomat held talks with Palestinian leaders as part of the effort to secure Mr Chambers' release. Consul-General John Makepeace, who is based in Jerusalem, said Mr Chambers' continued captivity remained of "great concern" to the UK, but repeated government warnings that they would not negotiate with terrorist organisations.

CHAPTER 9

The door slammed shut. Richard raised the blindfold and stared through the darkness and at the wall tiles, which were glowing blue in the moonlight. He entertained the possibility that, at the next opportunity, he might fly at his young guard with fists flying. He would render the Chain Man unconscious with a swinging right hand before dealing with Mr Friendly and the Second Coming. Then he would run into the street and freedom. He saw this imaginary version of himself, and his heart sank. He had never swung a punch in his life, and at his age, it was not a good time to start. He would be more likely to damage himself and, what was more, the pain in the soles in his feet would prevent him from running anywhere. Richard was forced to look at the facts.

The truth was that his life was overwhelmed and truncated by the number three. Three hours to live. It was a no-parole life sentence with a number attached to it. He could count it down to oblivion. Three hours. One hundred and eighty minutes. Ten thousand eight hundred seconds. Why did they not give him four hours or five? Perhaps the number three was random, in the same way that everyone's life span was random. Then he remembered that, in his case, the number three represented the hours till dawn, a traditional time for executions, and a time when life woke up, when people had control over themselves. So be it. If his last moments were to be in the glimmer of first light, he was determined to stand up straight and face the inevitable with arms spread out to greet the day. He did not want to die, but he was not afraid of death. It was the thought of the life he could never have that shattered him. The extra hours mattered, and he wanted them now. He could only guess at the sensations he would miss in the hours denied to him.

Richard clambered to his feet. He was aware of the pain, but barely made the connection between his stinging soles and his awkward gait. He was focused instead on the things that were rushing in to crowd his thoughts. There were so many things that each found expression in one word, and each word evoked worlds of feelings and emotions.

Family. He dropped into the plastic chair, steepled his hands together and raised the tips of his fingers to his nose. Family meant absolute security in early childhood. It represented never-to-be forgotten times and places, memories that could be conjured up as a golden age; Kellogs-Corn-Flake and sun-drenched mornings when mother stayed at home and father went to work. Family was also disappointments, youthful rebellion and escape, and the wounds of blame and guilt unhealing. It was the scramble in later life to return to the illusory security of the place where it had all started. No matter that the place had moved on or had never been. It was the guiding light, the northern star that Richard discovered in his later years, and now it was about to be extinguished.

Home. He saw the turrets and gables of his home near the Lakes. There had been a time when these characteristics of Victorian architecture were associated with his first home, Ashwood, and they prompted an emotional response to incidents in his childhood he had once been reluctant to revisit. No more. In his mind's eye he saw the light streaming through the windows of home, felt the pleasure of Ben's hand light on his shoulder, the comforting warmth of the coal fire on his cheeks, the reassurance of Nicole's presence: a flitting shape in the kitchen, a shadow on the wall, a hand on the door knob. Home was the place to fart with freedom, to walk naked or sing in the shower, the place where, sunken-cheeked, open-mouthed and snoring, he could sleep the sleep of the dead in front of the News at Ten.

Loss. A future denied. No more struggling with seeing Ben grow up and wishing there was a pause button to slow down his progression toward adulthood. For Richard, that progression would cease in two hours and some minutes. From then on, Ben would be cast adrift with just a memory of his father, and the grieving process would begin. Ben would cling on to every moment spent with his father; cherish every memory of him; of every walk across the fells, of every camping trip, of every model plane that never flew and of every bedtime story cut short by the call of sleep. But no matter how hard Ben tried, over time, and feature by feature, Richard would be removed from Ben's consciousness. Then, perhaps, he would clutch on to one of Nicole's photographs, keep it safe in his wallet until the day he took it out and saw it was faded and worn, cracked down the middle and, what was more, he realised he could no longer relate to the old-fashioned clothes or the hairstyle. The photo would then be allowed to disintegrate in some hidden corner of the wallet until finally, the word "father" became just the idea of a person who never was, and Ben would be fatherless. Then, and only then, would the grieving process come to an end. Nicole would help

Ben deal with it; show him that there was no need to feel any guilt at his father's disappearance.

Nicole would handle his death in her inimitable and compartmentalised way. She always gave 100%. She gave 100% while counselling her patients at the prison. She gave 100% to Ben when she was at home and 100% to her husband when Ben had gone to bed. She also gave 100% to her notebook. He saw her reaching for it at night, write her poems about grief and loss and then go, 100%, to sleep. And because he loved her Richard hoped that Nicole would find complete happiness in another man. He also hoped that she would carry him under her arm and look kindly on him from time to time as she flitted in the kitchen or put her hand on the door knob.

Apart from old photographs and memories, what was he, finally, going to leave behind? At some point in the future, his memorial stone would remain untended because there would be nobody left to remember him. With nobody to remember him, he might never have existed. Some of his articles had once created quite a stir but these would be superseded by other pieces written by scholars with access to more evidence. What about his students? Legions of them had passed through his lectures, but he would never know how he had touched their souls or altered their lives. Perhaps some of them were out there now and remembering him as he remembered Father Peter. Richard now regretted that he had never found the time to look the priest up and tell him just how much he had valued and appreciated him.

Richard was trembling. Perhaps he was afraid of death after all. But death, he told himself, could be an adventure. He raised his head and let his chin rest on his steepled fingers. He might soon be able to answer all those questions about the meaning and purpose of life, questions he had never been able to answer. He closed his eyes and tried to focus on the air entering and leaving his nostrils. He allowed himself to drift out of his body, to stand at his own shoulder and watch himself. His pain and his isolation were the same pain and isolation felt by all people who had once endured, and all people who were still enduring, the consequences of humans' worst qualities. The thought of their pain supported him. Their deaths comforted him. They would reinforce his own imminent death and give him a special destiny and a special power. Maybe this would be the power to change, the power to heal and to make a new life in this world without him. He experienced a moment of joyous energy. He was alive. And he was not alive because they had not killed him yet, not alive because he ate and drank. He was alive because finally and after all those years of life, he knew he could love and trust humanity.

Richard rose to his feet and paced around the room, his excitement anaesthetising his painful soles. Then he glanced at the tiles around him and he lay down on the mattress and stared at the ceiling. He was clutching at straws. His death would mean nothing except to those who loved and needed him. He put out both arms towards the ceiling as if he would stave off the executioner's sword. His spine relaxed. There was a pleasant tingling sensation in his chest and, with a heaviness weighing on his limbs, his breathing slowed to an even regularity, and he felt himself sinking into sleep. He thought he heard a voice, recognised its uncompromising urgency.

He awoke and remembered that he was at the end of his life. Sunlight was streaming through the window and someone was outside the door. Then there was a knock. On with the blindfold. The door swung open, and a voice cried out:

"Up, up, up." It was the Second Coming. "Sit down. Here on the chair."

"Is it time?"

"Yes, it is time."

"Should I face the wall?"

"Have you anything else to say to us?"

"No."

"You can save yourself. All you have to do is make the video – take it seriously."

Richard's mouth was dry. He was detached, not quite there as if the Second Coming had addressed his shadow while the real he stood in another place. He watched the detached shadow lift its chin and say:

"No. I will not help murderers."

Richard was aghast at this daring and defiant performance. The words had appeared as though by magic, and he was unable to identify the source of this refusal to aid and abet. His head told him to save himself, to agree to their demands and go back home to his family. But there were other voices, distant, murmuring but persistent. And then he thought he saw the speakers. Standing at the detached shadow's side was his father. Indistinct and ethereal, he was whispering words into his son's ear, and the shadow was repeating them like a ventriloquist's dummy. Beside him was Richard's young self. The little boy was staring at him and saying: *I am looking at what I have become. Please don't let me down.*

"I will not participate in terrorism," Richard said.

"You refuse to help us?"

"I will not cause pain to my fellow men."

"I take that as a 'no' then."

"Absolutely."

"Then there will be no reprieve. Your death sentence will be carried out."

"When?"

"Now."

"Can I write some letters?"

"You can write one letter."

"I need to write many letters – I have my family, my friends and colleagues."

"One letter."

"Only one?"

"If you can't help us, then we can't help you."

"Just one letter?"

"Yes, and be quick."

The Second Coming turned and walked from the room. Left alone, Richard felt just one step away from that eternity of darkness that would soon represent his future. He understood the need human's have for physical contact, or why some people needed the constant companion of noise – the radio, the television – anything to cover the silence, that echo of eternal darkness. Hope returned to him when he heard the knock on the door – but he had no need to push at the blindfold for he had not removed it. Two people came in. One was the Second Coming.

"So – write your letter."

The other man pushed a writing pad and a pencil into one of Richard's hands.

"You have ten minutes," the young guard said.

Both men left. Richard removed the blindfold and stared at the writing paper. He lifted the pencil and wrote:

Dear Nicole and Ben

He looked up. What do you say to your wife and child at a time like this? What words could express his feelings? Perhaps there were no words, and he would have to resort to comparison, use metaphors and similes to communicate his feelings. That would not do either. This was no time for poetry, and Nicole had never experienced the feelings that filled him now. He was wordless, voiceless and alone. His feelings were, quite literally, indescribable. He decided to focus instead, not on his feelings, but on hers, and show respect for her imminent grief.

I'm writing to you from my prison cell. This is a first and last letter from here and it isn't a very happy one I'm afraid. I'm telling you of my death sentence and execution, and I've got only a short time to live.

He lifted the pencil from the paper and his mind began to wander, to look for something meaningful to write. He was groping in a dark place, a vacuum in which his thoughts had no words and were shadows, and his words were without thoughts so that they were dead things and he was already living amongst them. Perhaps he was already shutting down. Maybe he was already dead. He shook his head and put pencil to paper again.

I ask you to have much courage. I'm going to die thinking of you, up to the last second, as I always have. Choose a good, honest man who will make you happy. Keep my memory as long as you wish, but I have to tell you one thing: no one lives with the dead. I had made beautiful plans for you and me and Ben, but fate has decided differently.

And now the lie.

I am well and in good spirits. I have done my best but I am sorry that my life must end like this. If you like, you should give something of me to Ben so that he can be aware of his father. This thing should always be with him.

But what? Given the opportunity, he would have given him a video, something to watch and listen to when Ben reached eighteen. But what would he say to him other than the usual parental platitudes: *I just want you to remember me with fondness? I wish you happiness?* Even that was a subjective concept. Happiness, for Richard, was an underlying sense of satisfaction with life in general and with specific areas of life such as relationships, health and work. But it was always relative to unhappiness and anyway, Ben might define the term in a different way.

Give him my walking stick. If he ever goes walking over the fells he might want to take it and me with him for a stroll over the tops. At least he will be able to feel my presence and he may even want to talk to me from time to time just to keep me company. Please give him the stick, the one with the badges from Mittenwald, and tell him why I want him to have it.

There were movements from outside the door. He scribbled down the first ending that came into his head.

I end in kissing you with all my heart, and your memory accompanies me to the end.
God be with you
Richard

And he folded the paper into three.

A knock at the door – blindfold on. Two men entered.

"Time is up," said the Second Coming.

He snatched the letter from Richard's hands and unfolded it. There were a few seconds of silence.

"Who is Nicole?" His voice was flat – empty of any emotion.

"My wife. Please make sure the letter is delivered."

"Umm."

The young guard said:

"I post it. You want eat?"

"No."

"You want last drink? Beer, whisky?"

"No. Perhaps a cup of tea."

The young man disappeared for a minute and then came back with a plastic beaker, which he placed between Richard's hands. He sipped at the tea. He had no regrets about the past. He had always done what he thought was right at the time. And yet, he did feel a deep sense of waste; wasted opportunities he could and should have taken while he had the chance.

Those wonderful flowers on Capri, their perfume came and went from him in a breath before his attention was diverted elsewhere. The sun, trickling through the cypress trees on the hills above Verona, passed him in an instant. The smell of snow on the top of Monte Grappa came and went like his own footprints. There had often been a voice in his head telling him to stay longer, that the time was now and would never return. But there had also been another voice telling him to move on, that there was always something a bit better just round the corner. Richard now knew that there was nothing better, that he should have lingered longer to enjoy those moments.

"You want more tea?"

"No, thank you."

The Second Coming cocked his pistol.

"Stand," he said.

"A few seconds please, to pray for those I love."

"Be quick."

Richard closed his eyes. Images and masks of the people he loved crowded his thoughts. He could only watch as his wife, his son and his father filed past, unreachable, untouchable, under the scrutiny of his inner eye. He wished Nicole and Ben happiness and a long fulfilling life and he asked them not to forget him – at least not completely.

"Are you ready?"

"Just one moment, please."

And in that one moment he tried to recall what he felt on his wedding day, at Ben's birth, and on seeing Ben's first faltering steps, and in that moment he floundered. What remained was the idea of a sensation but not the sensation itself.

"I'm ready."

"You want to say anything else."

"Yes."

"Hurry then."

He crossed his hands and lowered his head.

"God help me to fix my eyes not on what is seen but on what is unseen. For what is seen is temporary but what is unseen is eternal."

"Is that it?"

"Yes."

"Stand up then."

Richard struggled to his feet.

The young guard left the room. A few seconds later a radio burst into life and the words of an old song filtered into the room. *Let's dance together, let's dance all the night, let's dance until the morning light...*

He felt the Second Coming shift and tense and there was cold metal against his temple. Richard closed his eyes. The music was in the air around him. *But in the morning when you are gone, I feel so lonely I could fly.* He tried to fly with it and ignore the urine that was trickling down his legs, disregard his bowels, which were about to move. He wondered. Do you hear the shot? Do you feel the bullet enter your skull? Do you feel any pain or are you there one moment and flying unseen through eternity the next? *Fly away, fly away, baby...* In a second he would know. He would know.

CHAPTER 10

The gun nudged under the blindfold and pressed against his temple. Richard angled his head towards the window, and the daytime penetrated his blindfold and filled his eyes with an opaque light. The gun was removed.

"No, not this morning," said the Second Coming. "Later." Whether the man had planned this reprieve or whether he had made an impulsive decision was of no immediate interest to Richard. His body strength flooded from his legs, and he collapsed on the chair, an explosion of light celebrating his extra seconds of existence, and his mind wiped clean of everything except a savouring of life. As miserable as his life was at that moment, it was his, an unexpected gift at Christmas - he was alive and tingling from head to foot.

Richard heard the Second Coming settle the pistol somewhere in the folds of his *jalabiyah*.

"We can do something much better with you."

When Richard replied with nothing but a grunt, the Second Coming added, "Yes, something more suitable for a man of your standing."

There was a rustle of clothing and the sound of feet crackling on the concrete floor. Richard did not raise his head in an attempt to follow the man as he made his way to the door. He had learned by now to be a blind person, learned how to sense direction of movement, to feel emotions in the air, to hear a rapid heartbeat, to know hate in the tone of voice and to know when to be afraid. At that moment, Richard hardly noticed the Second Coming's feelings or his absence. He did not even remove the blindfold. He picked up nothing but a joyous sense of being alive, wanted to sing it out, cast its light upon the back of the world and tell everyone that this happiness was within their reach and waiting to be grasped.

Several minutes later, the door clicked open, and the smell of the young guard's aftershave and of the tea he was carrying drifted into the room.

Richard wanted to put out his arms and embrace the boy – to celebrate the fact that they were both alive, that he had nearly lost the youngster before he had even got to know him. He felt a sudden rush of regret at all the people he had never got to know when presented with the opportunity. Most of his encounters with others represented smothered possibilities, a wastage of his power to hold out a hand to someone different, to listen and to attempt to increase, even by a tiny amount, the quantity of humanity in the world.

The guard placed the tray on the floor. A real concern for Richard's ordeal and his fragile mental state was present in the youngster's reluctance to break the silence, and in the gentle care with which he arranged the teapot, the spoons and the paper cups. He could have been preparing breakfast tea for a sleeping king rather than for a desperate man whose trousers were soaked in urine.

"Don't you have a girlfriend?" Richard asked. "Perhaps you are married?" He needed to show the guard that he was all right, that his brush with death had not changed him. "Tell me about your family again. How old are your sisters? And your father? He has a record shop you told me."

The guard took Richard's hand and wrapped the thumb and forefinger around the cup. The youngster allowed the tips of his own fingers to linger for a while on Richard's wrist before lifting them away. Richard drank.

"Thank you."

The guard did not immediately respond, but Richard heard his lips smacking; and his breath, coming in short bursts, suggested he was having difficulty putting some thoughts into words. Eventually, and in a flat, controlled tone, he said:

"My mother here. Rest of family not here no more. Ten maybe twelve years ago - Israelis come one day and…"

His voice petered out, and while a wave of sadness rippled between the two men, Richard was flooded with perception. What was about to come was a confession. It was not an admission that he had lied, not a guilty plea that he had misled Richard into believing he had a family. The young guard's confession would be an acknowledgement to himself that he was coming to terms with a huge loss. Richard imagined he was with the boy and his memories, saw great pain in his life, saw through his eyes the screaming, the blood and the body parts.

"I'm sorry."

"Sorry? Life is a shit. It's cheap, yeah?"

Richard snapped his head towards the voice. Its tone had somehow weakened in a way that suggested the boy was still discarding the bits of himself his family had taken with them. Richard wanted to tell him that despite everything, life was the most precious of gifts, and he had nearly lost his. At the same time, the youngster's tragic loss prompted a strong need in Richard to sharpen his own memories: memories of his wife, his father and his son. He was afraid that their images were getting old, repetitive, and separating themselves from reality. What he needed now was a renewal of their touch, their smell, and the sound of their voices. Without that renewal they were all doomed to history.

"Life's not cheap if you can help people like you have helped me. And our lives don't belong to us. They belong to those who love us. You can help them too."

The guard said nothing for a moment, but Richard heard him fidgeting. Then, on one breath he said:

"Like I help sisters and dad, yeah? I don't know why they say goodbye when I say I need them."

"I'm sorry. I…"

"I tell you what they do to family, yeah?" Richard sensed the young man's face darken, and he had spoken sharply as though unwilling to hear empty apologies beside the agonising pain that was the loss of his family.

"Two bangs," he said, "quick - like bang, bang, the silver hammer, you know? I come quick. The shop is no touched. CDs and records are all there but my father is no there. Where has he gone?" His tone held a suggestion that his question required an answer, but Richard remained silent. He knew the boy had to say it himself, hear his own words expressing the inexpressible. "No, not there. He's not there. He gone somewhere and never come back home. One day he come home. He tell me he come home in the music. Every day I sit with him and listen music, yeah? Yes, one day – maybe when I'm old and grey."

There was a pause while the youngster gathered himself. Richard reflected that for years the boy's grief had been too much for him. Perhaps now he was on the edge of coming to terms with his loss so that the grieving could begin. Worse was to come.

"Then I go upstairs. Asma is on floor. She die, yeah? Ayah is in room too. She is in…." He paused, thrashing about for words he did not know in a situation he never understood. Richard heard him back away into a corner of the room. "She in here. How you say?"

"The corner?"

"Yeah, she in corner. She here and there and everywhere but head not there. Head not there no more. Head on the wall up there…." Richard guessed he had raised his eyes and was speaking towards the ceiling. "In head? What in head?"

Richard turned his face towards the floor and began sucking at his lips as though reluctant to release the word that hovered there. He said the word to himself as if to test his reaction to it.

"The brain."

"What? Rain?" said the young guard. "What that rain?"

Richard braced himself, closed his eyes on his already darkened world and said:

"The brain."

"Yeah, the brain on the wall. Ayah's brain. She wants be doctor, yeah? And now her brain all over…all over here, there and everywhere, yeah?"

His voice faded away as if an insulating curtain was falling over the images that haunted him. Richard knew from his own experience that you never got over something like that. You learned how to deal with it, incorporate it into your life and carry on. But your life is never the same again. There were too many regrets, too many what-ifs and too much guilt, and these would always return to taunt you when you least expected them. That was a fate that Nicole and Ben had just been spared.

"What are they going to do with me next?"

"No questions, please." His voice was distant, disconnected from feelings of any kind. Richard guessed he was still in the room in which he had found his sisters, and asking himself why it had to be them rather than him. He wondered if this survivor guilt was responsible for the boy's moodiness. He had gone on in life but not in living. He could not allow himself joy or happiness or anything that might let him return to a normal life. Perhaps that was why he had ended up in a terrorist organisation. These groups must have recruited a lot of boys like him. In some ways there was nowhere else for him to go. In that sense, he and his guard were both prisoners. Richard felt sorry for the boy but he had his own life and death to consider.

"Your leader said he would kill me later. How much later?"

"Later."

"When? Tomorrow? Next week? Next month?"

"Just later."

"But when? When?"

The young guard remained silent for a while, but his silence somehow contained an element of doubt.

"Perhaps never."

"You mean, they won't kill me?"

"To cooperate is life for you, yeah?"

"Yeah? If I cooperate with them, make their video, they do not kill me."

"Perhaps."

"No, never. I no help murderers and terrorists and I…"

Richard paused, catching an idea of the guard's face in his imagination; or was he feeling it? The youngster was staring at him, mouth open in disbelief, and incapable of believing his own ears. Richard's words, coming from another place, were putting his life at risk again after he had discovered just how much he valued it. Perhaps it was the conviction with which he uttered those words that had surprised them both. But where had this conviction come from? Was he a prisoner of an attitude of mind handed down to him from his father and his father's father or was he transcending himself and finding qualities he never believed he had?

Before Richard had the chance to change his mind, the guard, now sullen, left the room and locked the door. Richard removed the blindfold, and his gratitude for the light that streamed in through the ceiling window brought tears to his eyes. To celebrate his living body, he stood up and touched his toes. Then he lay down and raised his legs a few times. He sat up. Maybe there were no real convictions, and he was just a fool. Maybe he was just an ordinary man struggling to find a higher meaning in life by defending a set of principles – anybody's principles.

There was a knock. Blindfold on.

"You want video, yeah?"

Richard felt a combination of panic and hope stirring somewhere near his stomach. Later, the Second Coming had said, but at least there was time for a film. He nodded.

"Yes, I want video."

The guard approached and pulled at his elbow.

"Come with me, please."

He led Richard out of the room and along the corridor. The air was stale to his nostrils, his trousers were still wet and his freedom restricted to the space between the walls and the boys fingers pressing into the small of his back. But Richard was immune to these inconveniences. Life, he now saw, was much more than bodily comfort or discomfort; it was beyond that. It was a privilege to be alive.

They stopped, and the guard knocked on a door. Richard caught another glimpse of the young man's face in his mind's eye or was he just sensitive to the boy's moods, the smell of his emotions? They stood in an awkward melancholic silence until at last the youngster placed his fingers around Richard's wrist and pulled him closer. "Listen, *ustazz*," he said. "Let me whisper in your heart." His thumb caressed Richard's pulse. "Goodbye, *ustazz*. Goodbye."

Before Richard could reply, the youngster threw the door open, pushed Richard through and into a pungent smell.

"My pleasure is a hot gun," he said. Then he added, "Take off blindfold, yeah?" And as soon as Richard plunged into this other sensory world, his visions of the guard and his moods vanished. Richard knew where he was even before the door closed and he removed the blindfold. The camera was still on its stand, and the chair on which he had sat and made his pitiful act of defiance was still in place. Behind the chair was a green banner adorned with swirls of Arabic writing. A rifle and a grenade launcher were propped up against the chair back. An ammunition belt lay curled up on the floor.

The Second Coming was standing in spots of light at the back of the room. A curtain had been drawn back, and he was working at a bench below a small and barred window. He had removed his *jalabiyah* and was naked to the waist, but he had left the *kuffieh* wrapped round his face. In the fierce light, burn marks shone on his arms and torso. The Second Coming looked up and took the shocked expression on Richards's face with casual indifference.

"Dangerous work," he said. "These days we have better material to work with. Plastic explosives brought in from other countries."

On the surface in front of him were a number of cylinders. To Richard, they looked like water pipes.

"In the beginning we had to use acetone peroxide but it is very unstable – you see?"

He held out his hands and Richard saw that two of his fingers were missing. "Like most organic peroxides, acetone peroxide can detonate under impact, warmth, friction, spark or electricity." The Second Coming twisted his arms round, and Richard saw the extent of his burns. They travelled up his arms, across his chest and down each flank of his body.

"And today I am doing things the old way. I am preparing the old type of bomb. Why am I doing this?"

"I have no idea," Richard said. He was not interested in how to make bombs. Bombs were ready-made things that appeared out of nowhere in the skies above Dresden or Nagasaki. He had never associated bombs with active, people-led construction. He could not imagine making bombs for a living, or saying to others: *Hello. My name's Richard. I'm a bomb maker. But please don't be alarmed. I don't drop them and kill people. I'm not responsible for what other people do with them.*

A feeling of disgust with himself made Richard shiver. Was he guilty of intellectualising warfare or had he succumbed to government attempts to sanitise it? Richard knew that these attempts were nothing more than propaganda. And the purpose of that propaganda was to turn the unacceptable into something the public could deal with. In this way, the people could be persuaded to support their boys without grasping what it was they were supporting. The bombs that fell on Baghdad did not smash women and children. Those bombs were somehow pretty and holy and they represented a reasonable way of settling an argument with a ruthless enemy. The victims of those bombs never bled to death in agony. They expired gracefully. And they did this out of sight and away from the TV cameras. It was as if they had excused themselves and gone to the toilet.

The bomb under construction in this room was somehow different. It was dirty, evil and cowardly, made by murderers and killed innocent women and children.

"Can I see a video?"

The Second Coming was packing the pipes into what looked like the inner lining of a jacket. Attached to it were two straps that reminded Richard of his rucksack. Images of the Lake District flashed through his mind.

"Yes the old way is better," the Second Coming said. "Why is it better you may ask? TNT is, after all, a more powerful explosive." He was warming to his subject, sounded like an enthusiastic salesperson pitching his wares to an audience of housewives. "But acetone peroxide has a number of major advantages. It is easily available and the simplest to prepare. We can buy the components in any household store without provoking suspicion. As you know, hydrogen peroxide is used for bleaching hair, and acetone is used for nail polish as a solvent. Secondly, it can be easily plasticised and fitted to our belts. But the most important advantage is that acetone peroxide cannot be detected by their dogs."

He began brushing his fingers through a variety of objects that lay strewn over the bench. There were some ball bearings of various sizes, some nails and screws, and some washers and what appeared to be razor blades tied together with wire.

"Watch a video? Who said…? Ah, your guard…his English. He did not have the benefit of an international education. Maybe he did not make himself clear. You will help us make a video not watch one."

With both hands, he scooped up some of the metallic bits in front of him and cupped them into the pipes. He then selected a razor-blade wire and let in dangle from between his fingers.

"Look at this beauty," he said in a whisper. "This is the killing power. The explosion and its shock wave are rather small because of the amount of explosive used." He slid the razor blades into the pipe and clapped his hands together. "It is these objects that do the real work."

He then began running a piece of wire through the pipes and he did not look up when the door opened. Connecting the wire to a red button, he straightened his back and acknowledged Mr Friendly's presence with a slight nod. Mr Friendly was wearing shorts and a T-shirt. He examined the filled coat lining with his eyes and fingers. The *kuffieh* around his face made several movements before his voice emerged from its folds.

"So," he said, "we are prepared for our journey to paradise."

The Second Coming said:

"A good target has been selected by our agent. It's a wedding. Many army officers will be present. We need to send the best."

"And something special," said Mr Friendly.

"Yes indeed. Something very special. A very special bomb."

He picked up the lining and took up a position at Mr Friendly's shoulders - a gentleman helping a lady with her coat. Mr Friendly slipped the lining on and, turning his back to Richard, he spoke over his shoulder.

"Come, *ustazz*. Tie the straps together. Come…"

Richard put out his hands and let them hover as if the straps were flowing with powerful currents of electricity.

"They won't bite, you know. Yes, that's right but not so tight. You don't want to suffocate me too, do you? I must have space to breathe…"

He turned his attention to the Second Coming.

"How many triggers?"

"One. Just one trigger for one big bomb."

"It is short notice," said Mr Friendly.

"The mule has been notified. He's expecting you." His tone was official, communicating only the information while his emotional attention was elsewhere. He was filling more pipes with screws, ball bearings and shards of plastic. He picked several up, cupped them in his hand and examined them as if they were rare gems. His voice was quivering with feeling. "And these little needles cause endless problems for their medics. They don't show up on x-rays, you know." He poured them into a pipe and then allowed his voice to return to its official tone. "The mule will meet you on the other side and take you to the city. Paradise awaits you there."

He then angled his body over the bench and began filling another jacket with the pipes. To Richard he resembled a cruel and evil magician poring over his potions. He ran the wire through the pipes, and turned to Richard.

"Your turn," he said.

"What?"

"Put it on."

Richard did as he was told. The Second Coming fussed around him like a mother dressing her child. "Stand still. Still, I said. There…that's right." He took a step backwards and admired his work. "Now stand next to my friend here."

Mr Friendly had grabbed a rifle and was standing in front of the banner. The Second Coming went over to the camera and motioned to Richard.

"Sit behind him and say nothing – nothing." He raised his head above the camera and focused his attention on Richard. "You don't want another beating do you? Then do as you're told." And he buried his head behind the camera lens, raised his arm and then let it fall in the manner of a time-keeper.

At this signal, Mr Friendly began waving his rifle and chanting something in Arabic. His tone was grave but measured. Then he spoke in English. He stated the demands of his group – the withdrawal of US forces from the region and removal of US support for Israel.

"We are a double bomb for a very special purpose. To show that this is a struggle for real democracy against tyranny, both we and our western sympathisers are prepared to die as martyrs for the cause."

The Second Coming emerged from behind his camera and switched it off.

"So you see we have decided," he said. "What do you think?"

There was a long silence.

"Hm? We mean to use you as a weapon, you understand?"

A longer silence and then to Mr Friendly:

"He hasn't grasped it yet. We mean to use him as a living bomb, and he has nothing to say."

"You mean to use me as a suicide bomber?"

"Ah, he speaks at last."

"I won't go along with it. It's ridiculous."

"You have no choice. Choice is an illusion."

There's always choice."

"Not with us."

"Then I shall tear it off, I…"

"You will go with my friend here. You will be picked up over the border and you will travel by car to the city. Our mule will take you to a certain place and you will walk into the hall where the reception is taking place."

"And you expect me to detonate this thing?"

"No. My friend will detonate it for you. All you have to do is go along with him. But you will not leave his side."

"But you can't stop me from running away."

"True - you can run away but if you try and remove the belt, it will explode. Alternatively, my friend may use his trigger – boom!"

"Then I shall find a policeman…a security guard and warn them of…"

"And you will die anyway. What would you do if you were a policeman confronted by a man with a bomb belt? You'll be shot dead. And if they don't shoot you, my friend will press his little red button – here, look. You and your helpful policeman will both be blown to pieces. Whatever you do, you will die for our cause."

"I'll be murdered for your cause."

"As you like."

"And when will this take place?"

Not now – later, the Second Coming had said. *Not now – later*. How much later? Next week? Next month?

"Tomorrow," he said, "Tomorrow you will die for the cause."

British Council Newsletter – Middle-East

New study at University of Auckland suggests religion is not the primary motivation of suicide bombers. Between 1980 and 2006, suicide attacks made up four percent of all terrorist attacks in the world and killed 14,599 people. This number represents a third of all terrorism-related deaths.

Suicide bombing attacks are a favourite weapon among terrorist groups. These attacks are highly effective and they cause fear amongst the populace. Reports of suicide bombings appear almost daily. However, few reports attempt to explain why the bombings occur or what the motivations of the bombers are. The University of Auckland now has some tangible data which might help us understand why these bombings happen.

The data tells us that it is politics more than anything else that motivates suicide bombers.

The evidence from the database largely discredits perceived wisdom that religions or personality disorders cause people to blow themselves up. However, the research suggests that even though religion can play a vital role in the recruitment of suicide bombers, their real driving-force is a mix of motivations. These include: politics, humiliation, revenge, and despair.

CHAPTER 11

The late afternoon light struggled through the window, spreading its glow over the ceiling but failing to penetrate the floor light, where Richard rested his arms on his drawn-up knees. His head lay on the crook of his arm; his eyes were closed to approaching nightfall. He had never liked the twilight. The daytime was dying and the evening had yet to begin, and in the dreary interval morbid thoughts would move uncontrolled and uncontrollable in his head. Accompanying them was the monotonous hum of the fan, a constant reminder that time was running through his fingers and away from his grasp. The knock at the door was a promise of relief, a welcome interlude in the countdown to death; but when the door clicked open he did not immediately look up. A woman's voice broke through the silence.

"Are you afraid?"

She might have added the expression, "as well," for the emphasis on the word "you" was inclusive of both speaker and listener, suggested a bond of complicity that left Richard blinking in bewilderment at the shape by the door. In the uncertain light, her dark robe seemed to emerge from the darkness itself. She was as intangible and as delicate as a shadow. She muttered something under her breath, perhaps words spoken for herself rather than for public consumption, but Richard was sure he heard her say:

"We must be strong."

The use of the pronoun, "we" was too much for Richard. It appeared to draw him into a conspiracy about which he had never been consulted. A retort was on his lips before he could stop it.

"You dare come here and tell me of your school and your ideals about peace and good will – you who belong to an organisation that murders people."

The disappointment that accompanied these bitter words brought with it the realisation he had been feeling betrayed. This woman had convinced him of her sincerity. Then he had seen the bomb, the plastic needles that would not show up on x-rays. With an anger that came from hurt feelings, he added:

"How hypocritical is that? How dare you talk to me about being strong?"

"But it wasn't always like that." She spoke with tiny shakes of the head and with a calm sadness that rang with truth. "Until my husband's death we were reconciliatory. Then a few years later things got militant, and it became too late. When my son was old enough, he got involved. I still work for a solution by peaceful means. But the main reason for my presence here is to keep an eye on Hisham."

"Hisham?"

"My son. Your guard. He's a good boy but I'm losing my grip on him."

Richard allowed his gaze to slant towards the floor. Perhaps this woman was having difficulty cutting the umbilical cord. The unconditional love of a parent for a child was something he understood. He also knew that the process of letting-go would be difficult. Ben was nine, but the process was well underway. You let them go alone to birthday parties; you let them go for weekend sleepovers, but Richard had no experience of the point when a boy became a man, decided for himself what was right and wrong and refused to let others say "no" for him. He shrugged. None of this mattered anyway. Unless his kidnappers changed their minds, he would not live to see another nightfall, to experience the dreary interval between night and day, to watch Ben decide for himself what was right and what was wrong.

A movement by the door made him look up. Jihadi was looking around the cell as though she had lost some valuable object; perhaps a credit card or her wedding ring – but probably her baby, Richard thought. He wished he had not been so hard on her.

"My husband Jamal was a good man," she said. "If he was with us now, he'd help his son and solve our problems, may God be praised. Losing him almost killed me. He was everything in my life. We were friends as well as husband and wife. If I hadn't been strong I would've lost my mind."

She turned her head and looked at Richard for a second before sliding her eyes away to stare into the darkness.

"My son Hisham plants sadness in me. He has never accepted his father's death. He was six when his father died but he still doesn't want to believe his daddy will never come back. When he was very small, at the beginning, I took him to the cemetery, and he used to say, 'Let him out of his grave.' Now he just listens to his father's records and watches his father's beloved Manchester United on the television. When he does this, he thinks he is near his father. What terrifies me is the thought of the day he realises that his daddy will never come back. What will he do then?"

She did not look up expectantly, waiting for Richard to provide an answer to her question. Her eyes were locked on to some point in front of her but even in the darkness of the room Richard saw that the gaze was vacant. He also saw that her body appeared to have lost its foundation of vitality. She was the solid building after an earthquake, knocked off-balance and unsafe for human habitation.

"The idea of being a member of the People's Democratic Party never crossed my mind when I was younger and training to be a teacher. However, twenty years ago I thought this would be an opportunity to make the world hear the voice of the Muslim Palestinian woman. I wanted the world to know the Palestinian woman, what she thinks about, what her aspirations are. And Islam encourages women to be in politics. When Jamal asked me to join their party I agreed. We provided humanitarian support. We were a social and institutional movement that penetrated deep into the society. It was a grassroots organization, not an underground movement. A little money in our hands would do miracles, whereas millions in the hands of others would do little to change the situation on the ground. Our leaders lived with the people, not in ivory towers, and we earned respect and had impact among the people. The problem was that our democratic ideals didn't meet the world's desires, especially Israel, America, some Arab countries, and some organizations in Palestine. The PDP was met from day one with suspicion, and later, with attempts to overthrow the leadership. After the wars with Iraq the PDP got more militant. Does this make a difference?" She stared at nothing in particular and shook her head. "The occupation does not distinguish between guilty and innocent, men or women, democratic or undemocratic when it fires missiles. The Israeli occupation wants to tear us apart and annihilate our unity. Let us unite despite our wounds and achieve the Palestinian dream. I continue our work at the school. Peace is possible. Peace is one of God's names, may God be praised."

Richard raised his eyebrows.

"Peace?"

He managed to take a deep breath before continuing, to prevent some of the last words he might speak on this earth from being angry.

"Do you think peace is possible? Do you know what they are intending to do with me?"

But he had lost her. She had disappeared in a world of her own, a world not of her own making.

"I can't give up. Mothers have a gift from God of not surrendering. When such terrible things happen, you ask yourself where wisdom is. But I believe in God. We must keep this faith. My belief gives me some hope. Even before my husband's death our life was hard because the Israeli occupation detained him fourteen times. These years taught me to be the father and the mother at the same time. I was both the homemaker and the breadwinner. When he was killed, it was the most horrific thing imaginable but I had to keep on going. I still go to bed with tears in my eyes but in the morning, I have to live my life. People cannot imagine the sadness and responsibility I carry. The daily psychological pressure only adds insult to injury. My school is shot at sometimes."

She frowned as though she were looking at a place she thought she knew and realising that she would have to change her idea of what it was because the normal rules of civilisation no longer applied there.

"What happened to your husband?"

His question seemed to tap into the direction of her thoughts, which she now verbalised, but she could have been conversing with herself.

"Jamal used to joke with me. 'What would you do if I were killed?' I said, 'I would cry.' He said, 'It is okay to cry.' I said, 'The house is too small to accommodate mourners.' Mourners arrived in busloads. The march on the day of his death was the largest ever on the West Bank. People from surrounding towns and villages joined the funeral even though the Israeli occupation placed roadblocks."

"How was your husband killed?"

"It was July 31, 1996. I was at my school and Jamal was outside his shop. Israeli Apaches fired missiles around 1:30. One missile hit him in the head. He was the main target. He was killed with Jamal Saleem, another PDP leader, and two reporters, a cousin, and two children who were passing by. The other missile hit our house above the shop. My two daughters were doing their homework upstairs. They were killed instantly. They were fourteen and sixteen years old and studying to make something with their lives. Hisham found their remains, but Jamal's body was blown to bits."

She paused, and when her foundation slipped still further, Richard swung himself to a kneeling position, ready to catch her should she fall.

"The death of my husband was not the end; a woman can go on even if she loses a dear one. She can continue to give, to progress. Her life should not stop when she loses the dear one. But you need to be strong. You need to go ahead and to know what you want. But nobody can expect a human being to suffer a dreadful loss twice. This is why I must look after Hisham."

There was a movement from the folds of her robes – she was twiddling her thumbs and her face was moving from side to side as if still searching for the precious object she had lost. When she took an unsteady pace forward, Richard was about to jump up and support her when she put out her hand and said on a breath:

"No, no. Just tell me again about Father Peter." Her pause was long enough for her to regain her breath and her composure. "Please, I beg of you. I need to hear from someone who knew our founding father. Why didn't you follow his advice?"

"I've told you everything."

"I need to know more about him. He told you that if you could love at a distance, there'd be no chains of jealousy to tie you down and that you'd be free to dance for joy under the stars. Wasn't this good advice?"

She strained a smile but Richard heard the brittleness in the voice, saw that the edifice was about to topple again.

"Yes, it was good advice."

"Then why didn't you follow it?"

"Jealousy," he said.

"Don't you think now that you should've acted on what Father Peter told you?"

"You mean; do I have any regrets?" He shrugged. "I did what I thought was right at the time." Richard was dissatisfied with that. He had made a mistake. Why was he unable to admit it, even in the face of death?

"Tell me what happened."

She folded her hands in front of her. The prospect of hearing more about the founding father of her school seemed to steady her.

"I left Father Peter at the club and I was on my way home when the storm he'd predicted broke over the city. I made it to the Hotel Continental and decided to take shelter until the storm passed. It was there that I saw Khalid and Omar, and my fate was sealed."

Richard turned his eyes away from the door and looked into the darkness. He saw an idea of his younger self standing outside the entrance to the Hotel Continental, loitering on the pavement and squinting at the dark shapes beside him. Shaking and staggering in the wind, he submits to a howling gust that grips and then releases him and pushes him through a chaos of discarded vehicles and towards the hotel entrance. Inside, some people are beating the sand from their clothes, rinsing their mouths with bottled water or fingering their ears and nostrils to dig out the fine particles of grit. Outside, the flags adorning the entrance to the grand hotel make cracks like rifle shots in the wind.

Dicky pushes his way through the crowd, turns his shoulders to the fear and uncertainty that surround him, and enters the hotel's shopping arcade. He emerges near the end of the central walkway where the arcade deteriorates into unfinished units and coils of wire hanging through the ceilings.

"Love at a distance?" Richard muttered. "As free as the wind?" He glanced at Jihadi, looked away and wagged his head, assessing the pearls of wisdom Father Peter had given him. "Free to dance under the stars?" He pursed his lips while considering this question but he eventually shrugged, and his face betrayed nothing, expressed nothing but bone structure and an arrangement of features.

"Go on," she said.

Richard looked into the darkest corner of the cell, saw himself at the display window of some Western boutique. Dicky is concentrating so hard on the latest bags from London that he nearly misses the image of two boys reflected in the window at his nose. Passing like shadows behind him, their presence barely has time to ruffle the air, but something touches Dicky and disturbs him. He makes a slight movement of the head, a light shake of disbelief, and then angles it so that he can catch sight of the boys in his peripheral vision.

Exposed in the middle of the walkway, the two boys are hand in hand and swaggering, and daring the world to challenge them. They are swinging from side to side, as carefree as the wind as to which direction to take. At what seems to be an agreed signal, the boys swerve sideways and stop in front of *Clothes Connection*. One of the boys laughs, puts his arm round the other's shoulders and looks longingly at him.

"And that," Richard said, "was how my journey began its end. The tactile boy was Omar. The other, who was comfortable with the cuddling arm, was Khalid."

"So what did you do?"

"At first, I wanted to run away from the intimacy I had seen."

Dicky spins round and glares into his shop window. His eyes are blank and take in nothing except the reflection of his head. It is nodding, accepting or rejecting a parade of thoughts that present themselves for inspection before his inner eye. Taking a deep breath, he turns round, lets his gaze wander across the walkway to *Clothes Connection*. There is nobody at the shop window. The two boys have disappeared.

Dicky looks from left to right and sets off across the walkway on the tips of his toes. Every now and then he looks at the floor as though afraid it will swallow him up. When he arrives at the spot where the boys have been standing, he glances up and down the arcade and places himself in the space where Khalid has been. Dicky stretches out his arms, cups his hands and scoops the air towards him. He then intertwines his fingers and places them on his heart.

The colour rises from his neck to his cheeks when he catches sight of the boys again. They are walking arm in arm like two lovers wrapped up and protected from the world by their own feelings and heading towards the hotel exit. Omar removes his arm and nestles into Khalid's side while his hand rests in the small of Khalid's back and guides him through the doors. They are immediately engulfed in the sandstorm and whisked away as if by a flying carpet.

"At that point I forgot all about the advice I'd been given. What was I thinking? I guess I was looking for a sign that my eyes were deceiving me. But a horrible truth was unravelling, and I had to confirm it. At the time my immediate worry was that I'd lost them and that I'd never know what I was dealing with."

"Go on, please."

But Richard is far away with his memories. He watches Dicky turn and walk into the *Clothes Connection* window. He bounces off it, and the window sets up a low rumbling sound and quivers so that his reflection and the clothes on display shimmer like a mirage. He staggers backwards, his open knuckles held to his forehead. A passer-by rests his hand on Dicky's shoulder and says something in Arabic. Dicky gazes with disapproving eyes at the man in front of him, judging him and finding him responsible for Khalid's sudden absence. He waves the man away, scowls at the exit and mutters obscenities at the sun for not trying harder to shine through the debris in the air and reveal where the boys are going next.

He runs towards the doors and emerges in the parking area. The air is vibrating to a peculiar hissing sound as of a hundred snakes, invisible in the wind, the sand and the setting sun. He stands for a moment, rolling his head from right to left. The sun has disappeared but it has left behind a deep, red glow of great beauty. A number of people brush past him, and Dicky sets off with them, grappling with the wind that harries him, threatens to grip him, carry him off and dance with him across the city.

"Please," said Jihadi, "go on."

"I found the boys in the street. They were a single shape and some way in front of me. They seemed to be joined from shoulder to waist, swaggering and swerving through the wind and the sand. Two people in the fading light, they were moving as one."

No sooner has he spotted them than they veer to the left and drop from view. To all intents and purposes, the earth beneath them has collapsed or the two have been swallowed up in a large hole, unseen in the unstable balance between day and night. Dicky quickens his stride and arrives at a gap in the wall, just in time to see the two boys disappearing down a flight of stone steps and into the thickening darkness. The area at the top of the steps is covered in swirls and dots of Arabic writing that bubble from the mouths of an array of world leaders postered on the walls around him. Dicky pays no attention to these words of wisdom and speeds after the two shadows in front of him. He often bumps into water pipes or protruding bricks, but he does not notice. Nor does he mind when weeds, reaching out to him from the dampest corners, brush his face and lash at his eyes.

He stops his descent when forced to by a break in the steps. He peers downwards. Shapes are emerging from below, and occasional lights flicker from buildings while the sounds of city life, dampened by the storm, rumble up the steps towards him.

From above, rapid heavy footsteps disturb Dicky's concentration. The footsteps are followed by a swirling *jalabiyah* and sandaled feet that shoot out of the darkness and hit the stone landing beside him. A face rises in front of his. It carries suggestions of the Arabian Nights, of nobility and integrity and its eyes peer into his, question his presence there before disappearing through a tile-framed doorway in the wall. Dicky wobbles backwards, puts out a hand to steady himself and rests it on the tiles. They are pale, warm and blue with floral designs and inscriptions. The glaze is thin and transparent and holds a promise of what might be on the other side of the door.

"A sudden and unexpected easing of the storm cleared the air of sand," Richard said. "I backed into a doorway. Some way below me, the two boys had halted and were hovering on the steps."

For several seconds, the boys are transformed from vague and shadowy outlines to a tangible and three-dimensional reality. Dicky glances at the people who pass him by. Most of them are trudging upwards with heavy bags slung over their shoulders. Their dumb faces are silent but their eyes shout, *we know what you are doing here.*

"Then the wind picked up again," Richard said, "and the sound of rapid footsteps tapping on the steps from below announced the boys' departure. I set off behind them in the creeping darkness."

The bottom of the steps leads into a narrow alley. The wind is less intense here, and beggars have gathered along the walls on either side of it. Dicky brushes past the outstretched hands that grab at his trousers and steps round legless men on wheeled boards. With powerful thrusts of their arms, these men propel themselves in his direction and chase him to the end of the alley. Other hands appear from bundles on the pavement and grab for his ankles. He trips through piles of vegetables and arrives in the main street. He leans against the wall, panting, listening.

Somewhere in the hills surrounding the centre of town, an *imam's* call to prayer from the minaret of some mosque struggles through the storm. The entreaties fall on deaf ears. Relatively protected from the wind and the sand that blast the hill tops, the downtown streets are vibrating with busy people and loud, aggressive traffic. Inside shops, young men are carving rotating spits of meat. On the pavements, older men in red and white chequered *kuffiehs* twirl their prayer beads, and veiled women in black squint smiles at the hems of Western skirts and lift their eyebrows at the click-clicking of the pencil heels of the passing Western shoes.

"I found the boys again under some coloured awnings. Their heads were hidden in hanging beads, clothing and ornaments. I watched them from my safe distance but lost sight of them when a fight broke out around me."

Two floury-white bakers, unseen in the blowing dust, swerve to avoid a car and drop the board on which they have stacked their bread. The board tips over, and the bread spills over the pavement. Just as Dicky makes a move to help the bakers retrieve their bread, the beggars rush out of the alley to get a free meal. Dicky glimpses a scurrying figure with a piece of bread between his teeth while another stacks bread on to his board. His greed is his undoing. The two bakers and some sympathetic onlookers surround him, their fists and shoes smashing down on his head. Then they chase the others. Dicky trips and falls headlong into the melee. The beggars run around squealing like pigs under the beating fists and stamping feet. Dicky covers his head and, shutting his eyes to keep the horror away, he dives sideways, rises to his feet and stumbles away from the scene. Making a rapid pirouette he glances through the legs of the gathered crowd. Angry shouts and crying follow him as he completes his spin and trots down the main street.

Fighting through a tide of swinging arms, Dicky comes out into a space by the entrance to the *souk*. From his position, the *souk* is a dark place, full of darker corners. A red light hangs down from the centre of the entrance arch and makes the darkness even deeper. Down there, in the protection of the city centre, the sandstorm is reduced to a light rustling of wind and grit.

"It didn't take me long to find the two boys again," Richard said. "They were at a vegetable stand and raising tomatoes to their lips. They then disappeared inside the market, and I hurried after them to find the truth waiting for me."

Dicky pushes through curtains of beads, passes wooden stalls and rickety carts while the boys swerve between piles of rugs, urns and other trinkets. They stop and, to the sound of vendors singing over their produce, Omar leans closer to his friend.

"He kissed him on the lips," Richard said, "and everything changed in that moment. I didn't make a conscious decision but I knew I was going to punish Omar for what he'd done."

"Revenge for hurting you?"

"Yes. I see now that Omar had committed no crime. He hurt me and I hit back. It was an eye for an eye – only at that moment, I hadn't decided what his punishment would be."

Dicky spins round like a person who has been struck in the face. He turns and staggers towards the *souk* entrance. His feet fly along the street, and he arrives at the narrow alley. A police car and an ambulance are rumbling over the potholes to the bottom of the steps. He swerves around the gesticulating crowd and outstretched hands and makes his way upwards. Some of the beggars have collected on the bottom steps and throw suspicious glances towards the alley. Dicky barely shows any sign of noticing them and he steps around the figures beside the ornate gateway. These survivors from the fight are stretched out, their bruised heads angled towards the crowd and the noise below.

At the top of the steps, Dicky crosses the road and hurries into a narrow alley. He looks at each shop he passes but hesitates outside Megorian's theatricals and costumers. He looks up at the large leering puppet that hangs over the door, peers through the window at the masks, colour palettes, brushes and pencils, pauses for a moment with his hand on the door knob and then goes in.

"The idea came to me when I was outside the theatrical shop," Richard said. "I would punish Omar by making him lose face in the most public of places – the school play. I decided to put itching powder and sneezing powder in the lion's outfit. I really didn't know he was asthmatic. It was a childish trick to hurt the boy who had hurt me."

"Did it work?"

"Yes it worked. It was much more effective than I imagined."

"How do you think Father Peter would've reacted?"

"With forgiveness," Richard said.

Only Mr Megorian's black trilby is visible when Dicky appears. He wears it to remind himself that only heads under Western hats will think Western thoughts. But when he rises from his seat behind the counter, his white *jalabiyeh* falls in folds from his shoulders and tells him not to forget his Lebanese roots. He is versatile and urbane, can converse in English, French or Arabic on any topic from football to literature. His shop is often used by local intellectuals as a meeting point and a coffee shop - a place to while away a pleasant afternoon.

He greets Dicky like an old friend, listens to his request, and boasts of the purity of his powders while pulling out a variety of packets for inspection. Dicky is monosyllabic, makes his selection and pays for it without negotiation. Then he leaves the shop, clutching his purchase. Turning a corner, he finds himself in the crowded main street that leads to the school. Some people, wrapped up from head to foot, are staring at the evening sky and trying to breathe the coarse air. A few minutes later, Dicky enters the school grounds. The wind is still blowing. He turns his back on the wind and closes his eyes, apparently intent on joining the air, the sand, and flying far away. Then, he walks into the accommodation block, up the stairs and, wiping the sand from his eyes, he hesitates outside Wilf's room.

"I never stopped to think," Richard said. "How could I have known that my actions would cause me embarrassment so many years later?"

"Thank you for telling me," said a voice from the door. "How do you feel about it now?"

"In the face of death? It doesn't matter now."

"It matters to me. To be with someone who knew our founding father is comforting."

"Then we both need comfort."

"What advice would Father Peter give me?"

Richard closed his eyes. The silence in the room was almost tangible. He did not know when he crossed the tipping point of understanding. He rose to his feet and stood in front of her.

"He'd tell you this," Richard said.

They stood in the darkness of his cell, their memories of Father Peter joining them together.

"We need to be strong," he said.

"And we need to go ahead," she said.

And together they said:

"We must never surrender."

CHAPTER 12

An indistinct murmur arrived in his room with the moonlight. The sound was like a human breath rounding over some difficult word, and Richard listened intently, tried to identify its source. He was about to get up from the floor, to place himself nearer to the sound when it became audible as human voices from outside the door.

"Can we come in?"

In the middle of the night, these words seemed loud enough to wake the whole city, but a heavy silence surrounded them, and for the moment, the door stayed closed, and no light went on. Richard had recognised Mr Friendly's voice but the other person remained quiet.

A key probed for the lock. Richard slipped on the blindfold as the door clicked open. He was kneeling on the mattress when two people entered the room. One of them pulled at the chair, and the scraping of its legs on the floor was accompanied by a human sound. Whether it was a yawn or a sigh of resignation, Richard was unable to say, but nobody spoke, and into the silence Richard said:

"To what do I owe the pleasure of this visit?" He stopped for a moment, rubbing at his forehead with his fingers, wondering at the ironic tone of his voice. "Have you come to give me the last rites?"

"Maybe yes, maybe no. It's up to you," said the other man. It was the Second Coming and he had chosen to remain on his feet. "But whatever you decide to do, I have something to tell you, something that will make you happy in your last hours."

"Happy? And what will make me happy in the face of death? Are you going to tell me that scientists have discovered a cure for death? Perhaps they have proof after all that there is an after life."

Richard's dark humour and his comic division of the word "afterlife" seemed lost on the Second Coming, but the quality of the silence that followed his remarks was infused with the impatient tolerance he often recognised in himself while waiting for his students to settle at the beginning of a lecture. The Second Coming cleared his throat. He seemed anxious to get his news across.

"It's your young guard. He's gone." And then, as if to pre-empt any objections, he added: "It was, after all, his request."

A smile came to Richard's lips. At last, the youngster had seen the light, restrained his youthful need for rebellion or adventure and allowed his civilised self to break through. What he needed now was a proper job and prospects. He might even meet a nice girl, settle down and have a family of his own. Then he would learn to deal with his survivor's guilt and find happiness with Manchester United and the Beatles. His mother would be delighted. Suspicion appeared in Richard's head like black clouds in his peripheral vision.

"Gone where? America? England?"

"England?" The Second Coming picked up Richard's questioning intonation, and ran it into an extended hum that ended in an abrupt intake of breath "I don't think so. Right now he will be on his way to Tel Aviv with our colleague who chained you." The Second Coming now spoke as if he were dictating a letter to his secretary. He circled Richard with a measured, purposeful tread. "Both are wearing belts like the one you saw yesterday. In a few hours from now they'll both be in paradise. Posters of these martyrs are already printed. Our men are ready to plaster the walls of the city and the villages once we receive the news of their success. Videos of their proclamations will be available for rent in local shops."

Richard was appalled that such a caring and sensitive boy, one who would make a fine father, should end his life in such a fashion. He wanted to say how much he had come to like this moody individual. The boy had cared for him. He brought him tea and took care of his bodily needs. There were no words to express what his mother would feel about losing her son. She must have known what was going to happen when she had poured out her soul earlier that day. He wanted to ask how she was. But this would have been but a formality. He already knew. Still kneeling, and hemmed in by the physical presence of his captor, all Richard said was:

"But he was only a boy, for God's sake. I don't even know how old he was."

The Second Coming came to a halt at Richard's back.

"He was eighteen. That's old enough to know the misery, the mess, the power cuts, the wall and all the things that are festering behind it." His voice was cold, and Richard could feel the man's hunched shoulders and almost see his anger-contorted face. "And he was old enough to make his own decisions. I told you, it was his request."

Richard considered, tried to imagine the boy standing in front of his superiors and saying: *Excuse me but I request that you allow me to explode a bomb and blow myself to pieces in the name of the People's Democratic Party.* The boy was too intelligent to believe that vast numbers of oversexed virgins and copious amounts of food and drink would be waiting for him in paradise. Anyway, that was Western propaganda designed to explain an alien concept to ordinary people in terms they could understand. Richard reflected that the youngster's behaviour was not so very different from that of those other young men who, on July 1 1916, got out of their trenches on the Somme and walked into almost certain death. Perhaps the difference lay in the word, "almost." If the suicide bombers were fanatics, did that make our boys "almost" fanatics? Perhaps he was just playing with words, and the difference lay in the simple fact that the 1916 soldiers were ours; the suicide bombers were theirs. Perhaps Mr Friendly was right. Right and wrong depended on how killing and being killed were reported in the media. Well, whatever his young guard's motivation, perhaps now he was at rest in his octopus's garden by the sea.

The Second Coming had resumed his purposeful tread. It seemed to have calmed him, but the tone of his voice suggested that he was still hovering on the edge of anger. Richard knew that even a gentle shove might push him over the precipice.

"Enough of the young guard," the Second Coming said. "Let's talk about you. After all, you too hold the future in your hands. If you decide to cooperate with us and make the video we may respect your request and spare your life."

Richard sat back on his heels. A faint tone of irritation entered the words of his reply.

"You know very well by now that I can't do that."

The Second Coming took several steps towards the centre of the room and turned to face Richard.

"But you can you know?" The pitch and volume of his voice rose. "And you deserve to live. Your wife deserves to have you and so does your child. What right do you have to deprive them of a husband and father?"

Richard saw the logic of these words come towards him in a blaze of light. And in the light he saw Nicole and Ben with their arms outstretched. He blasted the image away with a roar of real anger.

"You dare use my family to blackmail me?"

Richard stared into the darkness waiting for a response that would match his rage. There was none; not a breath or a sigh acknowledged his outburst. The ongoing silence gave him the confidence to follow up and express his doubts. He tried a smile and in an artificially calm tone he said:

"What guarantees do I have that after I make the video, you won't kill me anyway?"

"There's only faith." The Second Coming pounced on the question in a manner that suggested he had been expecting it. "There are no guarantees and there is no pretending; no pretending about Israel and its aggression, no pretending about its air strikes, no pretending about our hopelessness. The situation is ready and hungry for real sacrifices."

Richard heard these words as if from a great distance. He had turned his head towards Mr Friendly, was listening to his silence and sensed discomfort. He thought that if he could exchange a look with him, he would see his secrets and concerns.

"Come with me," said the Second Coming. "Say you'll make the video. That's all you need to do to save your life and to see your wife and child again. What is stopping you?"

"No, thank you very much indeed," Richard said. His flat and impersonal tone surprised him. He had not intended to use it. It was a tone he might use when rejecting salvation from Jehovah's Witnesses. Perhaps it was a defence mechanism – a way of distancing himself from difficult decisions. "No really, I can't."

"What! Not to save your life for the sake of your wife and child?"

"It's impossible. I couldn't betray my family."

"You'd rather die instead? Nonsense. Come now and save yourself. It'll take a few minutes. Come…"

There was a gentle rustle as the Second Coming advanced across the floor towards him. He circled Richard a few times before coming to a halt at his back. He rested his thumbs on Richard's shoulders.

"Come with me, now," he said.

"And what would you have me do?"

"You must be seen to support our cause. You must be heard to denounce the West and its policies in this region."

"And if I do this, how can I be sure you will let me go?"

"You can't be sure. But you have no choice."

"No. It's really awfully kind of you; but I can't save myself that way."

That tone again. Those overstated words of refusal infused with irony. It was so English. So why was he using it here? There was another voice, a voice from the chair. It was soft and trembling.

"So I ask you to do it to oblige me personally."

Richard stiffened, felt the Second Coming's strength bearing down on his shoulders when he made a move to rise.

"Don't say that. It is dreadful to disoblige you." He realised then that his tone was not for the benefit of his listeners. How could it be? This display of flippancy would be lost on them. No, it was for him. He was laughing at death to give himself courage. "I must save my honour, you know."

"Honour," Mr Friendly said, "is that not such an old-fashioned concept?"

"Well, maybe reputation would be a better word. It is the thing that outlives us, and is the only immortality we can have. I couldn't allow my family to suffer on my account."

Richard felt the force of the Second Coming's anger. The swelling neck, the tension of the muscles travelled through his arms and into the fingers that pressed on his neck.

"This fear of damaged reputation is another consequence of your sick and corrupt democracy," the Second Coming said. "It has reached almost epidemic proportions. The cult of the individual forces you to fear other people's criticism to the point of obsession."

The pressure of his thumbs reduced and they now massaged his neck. Richard was in no doubt that the man was trying hard to control his feelings.

"But now it is all over for you," he said. "You are alone. Nobody can see you. There is no need to keep up appearances."

Richard began to stammer out a reply, but he was having difficulty finding his voice. The Second Coming was offering him a way out, and he had a brief thought, which shamed him as soon as it appeared, that he could accept the terms of his release, and he would be free to go back home and carry on his life as normal. Or would this normality be laced with guilt and self-abhorrence? He decided to try and leave his options open.

"Then if you can arrange for me to make a video that nobody sees then perhaps I will consider it." Richard realised the idiocy of his offer before the words were out of his mouth. There was no room for compromise, for giving in to temptation. "But if I must go into the arena with the rest, I simply have to save my reputation, you know. I must also think about my ancestors. How would they judge me and my actions if they could see me now?"

"And how much of this useless talk will you remember when we arrive tomorrow at our destination?" Mr Friendly said.

"And have you," the Second Coming added, "ever seen what happens to an exploding human bomb? No?"

Richard shook his head but he had heard stories – the head and the spinal column flying into the air like a rocket, and the aftermath – the blackened head falling back to earth, bouncing like a football and lying on the tarmac, the flaps of skin from the neck blooming open like rose petals.

"Don't forget that not everything always goes to plan. I have told you, have I not, that acetone peroxide is very unstable. Sometimes bombs partly explode and remove the legs or arms of the bomber. But if the bomb doesn't kill you, don't expect mercy from the mob around you, the people you were going to blow to pieces."

"No, really. I can't cooperate, but I have faith that what I am doing is the right thing."

"Faith? Which faith do you mean? There is our inner faith and there is the warrior's faith, the faith in fighting, the faith that sees God in the sword. Don't fight us. Make the video."

"Never."

"That is only pride."

"Only pride? I'm proud of my pride."

"I feel as if I were killing you," interrupted Mr Friendly. "Think of yourself, your wife and child and make the video. If not, you face certain death. Ask yourself. What are you dying for?"

Richard considered his answer, and a black and empty hole rose before his inner eyes and it hung there with startling vividness. At the same time, a vision of a future with his family and friends glistened in his imagination and self-interest began to disarm him. But inside his breast the voice of revulsion rang out: *I don't want to help them.*

"We all face certain death," he said, "and death is not such a terrible thing. Everything else fades away into insignificance in comparison to that great event. Even my ideals and principles have already faded away into nothing."

"So you admit you are dying for nothing?"

"Yes: that is the wonderful thing. It is since all the ideas and principles have gone that I have now no doubt at all that I must die for something greater than ideas and principles."

"But for what?"

"I don't know. For my son's future?"

"A future without his father? Come down to earth," said the Second Coming, "make the video and save yourself."

"My friend - would you respect another man who did that? What would my family think?"

He peered into the darkness of his world, waiting for a response. Eventually it was Mr Friendly who replied, his words penetrating Richard with a memory of some forgotten place and time.

"What nonsense it all is, and what a monstrous thing that you should die for nothing."

The Second Coming lifted his thumbs and moved towards the door.

"Die then if you must. Prepare yourself. We'll be back in one hour."

"Wait," said Richard.

"Ah, a change of heart. Good we will..."

"No, not that. It's my last letter home. Has it been sent?"

"Well, that depends on..."

"Yes," interrupted Mr Friendly. "That has been arranged."

He and the Second Coming swept out of the room with a busy rustling of their robes. Richard pushed at the blindfold and got to his feet. Sleep was out of the question. He walked to the wall, turned and walked to the opposite wall. The departure of the two men had ushered in a funereal stillness and the memory of another time when he had been given an hour to leave the city. In his mind's eye, Richard saw two figures tip-toeing down the stairs in the perfect stillness of early morning.

Dicky and Sandra draw shallow breaths, and both of them shoot quick glances at the face of the other. Their eyes do not linger for more than a second but they are thrown like a lifeline, a reassurance that what has occurred will not disappear like a dream on waking. They pause at the bottom of the stairs. She cuddles up to him, slips her arm through his, and they stand in the doorway, hesitate on the brink before stepping out and announcing their secret to the new day.

The shadow of the school lies long over the play area before them, and it retains the echoes of absent children, holds their laughter until ready to release it when the sun comes up the next day. Now it is bleak. Tyre marks draw patterns in the sand and bear witness to the previous evening's activity. They plunge into the school's shadow, and now and then a word or sound escapes from one of them to reveal how happy they are about their plans. Passing through Abu Haida's oleander Sandra rushes forward and places herself in his path.

"I'll be here in one hour." She wags a finger in front of his face. "Don't be late."

While she sets off down the street, a flicker of doubt touches Dicky's brow, and his eyes wander with her words as if they are drifting under his nose and taking him into unfamiliar territory. He turns into the stillness of the courtyard and straight into Abu Haida. The caretaker scans Dicky's face but at first, he says nothing. Instead, he lifts his arm and points at his watch in the manner of a young child learning to read.

"Mr Khoury will see you in half an hour."

Dicky hunches and squeezes his shoulders as though the school, its walls, its closed doors and silences are pressing around him. He goes up to his room. There is not much to pack. He fingers the cassettes, turns them over in his hands and throws them in the bin. Then he hauls his rucksack onto one shoulder and makes towards the door. Seeing his own reflection in the mirror, he hesitates and looks at himself expecting to see someone who resembles a no-longer-a-virgin-Dicky. He throws the door open and marches down the stairs and into the courtyard.

Mr Khoury is standing in the shade of the passageway to the cloisters and swinging at flies with a swatter. He does not acknowledge Dicky when he sees him walking across the play area but turns and strides through the cloisters and into his office. When Dicky appears in his doorway he is pacing up and down, his hands knotted together behind his back.

"Mr Khoury thanks you for coming, Mr Chambers." He is apparently studying the patterns on the rug and does not look up when Dicky walks in. He flings his arm towards a battered chair by his desk. The chair is covered in ink and decades of children's graffiti. "Do take a seat."

Khoury settles himself behind the desk. His round and shining face looms large above carved wood and velvet, and the desk spreads out between he and Dicky like a vast landscape. Shelves behind Khoury's head contain stacked boxes and a portrait of the king. He leans forward and rests his clasped hands on the desk.

"I think you must know why I asked to see you this morning. I see you have packed your things and left your rucksack by the door."

"I'm off to…"

"So let me get straight to the point." He leans back in the chair and swivels from side to side. An expression of mild distaste is in his eyes and in the set of his features. "What happened last night was a most terrible thing. You know what I mean don't you, Mr Chambers; I mean what happened to Mr Rifkin and, more importantly for you, what happened during the school play. It was an absolute disgrace. I must be seen to be doing something about it. So you know what is coming don't you, Mr Chambers?"

Dicky nods, is about to say something when Khoury stops him with a wave of his hand.

"Yes, I thought you did. But first, I have some very bad news. Perhaps this news will come as no surprise. I received a call from the hospital this morning. It seems Mr Rifkin had another attack of vomiting. Cause of death was heart failure, and we'll put this in his obituary. Nobody needs to know he was alcoholic and died of drink. It'd be difficult, you see, for the school. How could we have tolerated such a thing in a mainly Muslim school? What sort of example is that to set before young boys?"

"Absolutely."

"I'm glad you agree. Mr Khoury's been accused of being heartless. Do you think I'm heartless, Mr Chambers?" His pause is not long enough for Dicky to say a word. "Mr Khoury has a responsibility to the school. This is my first priority and governs all my actions and my decision about you. But we'll come to that in a moment."

Dicky has allowed his gaze to wander over Khoury's casual trousers, his tennis shirt and the white and hairy arms that protrude from it. He has clasped his hands together, holds them on his stomach while twiddling his thumbs.

"Yes, Stella was with him until the end. It's a tragedy for her don't you think? Mr Steele has already left. My informers tell me he took a taxi to the airport this morning. Where's he gone?" He shrugs his shoulders. "To London I suppose, and then to Bradford where he comes from."

Dicky starts to speak but Khoury raises his voice and Dicky's words are stillborn.

"Yes, it's the best thing really. Mr Khoury says he'll have to live with Rifkin's death on his conscience for the rest of his life. As for Mr Khoury?

I've never seen or heard of such behaviour. It was unbelievable, and our boys must be protected from such things. Mr Khoury says that we've had enough. Do I have to remind you that you're guests in this country? Your corrupt Western ways will not be tolerated here. What do I mean by corrupt? Do I have to spell it out?" He is invaded by a sense of fun, and it overflows into his eyes, which sparkle with enjoyment. "The drinking, the perverse sexuality, and these ridiculous notions of fair play and of doing the right thing – these have no place in our culture."

A question appears in Dicky's raised eyebrows and in his eyes but Khoury is overwhelmed by the sense of fun he is experiencing and he lets out a roar of laughter.

"I see you are asking yourself what the relevance of this is, am I right? Let me tell you."

"Yes, do."

"What you did yesterday evening was both stupid and unforgiveable. You've brought the whole school and me into disrepute by your actions. And did you know that Omar is asthmatic? No, you didn't. Did you care? But I warned you not to get involved with Khalid and you chose to ignore my warnings. Every action has a reaction, Mr Chambers, and one day you will see the folly of your ways."

"Folly?" Dicky screws up his face in an expression of surprised distaste. Then he sighs and says, as much for his benefit as for Khoury's, "I will not tolerate persecution."

"Persecution? You really think I'm persecuting you? No, not even discriminating. In throwing you out, I shall be upholding the interests of the school and the boys in it. Mr Khoury would draw your attention to the fact that you've not even apologised for your actions. Mr Khoury doesn't want you to suffer but you've only your folly to blame. If you can't apologise on principle, you might at least do so as a matter of good taste."

Dicky stares back, his eyes concentrated and empty, his mouth now closed.

"No, you can't even do that? Then so be it. You've no grounds for complaint and no grounds for accusing me of persecution. Now – you will leave this office, pick up your bag and leave. Good. One more thing, Mr Chambers. Please turn and look at me. Mr Chambers. Look at me I tell you. You will not speak to any of the boys and you will not speak to Khalid and he will not speak to you. If you do, I can't answer for the consequences. We've had enough of this with Mr Steele and Mr Rifkin. Yes, I'm sure you know what I'm talking about. So you're off to the seaside for a few days. I hope you enjoy the Arab hospitality there more than you've appreciated it here. Goodbye, Mr Chambers."

Dicky moves forward and reaches for Khoury's hand.

"So – you will at least shake my hand. Well – I wish you good luck and

142

goodbye."

Dicky closes the door behind him and walks along the passageway towards the boy's play area. A man emerges from the deepest of shadows and stands in front of him. Dicky stops and stares in disbelief. It is Friday, and the classrooms and the play area are deserted, and a silence hangs over the buildings as if they too are resting in the intense morning heat. With his eyes adjusting to the half light, Dicky lets his gaze settle on the man's frayed suit and on his hands that he is holding up in front of him, preparing them for some work.

"Thank you, *ustazz*. Thank you for sparing my son from disgrace. Thank you. Thank you."

Deprived of the full power of light, his face betrays no sign of the suffering that had lined it the evening before. "Khalid is a good boy. He has told me about you. Thank you, *ustazz*. Thank you." He steps forward and, stretching out his arms, he takes one of Dicky's hands and holds it while searching Dicky's eyes with his. "You have had a strong influence on him. And now he wants to study in England when he is older." He smiles and characteristics of his youth and family resemblances touch his features. "He has been told to stay away from you but he wants to say farewell in his own way." He squeezes Dicky's hand and, brushing past, he walks off in the direction of Khoury's office.

Dicky strides out into the play area. He looks at the Mercedes taxi waiting in the street by the school gate. Sandra is visible in the back seat, and there are two men in traditional Arab dress sitting beside her and sharing a basket of food. Dicky pauses for a moment, turns his head and listens for a sound. The hot, dry air plays with his hair, and the sunlight burns his face and forces him to screw up his eyes. He walks towards the taxi, and there is the faint plop of his plimsolls and the sound of the cicadas clicking against the stillness. Sandra winds down her window.

"Are you OK? Yes, get in the front seat and I'll sit in the back. I'm so looking forward to this holiday, aren't you?"

The inside of the taxi is very hot and smells of goat's cheese. As the car pulls away, a young boy in full Arab dress emerges from the oleander behind them. He stretches out one arm, grabs at a lamp post and leans sideways, spinning and waving his free hand in the air in a gesture of farewell. He then springs away, performs a pirouette and with a long sweeping movement he follows the taxi as it pulls into heavy traffic. The boy rises on one foot, rotates in the middle of the street, makes stylish poses and glides behind the car and waves his hand. The boy is Khalid. He is saying goodbye and dancing for his teacher.

The car accelerates along *Jebel Abweh's* main thoroughfare and then turns down a twisting road towards the town centre and the desert highway. Just outside the market, a cart has tipped its contents onto the tarmac, and the taxi driver swings at the wheel, and the car shoots into a side street. It slows to weave its way through wooden stands and carts that are lined up along high walls. They are all loaded with towers of bread, cigarettes, sacks of rice, sugar and flour. There are other sacks, full of lentils, spices and noodles. There are flasks of oil and cans of every sort. Vendors are shouting, customers haggling and chatting, and through this continuous noise comes the whispering cry of a little boy who has found them again: *"Ustazz, ustazz, goodbye, ustazz."*

Slow, slow, quick, quick, his feet travel sideways over the cabbage leaves, the paper and the remnants of fruit and vegetables. His head is turning to the left and to the right and he skips after them rotating onto his toes to raise himself above the crowd.

Then the car accelerates out of town and on to the desert highway. Sandra leans forward from the back. Her hand is on his shoulder again.

"Don't cry," she says "you'll be OK when we arrive."

Khalid is now but a figure in the wing mirror. He is standing on the edge of the desert and with an exaggerated movement, he raises his arm above his head and sweeps it down in front of him while he bows at the waist to take applause.

Pacing up and down in his cell, Richard bade a silent farewell to the cheeky grin, the shock of fair hair and the crackling blue of his eyes, and then watched as Khalid disappeared feature by feature from his memory.

Richard reflected that the week he and Sandra spent in Aqaba was one of the most healing of his life and had led the way to new worlds of feelings and desires. Freed from the conditions of English society, he and Sandra took ownership of their time and space. They were who they wanted to be and dreamed the dreams they chose to dream. They strolled along the sandy beach in the moonlight and imagined a future free of all the crushing constraints of parents and cultural expectations. And once, when they were eating by candle-light in the Red Sea Hotel and drinking wine to the sound of rippling waves, he managed to convince himself that he loved her.

Back in England, these single children slotted into the comfortable, the recognisable and the familiar: he to the second year of his university programme in London and she to home and horses in Bosham. Both tried to continue their relationship against the increasing reassertion of their respective backgrounds and parental expectations. Both did not realise, because they were too young, that in the Middle-East they had been able to live a life without restraint. No longer bound by the values of British society they were not expected to conform to Arab ones and their relationship could take root and grow in a social and moral vacuum.

When these social differences at first reappeared, they made light of them. She joked about his books. Her view that he always had his nose in them, was something she laughed at while plucking a volume from his hand

and throwing it to the floor during one of her sexual advances. Dicky noted, however, that the way she uttered the sound "book" suggested it was a word that she did not use very often. Towards the end of the relationship, the sound came out of her mouth with associations to things sinister or suspicious.

At first they saw each other every weekend. Either she came up to London by car or he went down to Bosham by train. As each was integrated back into their routines and life grabbed them with its commitments, they saw each other every fortnight, then every month until their relationship became an alien concept among other relationships – he with study, exams and career; and she with the world of horses.

Dicky thought, and Richard agreed, that Sandra's connection to horses was like an umbilical cord that her mother refused to cut. At the time of his arrival, Sandra's parents were hoping for foals. They were impeccably but coldly polite whenever he visited, but there was no doubt that any young man from outside their social circle was a threat that might carry away their child. Many years after his break with Sandra, Richard heard from a mutual friend that when the inevitable split with her parents came, it was angry and uncompromising.

After a few months in England, Dicky dreaded the visits to Bosham. Sandra's father, the Colonel, was suspicious of academic *wallahs*. Like most military men, he was a doer, a man of action and he wanted a doer and a man of action for his daughter. Dicky would sometimes arrive on a Saturday to find the house full of cavalry twill, regimental blazers, silk cravats and whisky. These men gathered in a closed group and talked and laughed about their wartime experiences while their sons congregated around Sandra. In reality, the older men were normal people sharing memories of abnormal experiences with people who understood, and before the diagnosis of post traumatic stress disorder.

Increasingly, Dicky found that the trip to Bosham was an irritation which took him from his books and his world of ideas. The journey became irksome and the weekends a waste of time. One day, he took the tube from Russell Square to Waterloo. He fell in with the jostling crowd and, with much irritation and tripping of feet, he extricated himself and made his way to the main concourse. He scanned the departure board and set off to the ticket barrier. There, he stopped. He watched the porters preparing for the departure of the Portsmouth train. He heard the doors slam. He heard the whistles announcing the train's imminent departure and he whispered the words of one of his father's favourite songs as the train lurched round the bend and out of sight. *First train to Bernadino, First train to Bernadino. If you get this one, you'll never need another one, Bee-dee-dee-dee-bom-bom to Bernadino.*

The words of the song were a warning. From that moment on, Dicky knew that the relationship was going nowhere. Never again did he take the train to Portsmouth and Southsea. He and Sandra met for the last time in the Friend at Hand pub near Russell Square. Her intellect was bland, and her voice increasingly displayed the understated displeasure of the county set, and he found it irritated him. A couple of days later, while he was still preparing for his exams, he decided to finish with the girl he might have forgotten had she not been the one to take his virginity. His rather long explanation of why he was dumping her was greeted by a long silence at the end of the telephone line. Pacing up and down in his cell, Richard recalled her last words to him, shaken from her mouth while she was on the point of tears. "But we're almost there, Dicky. We're almost there..."

There was a noise from outside his room, a loud knock, and the door flew open.

"It's almost time," said the Second Coming. "Prepare yourself to die."

BBC News Online

Video released of Richard Chambers

The kidnappers of university professor Richard Chambers have released a video of him in which he appears to be wearing an explosives vest. In the tape, Mr Chambers is sitting alongside one of his kidnappers, who is also wearing an explosive vest. His captors say they will detonate both vests.

The Foreign Office renewed its appeal for Mr Chambers' immediate release.

"It is very distressing for Richard's family and friends to see him being threatened in this way," a spokesman said. "We ask those holding Richard to avoid him being harmed by releasing him immediately. We are keeping his family fully informed and offering them our continued support."

A spokesperson for Mr Chambers' family said: "The family are obviously most concerned and distressed at this latest development. All our thoughts, of course, go with Richard in his present predicament. We earnestly request his abductors to release him, unharmed in any way."

In the tape, posted on a website used by militants, Mr Chambers is seen wearing a device around his torso and attached to shoulder straps.

The British Foreign Office said it deplored such footage of Richard Chambers.

"We condemn the release of videos like this which can only add to the distress of Richard's family and friends," a spokeswoman said. "They have not seen Richard for several weeks. Those holding Richard should release him."

Mr Chambers was abducted by a group calling itself The People's Democratic Party. The PDP has demanded the withdrawal of foreign troops from Arab lands and the removal of US support for Israel.

CHAPTER 13

Richard squinted through the windows of the old Mercedes. Dawn was about to break, and the sun waited, sent out an orange glow to announce its imminent arrival. On this, his last day, Richard would savour the moments of its hours, delight in its early-morning freshness, its pale light on distant and low hills, its promise of something else, of something better than the day before and better than what was to come. He tried to ignore the bomb belt. It had been fitted under his shirt and was tight to his skin, made breathing difficult.

The Second Coming filled the driving seat, his head swaying, riding the bumps and potholes in the road as the car rattled its way towards the edge of town. Mr Friendly and Richard were dressed in black suits and sitting like Siamese twins in the back seat. He could feel the ends of his captor's *kuffieh* hanging like a protective arm over his shoulders.

The last stars were retreating into the brightening sky, but spots and specks of darkness shifted in the landscape. Richard moved closer to the windows. These disturbing blotches were people and dogs, immune to the light, foraging through piles of dust and rubbish and fingering the broken bits of already broken bits. Other shadows flitted against the squat white houses, and Richard became aware of eyes that stared at the car from the edge of the twilit road. Children stood immobile beside the cancerous concrete of their dwellings, beside the torn and fluttering posters of yesterday's martyrs and yesterday's sons and brothers. Their eyes neither pleaded nor argued. They were lifeless and looked out from faces that had never known youth. Richard was appalled by their dumb immobility. They could have been born of the posters themselves and they seemed to say: Yes – stare at us, but soon it is your turn. Look - the twisted steel rods that you see rising from the concrete mark our gravestones and soon you will be amongst us.

Richard could not say where the city ended. The houses gave way to an iron railing that separated bushes and weeds from bushes and weeds. Several trucks, purged of all detachable parts were skeletal dinosaurs beside the road. They were reminders of another age, another war and another protective arm hanging over his shoulders to console him for another sorrow. The other war had been the Yom Kippur war of 1973, and the other protective arm had been Sandra's and it curled over his shoulder from the back seat of the Aqaba taxi on his day of dismissal and shame. And on that day he had seen relics from the First World War - the scavenged carriages of the *Hejaz* railway lying like upturned beetles beside the desert highway. The Second Coming's voice broke into his thoughts and woke him as though from a dream.

"We're almost there. On the other side of the border you'll be met by Abu Salim." His tone was jovial, the rhythm of his words almost bouncy. He could have been an approachable travel courier supplying information to a group of tourists. "He's an Israeli Arab but he's been well paid. He'll bring you to the city." His voice then flattened out, became brisk and business-like. "You will act quickly. You cannot afford to be stopped by the enemy. If they threaten to search you, the operation will end with you in paradise. My friend will see to that. The wedding reception is being held in the Hotel Vital, on the edge of the old town."

He fumbled in the glove compartment and his hand appeared over the top of the empty passenger seat. "Take this money and your ID. If you are stopped in the city you may say you are from Haifa and on your way to a wedding. Nobody will expect bombers to be middle-aged men." He inclined his head towards the back seat and smiled. "The belts have lock mechanisms - once activated they cannot be removed. Only my friend and I can do that. Any attempt to remove them will trigger an explosion."

The hills, low and hunched, closed around them, wrapped them in reeds and stunted trees. Here and there, rocks had rolled or tumbled and lay like fallen fruit on the edge of the tarmac.

"Perhaps," said Richard, "middle-aged men have more sense than to believe in an afterlife of milk and honey."

"You think our fighters believe this?" Mr Friendly snapped. "Be assured, my friend, that may be how the West portrays them. The truth is very different. Let me tell you a story."

Mr Friendly leaned sideways, and his *kuffieh* slipped off Richard's shoulders and dangled between them.

"On October 4, 2003, my very good friend exploded her suicide belt in the Maxim restaurant in Haifa, killing twenty people and wounding many more. She was twenty-nine years old and studying to be a lawyer. According to her family, her mission was in revenge for the killing of her brother and her fiancé by Israel's security forces and in revenge for all the crimes Israel had perpetrated in the occupied West Bank."

"One such case," Richard said, "hardly constitutes evidence."

"Perhaps not," said Mr Friendly, "but my experience tells me this. Contrary to the popular Western image that suicide terrorism is an outcome of religious fanaticism, suicide bombing attacks are politically motivated. But that is not all. They are motivated by an explosive mix of desperation, pride, anger, and a sense of powerlessness. And let me tell you, *ustazz*, there is no shortage of recruits."

"Of people with some kind of personality disorder, perhaps."

"No, *ustazz*, the majority of suicide bombers I have known are psychologically normal, deeply integrated into society and emotionally attached to their national communities. Labels that the West randomly attaches to the bombers, such as 'mad,' merely reveal an inability or unwillingness to fathom the deeper reasons for their actions. Until the West understands and fully grasps this, the killing will continue. And it will be the young who carry out these attacks."

Richard found no answer to this. Mr Friendly put his hand on his shoulder.

"Do not worry, *ustazz*, we will not be detected."

Richard heard the falling note of the engine, felt the old Mercedes pitch and role, and watched their own dust cloud swirl around them, heard the car's tyres crackling on stones and gravel. The Second Coming had swung off the road. He pulled up in the middle of a grove of gnarled trees, slid his arm over the passenger seat and turned his head towards the two men in the back.

"Get out," he commanded, "and come with me."

It took Mr Friendly a while to push the door open, and the Second Coming was already shading his eyes from the sun and scanning the desert behind them when Richard and Mr Friendly joined him. He bade them silent by raising a finger to his mouth. He cocked his head to catch the direction of the breeze and angled his head to listen. After a while he said:

"OK - this way. Follow me and keep low."

The three men clambered up a stony, man-made slope and raised their heads over the top.

"Wait here and keep down," the Second Coming said before setting off again. He was on all fours, crawling through long grass and in the direction of a fence rising from reinforced concrete blocks. Crouching beside Mr Friendly, Richard looked out over the tips of the grass. It was swaying to the clicking of the cicadas and dancing to the gentle music of a light breeze, and made Richard feel he had shrunk - a little boy surrounded by an ocean of magic.

The Second Coming was still on his knees and some way in front of them. He was holding his arm straight out behind him like a bird with a broken wing. With a tickling movement of his fingers, he signalled to both Richard and Mr Friendly that they should join him.

Richard heard metallic noises coming from the direction of the fence. It was some moments before he saw the huge tear hanging sideways from the fence like a flap of skin. Two men were standing at it, and the wire pinged and pocked while the cutters did their work. Beyond the fence were more hills, lush and green, and there were some settlements – clusters of white dots joined together with winding white strings of roadway. That, Richard knew, was Israel.

When the two men arrived at his side, the Second Coming whispered, "It's not time. Wait back there by the car until I tell you to come. Keep your heads down and keep still. Don't give our position away. The enemy are around."

Richard and Mr Friendly backed away through the grass, slid down the slope and found a spot of shade under a stunted tree. They lay on their backs staring at the sky.

"Are you sure about this?"

Richard's voice sounded strange to him. He should have been pleading for his life, appealing to his captor's sense of right and wrong. Instead, he was defensive.

"Have you thought about the consequences?"

There was a long silence. It was the silence of the countryside after the traffic, the silence that evoked the presence of nothingness, a silence that reminded Richard of the presence of death. He turned his head and looked at his companion, tried to find his eyes. Mr Friendly had rested his swaddled head on the crook of his arm, while the fingers of his other hand played with his nose. His body was speckled in sunlight and shadow.

"Don't talk to me of consequences." He spoke low and slowly as though trying to master the shakiness of his voice. "Consequences are in my blood." He made a slight movement of the hand that now covered his eyes. For some time he remained silent while apparently communing with some thought, idea or memory. Then he turned his head towards Richard's and contemplated his face for a moment before saying, "Let me tell you how it was for me and thousands like me. A condemned man has a right to know his killer's motive, don't you think?" He allowed his eyes to wander for a while before turning his head away and covering his eyes again. "I was born in a refugee camp and just five years old when Israel's victory in the six-day war sent thousands more refugees pouring over the border. But I was one of the lucky ones. I was lucky because my father worked hard and was able to buy a very small piece of land and build a house of concrete. Before that, we lived in a house built from clay." He was speaking very low again as though unwilling to disturb his fragile memories. "Living in the camp meant that you had limited options: no garden, tiny streets and poverty everywhere. My father was also full of energy, hope and enthusiasm and he earned enough money to send me to a good school. You see, don't you? What motivated him was the opportunity to give me the education and the chances he never had. He quite literally killed himself in order to achieve it."

"All the more reason why you should live."

Mr Friendly considered the comment for a moment and then exclaimed:

"No, *ustazz*. Listen. In 1979, my father was able to provide me with enough money to study at the LSE in London. Imagine the thanks that are due to him. He was a peasant, a man who had never been abroad. What did he know about England or about university? I do know that he loved me, and that he knew education was the only way out for me."

He touched at his eyes with the fingers of one hand. He was silent for some time, and Richard guessed that he was revisiting never-to-be-forgotten times and places from his youth. After a while, Mr Friendly became aware of Richard's intrusive eyes and he changed to a more neutral topic.

"Your country and its people have taught me many things; things like fairness and decency, and doing the right thing, and acting according to your principles."

He lifted his hand so that it hovered over his face a moment before dropping it into his jacket pocket. He extracted a small packet, unwrapped it and passed it to Richard.

"Eat this," he said, "your last breakfast."

Richard took a piece of cake from his hand and put it in his mouth. So this was his last meal and he had not even been given a choice.

"But murder is not acting according to any principles I know of," he said through the half chewed cake. "What you are doing now is nothing more than revenge for what they did to you, your father and your people. If you kill Israelis, then there's no difference between you and them."

Mr Friendly drew in his feet and raised his knees. He altered the position of his arm and curled it upwards and rested his head on the palm of its hand. The fingers of the other arm drew circles on his chest.

"So – if we cannot live as equals then we must die as equals."

"Then you must find a way to be equals in life and not only in death. All you are doing is giving them an excuse to carry on killing."

With an excited flourish, Mr Friendly raised his arm from his chest and made circles in the air with his hand.

"Do they need excuses? Do they have any morals? The world sees what they are doing and it watches with indifference. Israel behaves like an adolescent. It is convinced that it can do as it wishes, that its actions carry no consequences and that it will never die. Israel's triumph is that they have convinced the world that they are the victims, while they kill us. How can this be?"

There was a long pause while the sun burned on their faces. The cicadas had set up a high-pitched drone which crackled through the air like sizzling fat. From far above, the wire continued to pop and ping. Mr Friendly had let his hand drop to his chest again. He was making circular movements over his sternum and punctuating the movements with agitated taps of his fingers.

"It is true that the continuing occupation of Arab lands has shifted the international balance of opinion, but this is still offset by the memory of Europe's dead Jews. They have used the fact of six million deaths and they have used it well to trade on the world's guilt."

"Then you need to wage a moral war. You need to show the world that your cause is a just one, that it is they and not you who have no morals. Your cause needs people like you. You are throwing your life away, aren't you?"

Mr Friendly turned his head to one side, stilled his hands and clasped them together as though saying his prayers.

"And perhaps our cause needs people like you, my friend. You are the historian. You are the one to tell the world that Israel should no longer have any special claim upon international sympathy."

"You aren't answering my question. You…"

"You are the one who should tell the world that the US will not always be there. But above all this, it is you who must tell them that weapons and walls and barbed wire fences like this one here can no more preserve Israel than they preserved the German Democratic Republic or white South Africa and that their colonies are doomed unless they are willing to exterminate the local population."

"Perhaps if you can't answer my last question," Richard said, "you will tell me this." He paused, aware that the last time he heard this tone in his voice was when he accused a student of plagiarism. "What are you dying for? Did your father sacrifice his life so that you could throw yours away? Do you think he wanted that?"

Mr Friendly turned his face away from Richard's but as he did so his face betrayed a flickering grimace as though he had experienced a stabbing pain in his teeth. His mouth appeared to tighten.

"He taught me by his example that I should stand by my principles." Mr Friendly's tone was defensive. "I know that if you fight for democracy, then you must be prepared to die for it. My father sacrificed his life for me, and I am prepared to make sacrifices for something that is bigger than either of us." He paused and twisted his head still further away from Richard's and when he spoke again the anger in his voice seemed directed at his armpit. "Someone must make a sacrifice for the rightness of our cause."

Richard allowed his eyes to flicker over Mr Friendly's chest. He felt offended by the man's tone. It seemed to betray him as it betrayed their relationship. Richard reflected that he and his captor had got to know each other quite well. Richard had grown to respect his sincerity, to recognise it rounding every vowel and consonant of his words. But now these words were hollow and empty of meaning. Something alien had taken control. The man was lying. He stared at this revelation in mild shock and disappointment.

"But it won't be you making the sacrifice, will it? No I don't believe you," said Richard. "Undo your shirt and let me see you belt. No? Then it's me alone who's going to die, isn't it?"

Richard was about to rise to his feet when he felt himself shift sideways as though along a fault line deep inside himself. For what seemed an eternity he tried to come to terms with the feeling that he was not there. He was oblivious to his body parts, oblivious to the bomb belt, and his head was floating in space. Mr Friendly straightened his legs and pushed himself to a sitting position.

"So the drug's taking effect," he said. "Your last meal was very special. It will help you during your final hour."

Two rocks cracked together and rolled down the slope. They were followed by the Second Coming. Richard looked down at his shoes to reassure himself that he was connected to some physical entity. Something terrible was about to happen but for the moment he was incapable of remembering exactly what. He heard someone say:

"They are prepared. Abu Salim is waiting on the other side to take you to the city. We must wait for his signal. Are you ready? Follow me to the top of the slope?"

The three men clambered back up to a position on the edge of the grass. Richard was lying beside them and without any recollection of how he had got there. The desert seemed to stretch before him for an apparent eternity. He rose to his feet and took a step towards it, but the Second Coming grabbed his arm and tugged him back down to earth.

"No. Wait for Abu Salim's signal."

Richard stared out into Israel along with the others, scanning the area for a sign. It seemed to Richard that he had now moved out of time. At one and the same time he was the person he had been and the person he would become. While in this state he thought he heard someone call out to him. It came at a moment of stillness when all movements in the desert seemed to freeze. Mr Friendly put his hand on Richard's arm.

"Just stay close to me."

Richard looked towards the desert expecting to see someone but there were only the tips of the grass waving back and forth in front of his eyes and a strong sensation of connection and of intimacy. There was nothing else: no sound of a voice calling to him; no sound of anything except that of the sun baking on the scorched earth and the clicking of the cicadas. Richard wondered whether he was asleep and walking around in his own dreams. He was filled with an emotional response to some long-gone incident in his life. The event was beyond recall. Still wandering in his memory though was this feeling of connection, this sensation of intimacy – the intimacy of loss.

"He's here," said a voice.

It was there. A flash of headlamps from the car that linked him with death.

"Follow me," said Mr Friendly.

They dashed towards the fence, ducked through the hole and ran towards the car. Bent double they ran across no-man's-land and dived into the back seat. The car reversed and pulled away in a cloud of white dust.

And then Richard heard again the voice calling his name. He turned and gazed through the back window. At first there was just a cloud of white dust but as the car hit the tarmac and accelerated, the cloud thinned and settled down on the road. There, as though materialising from the dust itself, a boy was standing. He was as still as a statue and he was staring in Richard's direction as if he knew him, as if he was about to spring forward and introduce himself. But between Richard and the boy was the fence. It was bent at the top and reminded Richard of the pictures he had seen of concentration camps. This was where Richard was, on the last road, the road to heaven. The boy was now on the other side.

CHAPTER 14

"Get out of the car," said Abu Salim. "You must hurry. There are no guards now."

Richard was floating – incapable of thinking and without any recollection of how he had arrived in this glittering place where pampered dogs trotted at the heels of their owners, and tennis stars smiled from giant hoardings and told the world that happiness was an accurate timepiece. Mr Friendly rounded the bonnet and pulled the back door open. Prising Richard out of the car, he held his arm while buttoning up his jacket. Richard recalled something about a wedding. A wedding? Perhaps it was anticipation of this event that prompted the tightness across his chest, the heaviness on his body.

"What's the matter with your friend?" Abu Salim said.

Richard felt the man's eyes penetrate to his core, play with the excitement of this special day and the knowledge that he was its king. Until then, Abu Salim had been a sketch, a vague angel of mercy adorned with gold chains and silver rings and sitting on a cloud of after-shave and tobacco smoke.

"He's eaten the cake," Mr Friendly said.

Already eaten the cake? What a thing to do, Richard thought. No wonder Abu Salim allowed his eyebrows to draw down in an expression of disapproval. No surprise that his eyes were half closed and seemed to be assessing the outside world and judging it according to some inner code which said, "Don't trust a person who eats the cake before the ceremony."

"That's the hotel," he said. "Go quickly."

He was pointing to the left of a large gateway cut into the city wall about 100 metres from the car. The hotel, which seemed to hang on the end of Abu Salim's finger, was a mixture of styles: a graft from the stone of the old wall and an alien implant of shining glass and angular steel. The flag poles, jutting out over the entrance, reminded Richard of gun barrels. But he knew he liked this city, had been here many times before. There was a sense of comfort in the place. It was present in the bearing of the people, in the gentle purpose of their stride and in the ease with which they rubbed shoulders with others. Richard guessed that this comfort stemmed from the simple fact that he and the rest of the population were where they felt they should be. The next stop on their journey was the afterlife, and this city was their waiting-room. There was nowhere else they wanted to be.

"I'll wait for you here," Abu Salim said to Mr Friendly.

Richard was jolted back to the present and allowed his thoughts to drift to what was going to happen now. He and Mr Friendly were about to do something together. Someone was getting married, but who was the groom, who was the best man and where was the bride? Was his friend having second thoughts? The two men set off like competitors in a three-legged race stepping over the road towards their destiny. Richard drifted in and out of time. He was restless and irritated, his mouth was dry, and his breathing was coming in short and sharp gasps. In an attempt to place himself in the perspective of time, he turned his thoughts inwards. He found confused fragments of childhood memories: *Where are we going? We don't know. Does it matter where we go? Down to the forest where the flowers grow – anywhere, anywhere. We don't really know.*

A passing woman looked at him, and Richard looked back, let his gaze travel from her *Gucci* shoes to her dress and to the stone-studded watch on her wrist. She was young and beautiful and she had to be happy with a watch like that because the tennis star said so. Richard was surprised when he saw a look of compassion in her eyes. Perhaps he should reach out and talk to her, tell her that something terrible was about to happen and that he needed help. But he knew he had forgotten the script, and there was nobody there to prompt him, and anyway he was walking to a wedding not to the gallows tree.

They approached the hotel's revolving glass doors, and the pavement filled up with suitcases and people who had come to see the spectacle. He was the centre of attention and no sooner had he appeared than heartfelt words of greeting and farewell rippled up the pavement and lingered in his ears as an expectant hush. He was standing on stage again, but he had forgotten the part he was to play and he struggled to find the words he had never learned. He tried to bury himself further in his own thoughts.

"If I am going to the gallows," he said to himself, "it won't be painful. Here one moment and gone the next."

Both he and Mr Friendly pushed through the revolving glass, the door patting Richard's posterior and ejecting him into the entrance hall. He looked around him with his eyes only. There were a few pieces of baggage in the hall, and hotel staff in red jackets were running about and shouting.

After what seemed an eternity of standing on the spot, Richard involved himself in the action around him. A few people were gathered in a glittering bar for a farewell toast, and a line of children appeared. Dressed like angels and holding wands, they were curling round the baggage, ducking and weaving under arms and elbows and making noises like steam engines. Then, as though lured by the pied piper, they disappeared into the reception room, their hoots and screams of laughter hanging in the air. Where was Ben? Was he here to see the spectacle?

Richard had floating thoughts – the razor blades, the ball bearings and nails, and plastic needles that wouldn't show up on x-rays. *Somewhere on the stairs is a place I go. There isn't any other place I know, and boom – your head and spinal cord splatter over the ceiling.*

Richard approached the reception room and stood in the doorway. The room seemed to stretch before him. Some of the people were in formal dress and standing in small groups, talking, gesturing, and seeking out eyes with their eyes. At the far end of the room hundreds of people were dancing in the darkness. He wanted to kneel and say his prayers but his thoughts drifted to what he was doing there. Something terrible was about to happen but he was incapable of remembering what. He knew he had to turn round and run away but he had forgotten what he was running away from. He would ask Mr Friendly.

"What are we doing…?"

It took several seconds for his mind to register what his eyes were seeing. There was nobody at his side. His friend must have had second thoughts after all and bolted before the bride arrived. Richard felt vulnerable. Mr Friendly was his connection with this place and without him he felt exposed, and had no right to be there. He was an intruder who might, at any time, find his presence challenged. He muttered thanks to God when he caught sight of his erstwhile companion. He was now a long way off and talking to the angel of mercy on the corner of the street. Their movements were agitated, and their rough talk and aggressive language were attracting sidelong glances from passers-by. Then Mr Friendly darted back towards the hotel, and the angel of mercy set off in pursuit plucking at the tails of his jacket.

Richard shook his head as though to throw off the protective blanket that was trapping his thought processes. And something had happened to his hearing. People appeared to be laughing and talking, but to him there was just a distorted babble, rising and falling in waves. Richard tried to assess its mood. Babbles had no language but they had defining characteristics of tone. There were babbles of expectancy, babbles of disappointment and babbles of irritation. Lecturers were experts in babbling voices. But he was no longer a lecturer and everything in the room seemed to be happening in slow motion, and the sounds were merging into one prolonged and muted roar. And why was everyone so excited? He peered into the reception room. The children were turning in circles, and the music and coloured lights seemed to follow them like searchlights. He thought he heard the strains of an organ, and the joyous cries of children whirled round his ears. Of course! They had heard it too. It was the merry-go-round. It came every year at this time to take the children on safe and easy riding throughout the world and now he was old enough to ride on it. His pulse raced. G Turnbull proudly presents Golden Victorian Galloping Horses, and here they were in the hotel.

Watching the dizzy blur of faces spinning and scarves and coat tails flying in the wind, Richard dug into his pockets in search of a threepenny piece. He shivered in anticipation and pulled some coins from his pocket. There was Dazzler with his flared nostrils, Honey with her flying mane and Ned, Silver and Dan, Tap, Tim and Lucy, each one saddled and ready for the next trip. Head and shoulders above them all stood his favourites. Painted in gilt from the ears to the hooves was Gold and directly opposite, with a bridle of carved hearts and a painted ribbon between the ears, was Love. Richard made his way forward. He ignored the gasps and protests of people pulling at his arm and he pushed through the people to get on the merry-go-round.

"Are you ready?" said a voice. "Shall we go?"

Richard covered his face with his hands and opened his fingers. In this last moment, he would keep his eyes open so that he could see the children. "God bless them and God bless me," he was whispering when a gleam like that of sheet lightning passed across the dance floor. He span round as though to escape the blast – hoping to see more than the eye could see, something beyond the present and into the infinite distance, a glimmer of light in the darkness. Mr Friendly was at his elbow and tugging at his arm. His eyes were sparkling and his face seemed scrubbed, purged of pain, was almost angelic. He leaned forward and shouted in Richard's ear.

"I can't do this. We have to leave - now."

He took Richard's arm and led him towards the exit. Richard was stumbling over the carpet when he noticed the angel of mercy on the other side of the revolving doors. It occurred to Richard that perhaps he was on his way to paradise. But the angel of mercy was real, he was present, ferociously angry and he had one hand on the butt of a revolver tucked into his Chinos. Mr Friendly bundled Richard through the revolving doors and straight into the blast of Abu Salim's anger and an ever-increasing circle of emptiness that surrounded him. People were walking past him as though he was contaminated with some terrible disease.

"No, you must go through with it," he was shouting, "send him back in."

Mr Friendly pushed Richard past him, but Abu Salim was not going to be put off so easily. He was tugging at his revolver, pointing at Richard and screaming.

"The man must die, die. You must send him back or…"

A further tug at the gun brought its barrel into view. Mr Friendly dropped Richard's arm, stepped in close to Abu Salim. Mr Friendly appeared to crouch, lowered his arm to his belly and brought his fist up to land on Abu Salim's chin. His head snapped back, and he fell to the pavement and rolled over, his hand still on the butt of his revolver.

"Quick," said Mr Friendly, "follow me."

They rushed away from the increasing noise, along the pavement and into an ecstasy of colour and motion. Cars and bicycles passed by and a vast river of people ambled or paused around the cafes and kiosks. They were all gesticulating and conversing loudly as though excited by some news event. Most were fashionably dressed while others, conspicuous by the speed with which they walked, chose to wear the black clothes and the skull cap to show their respect for God rather than for Gucci or Benetton. Richard and Mr Friendly weaved their way through this active and bright energy and ran across the road towards Abu Salim's car. Someone behind them shouted, and Richard stumbled. He could not run fast enough. His chest felt constricted, and there was a weight there that disturbed his natural balance, and his legs were heavy as if stolen from a bad dream.

"Quick," said Mr Friendly through half-closed teeth, "before Abu Salim betrays us."

He stopped at the car and turned round. In the midst of the current of people a wide space had opened up at the entrance to the hotel. In the middle of that space, like a street entertainer, Abu Salim was on his feet and waving his hands in the air. He was surrounded by young men in dark suits. Some of them had disconnected themselves from the crowd and were making calls on mobile phones. Their faces were as calm as the air, and their heads were turning like antennae, their eyes taking in every movement around them, their ears hearing every sound, and their noses sniffing out the direction of the prey. With an almost unnatural calm, Mr Friendly said:

"The mission will go on. I need your belt."

"You have a belt."

"I have no belt."

"But you told me…"

"*Ustazz,*" there was real anger in his voice, "I tell you I have no belt. We lied – we lied. Only you have the belt." He began to make noises that landed somewhere between laughter and pain and all of them to the tone of disbelief. "I was to lead you here and I would detonate the bomb. You understand? It was Omar's idea. But I can't kill children. And I can't kill the man who once saved me."

"Omar?"

Mr Friendly grabbed the lapel of Richard's jacket and dragged him past the car and towards a half-constructed building of glass.

"Quick – over here."

The building rose from the old city wall in a way that suggested it was growing on the foundations of the old but reaching out towards something new. They entered the site to the sounds of sirens screeching and footsteps thrashing over the roads around them. Mr Friendly halted and used Richard's momentum to swing him down to the floor.

"We haven't much time. You must give me your bomb belt. You will live, and I will die."

"You must save yourself, too."

Mr Friendly shook his head.

"No, *ustazz*. You are the one who put the words into my mouth. Remember Androcles? I've never forgotten them. I must go in to the arena with the rest." He smiled thinly. "My honour you know."

He threw off his jacket and shirt and stretched out his arms.

"Give me the belt," he commanded.

"I can't touch it. You said I can't touch it. You said…"

"Just take it off."

"No, I won't let you die."

Mr Friendly was staring down at him, had raised his fist. Richard was turning his head to one side when there was an explosion and darkness began to descend. He heard a voice as if from some place far away.

"You were right, *ustazz*. In 1973, you helped make me what I am and what I believe. It was your values that impressed me, you see? That sense of fairness, of honour and of doing the right thing. I see it all now. I forgot it for years and then it came back to me. I didn't ask for it but something made me remember. It is my life. It is the truth. It is the truth of my life. When I go, it will not go with me. You will survive. But I want you to see the results of your actions before I go."

There was a commotion outside. Mr Friendly glanced through the glass frontage. People were spreading out in all directions and men in uniform were running around. It must be the grand old Duke of York, Richard thought. After all, he had ten thousand men. *He marched them up to the top of the hill, and he marched them down again.*

Mr Friendly was pulling at Richard's shirt, ripping it open and fumbling. And in that instant, the weight on Richard's chest was lifted, and he took, as if for the first time, a breath of cleansing air. Mr Friendly was then standing over him with Richard's bomb belt in his hand. There was more shouting, more footsteps and the sound of automatic gunfire. Mr Friendly stepped away from Richard and raised the belt into the air. There was more gunfire and Mr Friendly waved his hand in front of his face as though to brush away flies. He staggered. Something red exploded from his shoulder, his chest and stomach. He fell backwards and lay on his back with his legs extended and with one arm coiled around his neck. A hollow flapping sound came from the area of his chest and a pinkish foam was coming from his mouth while he gasped for air. Richard sprang to his feet. What was going on? Why was Mr Friendly lying here? He bent over to pick up the bomb belt. He had every intention of throwing it as far as he could but a strident command from behind stopped him. He turned round. What was going on? There was a line of kneeling soldiers. Their guns were raised and pointing at him.

He saw Abu Salim raise his revolver. He saw a flash, saw the gun jerk sideways, the smoke curling out of the barrel. He heard nothing. The bullet must have missed because he was still standing. But he was somehow rooted to the spot and incapable of moving a finger. He was feeling like a fool and wondering what everyone would think of him when he thought he had been struck by lightning and he began to vibrate from head to toe. Then he saw a bright light over him and the golden dome of a mosque rising from behind the city wall. It was topped with a crescent and it glinted in the sun. Richard reflected that it was the same sun that had warmed him thirty-five years earlier, but this time it was different. He was lying on his back and could not move. He saw the white city walls through the glass and he saw that the walls were confusing him with memories of similar walls, and the memories were clouded by the ghosts of people he had once known. Gradually the memories took control. He was backstage and reading Androcles' lines to a little boy in trouble.

"I must go in to the arena with the rest. My honour you know."

A tingling sensation spread over him. It was worse in his upper back, and he tasted blood. He reached up and touched the back of his neck. It was painful and he felt a knot like a tennis ball on the back of his head. There was a huge amount of blood. Where was that coming from? He put his hand up to his cheek. There was nothing there – a large part of his face was hanging down to his shoulder. He pushed it back up in an attempt to hold himself together. What had happened? Had his bomb gone off?

He was looking down at his hands just to make sure they were still connected to the rest of him when the strains of a familiar song drifted over the city wall.

When I am old and my hair is grey
Will you remember me?
Will you still remember me the way I was?
The way I was back then?

Then he heard sirens, tyres sliding and complaining, footsteps slapping and people shouting. Why was nobody coming in his direction? He tried to shout out but no sound came. Did nobody know he needed the warmth of a human hand? Could nobody see that he wanted to hear reassuring words telling him he was going to be alright? He turned his head. Mr Friendly was no longer gasping for air and the strange slapping noise had stopped. Richard allowed his hand to walk crab-like over the cemented floor. *Wait, Dicky, wait! It's too late, it's too late.* He found the dead man's warm fingers. They were delicate, and Richard held them tight while images and masks of people he had once known and loved passed in front of his inner eye as though to say goodbye. There was his wife, his mother, his father and his beloved Ben. He should be picking him up from school at this time and not lying around on the floor and holding a dead man's hand. Then he would need to start the dinner. It really was time to get up.

As I was back then
Young and free

Richard jerked. He was trying to turn his head, to find the dead man's eyes with his, when the light began to change - a rippling curtain falling over the stage at the play's end.

Will you still remember me the way I was?
The way I was back then?

There was a hush from without. There was the fading warmth of a man's hand in his, and a rushing sound in his ears like a mountain stream - whispering, whispering to stillness.

"Khalid," he said.

And there was silence.

EPILOGUE

Ben picked up the walking stick and set off towards Ambleside. It was now that time after noon when the light mellows and the mountains whisper to those who listen. The browns and greens fade, as colours will in the light of dying day, until the furthest hill weighs low and darkly on the horizon. At this time of stillness, when the air of invisible things brushed the tips of the long grass, the boy thought he heard a distant cry. From some place beyond the vanishing point a person was calling him. The voice seemed familiar and had a questioning tone, but no sooner had it come than it was taken by the wind and carried away into approaching night.

"What about the nice man who saved you, dad?" Ben said. "I saw his face on the television and in the papers. He looked such a good person. You said that he was a reasonable man, and that you and he just saw things differently. So why did he have to die, dad?"

Ben moved still further down the ridge towards the town. To the right, between the massive gnarled humps, a stream ran chill and cold. Foam-speckled and tumbling, it cut down the beck and it seemed to challenge him by saying: *I shall arrive at the bottom before you.* And at some unseen place, as if playing a game of hide-and-seek, the stream merged into the still lake. The boy was alone in the twilight. There was just a stirring in the air of someone or something that had come, whispered in his heart, and passed by.

"Tell you what, dad, the next time I meet an Arab or an Israeli I won't spit on them or tell them I hate them. I'll hold out my hand and listen to what they've got to say. I think you'd like that, dad. I think that you of all people would like that. I'll listen and I'll try, if only by a little bit, to increase the quantity of kindness and humanity in the world. What happened to you might be someone else's gain."

The wind freshened in the tree tops, and the leaves at the boy's feet looped happily in the wind. Ben skipped down the street to his house.

Opening the front door, he slotted his father's stick into the stand and threw off his jacket.

"Dad," he shouted, "I'm home."

There was a rustle as his father spun round in his chair and appeared as a shape in the doorway with the sunlight at his back.

ABOUT THE AUTHOR

Robert John Goddard was born in London in 1952. He has a BA in the History of the Middle East, a Postgraduate Diploma in International Marketing, and a Masters Degree in Education. He has lived and worked in Italy, Portugal, Jordan and Germany. All of his novels and stories contain elements of his experiences in these places. He currently lives near Frankfurt with his German wife and 8-year-old son, Anton. He also has a 33-year-old son, Alexander, from his first marriage. Robert has written five novels, several short stories and a book for university teachers entitled: "Teaching English for International Business." He is currently writing his sixth novel.

Printed in Great Britain
by Amazon

38392282R00096